# Fighting for the Edge

by
Jennifer Comeaux

**Fighting for the Edge**
Copyright © 2016 Jennifer Comeaux
Cover Designed by For the Muse Designs
ISBN 978-0-9904342-6-9

*To all the readers who've loved this series and these characters as much as I have. Thank you for always inspiring me! You have no idea how much it means to me to have your support!*

# CHAPTER ONE

*December, 2005*

"THIS NOR'EASTER COULD BRING UP TO twenty inches of snow to Cape Cod by morning. With expected wind gusts up to fifty miles per hour, power outages will be likely."

The silver-haired weatherman on the TV pointed to the radar covered in white, and I paced across the rink's lounge to the window. While my partner Chris and I had practiced all morning for the upcoming Grand Prix Final competition, a layer of snow had blanketed the parking lot.

I turned to my husband and coach Sergei, who was pouring coffee into a paper cup. "Maybe you should cancel your afternoon lessons. The roads might get bad soon."

His deep blue eyes peered out the window. Before he had a chance to answer, our rink manager Logan flipped off the TV and said, "Don't worry, Emily, I'm closing up shop. I don't want to be stuck here later."

"Guess we're going home then." Sergei covered his coffee with a travel lid.

I left Logan and Sergei discussing the weather report as I

jogged down the narrow staircase to the lobby, where my best friend Aubrey stood on the rug, shaking snow out of her long blond hair.

"I ran out to get my ballet shoes, and the snow started coming down harder," she said.

"Ballet class is cancelled. Logan is closing down for the day."

Aubrey's green eyes lit up. "Excellent! I need to start packing for Tokyo."

I laughed. "Why am I not surprised you haven't started yet?"

"We don't leave until Sunday. There's a whole day between now and then. We're not all organized freaks like you, Em."

"I hope you have a flashlight cause you might be packing in the dark."

My cell phone rang, and I pulled it from the pocket of my warm-up jacket. Upon seeing my mother's number, I said, "Want to bet my mom will give me detailed instructions on preparing for the storm? I swear, sometimes she acts like I'm a kid instead of twenty-four and married."

Aubrey snickered and went toward the locker room while I answered the phone. Mom launched into a series of reminders to which I replied, "Yes, we have plenty of candles and a portable heater. We've been through a nor'easter before."

"Well, they're saying this could be one of the worst," Mom warned in her patented worried voice. "It's going to be a long night."

AUBREY DROPPED ANOTHER HANDFUL of spinach leaves into the sauté pan and sprinkled them with a dash of salt. The wind howled outside her apartment, but she still had electricity.

She'd thought about calling Em to tell her she'd finished all her packing before dinner, but she was probably busy snuggling with Sergei in their townhouse.

A twinge of jealousy nipped at her. She and Em were the same age, and her best friend had already found the love of her life. Meanwhile, she'd never been in a serious relationship. *That's your choice*, she reminded herself. Keeping things casual with guys had let her stay focused on skating and free of all the romance drama. She'd listened to her ice dance partner Nick's love-life problems for enough years to know relationships were often more trouble than they were worth.

Her cell blared "Mr. Brightside" and vibrated on the laminate countertop, and she knew from the custom ringtone it was Em's happy-go-lucky partner. She cradled the phone to her ear as she tossed the wilting spinach. "Hey, Chris."

"Hey, do you have power?"

"Yeah, you don't?" Chris's apartment was in the building across the parking lot from hers.

"It went out a few minutes ago right when I was getting ready to eat. Can I come over and microwave my frozen pizza?"

"I have extra roasted chicken and sautéed spinach if you want some."

"You have to ask?" Chris laughed. "I'll be there in a minute."

She placed the phone on the bar between the kitchen and living room and dumped more spinach into the pan. It would be nice to have the company, but she hoped Chris wouldn't pepper her with questions about his ex-girlfriend Marley. Aubrey still kept in touch with her good friend, a fellow ice dancer who'd moved to Seattle the past spring. Marley had broken up with Chris a few months later, and though he claimed to be over her, he always wanted to know what she was up to. A perfect example of how relationships often led to nothing but angst.

When a loud knock sounded, Aubrey turned off the stove and hustled to the door. She opened it wide, and a blast of cold air rushed into the living room. Chris hurried inside and pulled back the hood of his black Baltimore Orioles sweatshirt, which was covered with snow. His thick dark hair stuck up in spots.

Aubrey shut the door. "Don't drip all over my carpet."

"Yes, ma'am."

Chris tugged the sweatshirt over his head, lifting the white T-shirt underneath above his stomach. Aubrey's eyes drifted to his perfectly cut abs. Nothing she hadn't seen before at summer beach trips with their group of friends, but she couldn't help but appreciate a fine physique when she saw it.

Chris dropped the hoodie onto the small square of tile in front of the door. "Man, it smells good in here."

"I learned a few tricks, living with Em for four years."

They walked into the kitchen and Chris bent over the half chicken resting on a platter. "Did you roast this?"

"No, I bought that at the store, but I did sauté the spinach."

"Em would've cooked the chicken and made gravy from scratch." Chris folded his arms and leaned against the counter. The serious expression he wore was probably meant to intimidate, but Aubrey knew him too well for that.

She took hold of his broad shoulders and aimed him toward the door. "You can always go back to your frozen, uncooked pizza."

He turned and smiled, showing his matching dimples. "Your dinner looks *fantastic*."

He hopped onto a stool next to the bar and tapped on her laptop while she put her attention on slicing into the juicy chicken.

"What's the latest on the message boards..." he mused out loud as he scrolled. "New interview with Madeline Hyatt and Damien Wakefield. No thanks. I've had enough of

Damien's mouth."

Aubrey paused mid-slice and lowered her head further. The Canadian pair champions weren't Em and Chris's favorite people, and her own dislike of Damien had grown stronger recently after a certain night she desperately wanted to forget. She was *so* not looking forward to seeing him in Tokyo.

"No way," Chris said. "Marley and Zach pulled out of the Final."

"What?" Aubrey's head shot up. "Where do you see that?"

"It's on IceNet." Chris read silently and then said, "Zach has a sore neck."

"Marley didn't mention anything when I talked to her this week." She peered at Chris and saw the same curious gaze she was giving him. "You think Zach might not really be hurt?"

"Faking an injury so they won't have to face you and Nick before nationals? Wouldn't be the first time their coach was suspected of doing something like that."

She set down the knife. Part of her reveled at the news, knowing she and Nick wouldn't have to contend with two of their toughest competitors, but the other part felt disappointed. She loved a challenge, and competing against the United States' other top team would've been a fierce battle.

"I'm gonna call Mar later and see what's up," she said.

Chris remained quiet, his eyes focused on the computer.

She resumed cutting into the chicken and asked, "Are you bummed she won't be in Tokyo?"

"Huh?" Chris looked up. "No, I'm… I'm through thinking about her. I've spent too much time dwelling on the past when I should be moving on."

*And my point about relationships is proven yet again*, she thought.

Chris slid off the stool and came around into the kitchen. "Maybe you had the right idea all along — not getting serious with anyone. I mean, we're young. We should be having fun."

"So, you're gonna be a player now?" She laughed.

"Hey, I can be—"

A loud whistle of wind rattled the kitchen window, and darkness fell over the apartment. The glow from the laptop screen provided the only light.

"At least I finished making dinner," Aubrey said.

"Yeah, I don't need to see the food. I just need to taste it," Chris said.

"Can you grab all the candles from the living room?"

"Why do girls like candles so much? Mar used to have—" Chris stopped midway through the living room and then continued on in silence.

Aubrey fumbled in a drawer for the lighter while Chris set two of the big candles on the bar and two on the small round table in the dining area. Once they had sufficient light, they filled their plates and grabbed a couple of bottles of water from the refrigerator.

Chris sniffed the candles as he sat in one of the dining chairs. "They smell like birthday cake."

She sat across from him. "It's yummy, isn't it?"

"Now I get the appeal. I need some of these for my place."

She laughed. "I'll tell Em to make that your Christmas gift."

"What's Santa bringing you for Christmas?"

There was no gift that could make the holidays at her house bearable. Unless her parents received a marriage makeover. But she wasn't going to get into all those issues with Chris.

"Hopefully, not another year of listening to my dad complain about how much money my mom spent on presents and my snotty sister-in-law making rude comments about skating."

"My parents aren't even coming up this year. They said

6

FIGHTING FOR THE EDGE

they'll see me at nationals two weeks later, so they weren't making another trip. You know, because traveling from Baltimore to Cape Cod is such a long haul." Chris's sarcasm dripped thicker than the wax from the candles. "So, Em invited me to go to her big family dinner in Boston."

"Oh, you're gonna love it. They go all out. You'll be in a food coma from all the pasta and tiramisu and cannoli."

Chris finished chewing. "I know, I hear about it every year. I might tell my parents to stay home every Christmas from now on."

"Do you think you'll live here after you and Em retire?"

"It sounds weird to say 'retire' when I'm only twenty-five. Like I'll be collecting a Social Security check." He chuckled.

"Well, how about, do you think you'll stay on Cape Cod after you conclude your skating career?"

"I like it here, but there aren't a lot of opportunities if I go back to school."

"You could move to Boston. That's probably where I'll look at colleges."

"And what do you want to be when you grow up?" Chris asked with a smile.

That was a question she'd been pondering a lot lately. As the days ticked down to her probable retirement, she realized she needed to start making some decisions about the next phase of her life.

"I've been thinking about studying interior design," she said. "Put my HGTV obsession to good use."

"You've got great taste in candle decoration. Who wouldn't want their house to smell like cake?"

She laughed. "I think it's a little more involved than that."

"Are you 'concluding your skating career' after the Olympics, too?"

"I think so." She picked at the label on her water bottle with her fingernail. "If Nick and I don't win a medal in Torino,

I'm not sure I want to stick it out four more years for another chance. The closer we get to the Olympics, the more I feel like this should be our last hurrah."

Her cell chirped from the kitchen, and she rose to check it. She read the text as she carried the phone to the table.

"You'd think the fact that I haven't responded to any of this guy's messages would tell him I'm not interested, but he keeps texting me."

"Who is he?"

"Just a guy I met at the gym. He's hot as all get-out, but we went to dinner and all he talked about was his ex. No amount of hotness could get me past that."

Chris's forehead wrinkled. "Is this what I have to look forward to on the dating scene?"

"Oh, yeah, we were talking about how you're gonna be a playboy when the lights went out. Haven't you only ever had serious girlfriends?"

"One throughout high school and then Marley. But since I got dumped both times, I figure it's time to try something new."

Aubrey studied him through the dim candlelight. With his warm brown eyes and lightly-freckled ivory cheeks, Chris perfectly fit the image of "the boy next door." And it wasn't just his looks that made him a great catch. She'd seen how he'd treated Marley all the years they were together — like she was the most precious thing in the world.

"I don't know if you're capable of being a casual dater." She tilted her head to one side. "I think you're the type of guy who falls hard and fast for a girl and wants her all to yourself."

"Well, you make staying single look easy. Maybe you need to tell me your secret."

"If a guy starts getting clingy, I let him know I'm not looking for anything serious. Having the 'I'm training for the Olympics' excuse makes it a lot easier."

"You think girls will fall for that excuse too?"

"Once they get a look at your abs, they won't care what lines you feed them."

Chris sat back in his chair and grinned. "So, you've been checking me out."

She smirked. "You know you're in great shape."

A car alarm sounded in the distance, and its wailing filled the silence as they turned back to their plates. Chris chewed with a pensive look. "How come it feels like we're talking for the first time when I've known you for seven years?"

"Probably because we've never hung out... just the two of us. Mar was always around or Nick or Em..."

"We should hang out more often. You can be my wing woman and teach me all the finer points of serial dating."

"I gladly accept that position." She smiled and lifted her water.

Chris raised his bottle. "To keeping things casual."

She tapped her drink to his. "And Bah Humbug to relationships!"

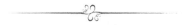

"DO YOU THINK WE should've gone to my parents' house?" I asked Sergei as I sat beside him on the couch. "If we were in Boston, we'd be closer to the airport. It might be rough getting out of here Sunday morning."

He slipped his arm around me. "Everything should be clear then. All the reports say the snow will let up tomorrow."

"I just don't want to miss our flight and be late getting to Tokyo. It takes my body so long to get acclimated to the time change in Asia, and I need to be one hundred percent with the Canadians breathing down our necks and—"

"It will all work out." Sergei locked his eyes on mine. "I promise."

I smiled. "Early competition jitters, I guess."

He cuddled me closer. "I am totally confident we'll have no trouble making it out of here. Besides, if we were at your parents' house, we wouldn't be here alone… and snowed in."

His lips brushed against my ear, setting off a tremble of goose bumps all over my skin. Even though we'd been married two and a half years, I felt like we were still newlyweds. I'd worried that working together at the rink every day might make us weary of each other when we came home at night, but there'd been no such problem. I couldn't get enough of Sergei, and from the way he was looking at me now, he obviously felt the same.

I tilted my head up and let my gaze travel over Sergei's face, starting with his hypnotizing eyes down to his slightly crooked nose and stopping on his oh-so-kissable mouth.

"What can we possibly do to entertain ourselves?" I asked.

"I may have an idea." Sergei reached into the back pocket of his jeans and pulled out a deck of cards. With a crooked grin, he said, "Strip poker."

"Strip poker?" I laughed. "How did you come up with that?"

"I saw it on TV last week when I couldn't sleep."

"What kind of late-night TV were you watching?" I raised an eyebrow.

He laughed. "It was a regular movie."

I looked down at the cards and then up at Sergei. "This will be normal poker, right? Not some fancy version you played in Atlantic City?" When we'd attended Skate America there in October, Sergei and Chris had spent a lot of time in the casinos.

"Regular five-card draw poker. Nothing fancy." Sergei stood and put the deck on the coffee table. "I'll get some wine. You can inspect the cards in case you don't trust me." He gave me a wicked smile as he walked backward to the stairs.

I examined my outfit. With a cardigan plus a camisole

topping my jeans, I had a slight advantage in the number of starting items. But I wanted a bigger edge. My eyes zeroed in on the Santa hat under the towering Christmas tree in the corner.

I jumped up and squeezed the floppy hat over my long, wavy hair. Sergei returned from the downstairs kitchen and set the bottle of wine and two glasses on the table.

"Hats aren't considered clothing."

"I was not informed of the rules when the game was proposed. Therefore, my hat will be considered an item in play." I flicked the white pom-pom.

Sergei pulled me into his strong arms. "You're lucky you're so cute when you get all competitive."

"Remember that when I kick your butt." I flashed a smile and kissed his stubbly cheek.

We sat across from each other on the carpet, leaving just enough space to place the cards. I poured the wine while Sergei shuffled. He dealt the first round and took a sip of his drink.

"You know where we need to go in Tokyo?" he said. "That nightclub we went to the last time we were there."

"Ah, yes, that was a very memorable night. The night you tried to seduce me."

"Unsuccessfully." Sergei laughed.

"Maybe we can do a reenactment next week. You might get lucky this time." I winked over my cards.

A gleaming grin spread across his face. "I definitely like the sound of that. And I'm feeling pretty lucky right now with this hand."

He displayed three kings, and I groaned, showing my measly pair of nines.

"First item of clothing must now be removed," he said in an official voice.

I frowned and then slowly unbuttoned my red cardigan, watching the admiring glow in Sergei's eyes intensify. I paused with the sweater pulled down over one shoulder.

"Enjoy this because you'll be doing all the stripping from now on."

"That's quite a statement." Sergei poured more red wine into my already half-filled glass.

"Is your plan to get me tipsy so I'll make bad decisions?"

"No, I can beat you without any tricks. I'm just taking care of my wife." He rubbed his hand over my outstretched leg. His touch heated my skin through the denim.

"Mm… also trying to distract me with affection. Very nice strategy." I closed my eyes for a moment as he moved to massaging my bare foot. "But it'll take much more than that to throw me off my game."

"I suppose I'm partly responsible for you being such a focused competitor."

"If it wasn't for you, I'd still be an anxiety-riddled head case on the ice. Have I thanked you for that lately?" I leaned toward Sergei and gave him a soft kiss.

He licked his lips. "Now who's trying to be a distraction?"

I giggled and sat back to play the next round. Sergei's two pairs didn't stand a chance against my three eights, and I did a little jig. "Shirt's coming off!"

Sergei's gray thermal shirt showed off the contours of his lean muscles, and as he pulled it over his head, the view became even more delicious. I'd teased him about being an old man when he'd turned thirty the previous year, but twenty-year-olds wished they had his body. I sighed and resisted reaching out to run my hands through his short golden brown hair, across his sculpted shoulders, down his firm chest…. *Stay focused on the game!*

Sergei shuffled the cards, and luck turned back in his direction as he easily won the next round. I huffed and removed my camisole, careful not to knock off my hat.

"Now we're almost even," he said, looking me over as he

dished out new cards.

"Not exactly. I have four items left to your two."

"Not for long." His eyebrows danced.

Branches of the big elm tree next to the townhouse rapped against the siding, and I sent a worried glance toward the large picture window. Sergei squeezed my foot. "It'll all be over tomorrow."

I gave him a little smile and concentrated hard on my cards, swapping three and trying not to smile when I received the new ones. Sergei placed his on the beige carpet for me to see. They were full of red hearts.

"Let's see you beat a flush," he said.

I made an exaggerated pout and then turned it into a wide grin. "Four of a kind!" I declared, fanning out my cards next to his.

He gaped at me, and I threw my head back with laughter. "Pants coming off!"

Sergei wore a half-annoyed, half-amused look as he stood. I rested my elbows behind me, reclining so I could take in all six feet of him. He popped open the button of his faded jeans and removed them at a teasingly slow pace. In nothing but his gray boxer briefs, he looked like a Calvin Klein underwear model. Only heart-stoppingly better.

"If you need help staying warm, I'd be happy to oblige," I said.

He returned to sitting across from me. "You're trying to distract me again."

"I just want to 'take care of my husband,'" I said with a sweet smile.

After another shuffle and a few quiet moments of decision-making, we readied to play our hands again, and my poker face threatened to crack. I had a good feeling I was about to do one of my favorite things — win.

Sergei spread his cards and announced in a confident tone, "Full house."

I shook my head. "You're making this too easy."

With a flourish, I presented my handful of diamonds. "Royal flush."

Sergei peered at me. "Are you hiding cards in your back pockets?"

I gasped in indignation. "I don't cheat. I won fair and square and now it's time for you to pay up, my love."

He took his time rising to his feet and then pointed to his briefs. "You want these off?"

I nodded and hummed in response.

He gave me a slow, sexy smile. "Then you have to take them off."

Desire burned deep within me, and I stood to face him. Lightly touching my fingertips to his chest, I trailed them down his smooth skin to his hard stomach. His eyes didn't leave mine, thrilling me with their passion.

I slid my thumbs inside the waistband of his shorts and whispered in his ear, "You just made my victory even sweeter."

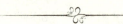

MY EYES FLUTTERED OPEN at the sound of music, and I hit the off button on the clock radio beside the bed. The music continued, and I realized it was Saturday morning and the noise was Sergei's cell ringtone. Slipping out of his warm embrace, I reached farther across the nightstand to grab the phone. The slight movement resounded in my head and made me wince, and visions of an empty wine bottle and scattered cards and clothing flashed through my memory. I picked up the phone and squinted at the small screen.

"Logan?" I muttered to myself before answering hoarsely, "Hey, what's up?"

"Em, I'm at the rink. The fire department called me."

My heart leapt into my throat, and I sat up straight. Next

to me, Sergei stirred under the blanket.

Logan breathed deeply over the line. "The roof caved in. Em, the rink is destroyed."

# CHAPTER TWO

I POPPED TWO TYLENOL CAPSULES INTO my mouth and washed them down with a gulp of water. The dull ache in my head had been worsened by Logan's grim news. Our rink, the place I considered my second home, was in shambles.

The stairs creaked, and Sergei appeared in the doorway of the kitchen with his cell phone in hand. "I talked to Logan, and it's probably going to take months to finish the repairs. I'm making some calls, seeing what our options are."

"None of the other rinks on the Cape have the ice time we need."

"I know, we're going to have to look a bit further. I'm calling around Boston, and Peter and Natalia are calling Providence."

Aubrey and Nick's married coaching duo were the only other coaches at our rink with elite-level skaters, so it made sense they were also anxious to find a temporary home.

I set the glass of water on the counter and massaged my left temple. "Boston and Providence would both be long commutes for everyone to make every day, especially when the weather could be iffy. We can't afford to lose practice time because of people getting stuck in traffic or stranded by snow storms."

"Those rinks are really our only options, though. The ones here on the Cape aren't set up for the level of training we do."

"This is just... unbelievable. One month from nationals, two months from the Olympics, and we don't have a place to skate."

Sergei joined me at the sink and swallowed me in a warm hug. I rested against his soft sweater and breathed in his fresh-from-the-shower scent.

"We'll find a place." He stroked my hair. "Might have to make some adjustments the next few months, but it wouldn't be an Olympic season if we didn't have drama, right?"

I smiled halfheartedly. When Sergei and I had started dating, we'd kept our relationship secret because the U.S. Figure Skating Federation wouldn't have approved of it. They eventually found out and threatened to suspend Sergei from his coaching duties for violating the Code of Ethics. After the 2002 Olympics, the Ethics Committee ruled in Sergei's favor, but the ordeal had made the weeks surrounding the Games a nightmare of stress.

"At least this time you're not in danger of losing your job and your whole career," I said.

"That's right. This is easy stuff compared to that." Sergei kissed the top of my head. "We'll figure it out, Em."

I gave him a peck on the lips and climbed up the four flights of stairs to our bedroom. I loved the townhouse, my parents' summer home that they'd been letting us use, but I was looking forward to living in a place with fewer levels. As soon as I retired from skating, Sergei and I planned to buy our own home, and my parents could finally have their summer retreat back.

Before I entered the bedroom, I stopped across the hall and took a peek through the glass doors to the terrace. Piles of snow hid the wrought-iron patio furniture, and not an inch of the knotted wood floor was visible. Thankfully, the sky was clear, so the storm seemed to have passed as predicted. But not before ruining a very special place in my life. My heart grew heavy thinking about what the destruction at the rink must look like.

I walked through the bedroom to the bathroom and stared at the blue eyes watching me in the mirror. The closer we got to the Olympics, the more anxiety crept into them. After coming so close to winning four years ago, I wanted to turn silver into gold so badly. It was what I thought about every time my legs felt like hundred-pound weights after triple run-throughs, when I had to push through a long and grueling workout in the gym, when my entire body ached from practicing a new jump combination over and over.

I pulled the ponytail holder from my hair and let the dark blonde waves fall over my shoulders. I needed to focus on one challenge at a time, the first being Grand Prix Final. Winning in Tokyo wouldn't guarantee a gold medal at the Olympics, but I'd feel more confident about our chances. And any competition where Chris and I could defeat our arch rivals Madeline and Damien was a joyous occasion.

A long, hot shower eased some of the tension in my body. Leaving my hair wet to air dry, I put on a T-shirt and a pair of yoga pants and went to find Sergei. He was sitting on the sofa with his computer on his lap, typing amazingly quickly with just his index fingers.

"Any luck with the calls?" I asked as I gathered the playing cards still strewn over the carpet.

He punched one more key and looked up. "Skating Club of Boston is taking us in. I was just emailing all my students the schedule there."

"Wow, going back to my old rink. Never thought I'd train there again."

"They were happy to help. Said as soon as we get back

from Tokyo, Peter and Natalia and I can bring all our teams."

"What about the drive? We'll have to leave before the crack of dawn to get there for the morning session."

Sergei pushed up the sleeves of his sweater. "I was thinking about that. Doesn't your Uncle Joe have some furnished rental apartments in the city? Maybe there's a vacant one we can use."

My heart leapt at the glimmer of hope. "I can call him. I wish he'd have two open so Chris could have a place, too. And then there's Aubrey and Nick…"

"We'll have to see what we can find for all of us. Most of my kids won't have a choice but to make the drive since they're in school here."

I packed the deck of cards into their box and gave Sergei a thoughtful look as I moved to the couch. "We could stay with my parents if we need to."

His eyebrows arched. "For months?"

"You get along great with them. And we can come home on the weekends."

"Sure, we get along, but living with people is a different situation. Your dad would be easy, but you know how particular your mom is… and how nosy."

"I'd make sure she respects our space."

"Don't forget Liza will be with us for two weeks. She'll need her own space, too."

I hadn't forgotten that it was our year to spend the holidays with Sergei's eleven-year-old daughter. She lived with her mother Elena, Sergei's former skating partner, in New York, and we spent as many weekends and holidays with her as possible.

"My mom and dad love Liza. They'd be glad to have her, too. She could use the guest room, and we could sleep in my old room."

Sergei stared at the laptop screen, not appearing convinced. "Let's see what your uncle says first."

AUBREY STEPPED INTO THE townhouse and wrapped her arms around Em. "Can you believe this craziness?"

Em returned her hug with a firm grip. She might be petite, but she had some serious strength.

"It's totally nuts," she said.

Chris shut the front door behind him. "So, we're Team Boston now?"

"We'll always be Team Cape Cod," Aubrey said.

She and Chris draped their jackets over the banister, and they all took the steps up to the living room, where Sergei was texting on his phone. Em sat in her favorite oversized chair while Sergei perched on one of the pillowy arms.

"I talked to Uncle Joe," Em said. "He has one apartment available in Back Bay that he said we can use for free. It has two bedrooms and a sofa bed."

"You're thinking we can all live there?" Aubrey asked as she and Chris sat on the couch.

"No way." Chris shook his head. "Em, I love ya. Sergei, I'd walk through a wall for you, man, but I do not want to be all up in your private business."

Em laughed. "It's not like we'll be doing our private business in the living room."

Sergei turned to her with a grin. "Well, last night…"

She slapped his thigh, and Aubrey snorted.

Chris held up his hands, palms outward. "Way too much info."

"I think Chris has a good point," Aubrey said. "I wouldn't want to live with Nick. He already got an offer to crash at a friend's place anyway."

Chris propped his boot up on his knee. "I just think we should keep some separation. We don't need to be getting on each other's nerves at this stage of the game."

Em leaned her head back against the chair and looked up

at Sergei. "I guess we have to go to Plan B then. You and I move in with my parents."

Sergei could barely hide his grimace. Knowing how overbearing Em's mom Laura could be, Aubrey didn't blame him for being less than thrilled.

"So, we get the apartment?" Chris asked.

"If you two don't mind sharing the space," Em said.

Aubrey tilted her chin upward and peered at Chris. "You don't have any weird habits, do you? Like sleepwalking… watching The Weather Channel for entertainment…"

"I'm the most perfect roommate you could ever ask for," Chris said with his palm pressed to his broad chest.

She laughed. Having Chris's humor around might be exactly what she needed with the stressful months coming up. And she'd shared a bathroom with her brother growing up, so she was used to messy boys.

"This'll be good," she said. "I can monitor your playboy progress. The pool of eligible women will be much larger in Boston."

Chris pointed at her. "Way to find the upside to all this."

"I don't even want to know," Em said.

Sergei's eyes were focused on the carpet, and he didn't seem to be paying much attention to their banter. He rubbed his chin and shifted slightly on the chair.

"Maybe we can find a place to rent that's not too expensive," he said to Em.

"Anything short term will be pricey. Why waste money that we can use for a down payment on a house when we can stay with my parents for free?"

Aubrey sensed tension between them and didn't want to stick around for the potential argument. She rose to her feet.

"I need to get home and take a nap… try to get myself on Tokyo time. You'll thank Uncle Joe for me?"

Em stood and nodded. "He said the apartment has everything — furniture, kitchen stuff, towels — so when we get back, you can move right in."

Chris got up and gave Em a quick hug. "Thank him for me too."

They made their way out to Chris's truck, and he pumped up the heater. "Good call getting us out of there. There's nothing more awkward than watching a couple fight."

Aubrey faced the window. "Yeah, I've seen enough of that with my parents."

Chris paused as he put the truck in reverse, and Aubrey turned and saw concern in his eyes. She hadn't meant to get all personal, so she hastily said, "Why don't we drive by the rink and see how it looks."

Chris's gaze lingered on her a moment before he curved the steering wheel and shifted into drive. "Sure."

They traveled down Route Six to South Dennis, noting the signs and trees that had toppled in the storm. When they came upon the turn for the rink parking lot, they were halted by barricades and yellow caution tape. Chris pulled the truck onto the shoulder of the road, and Aubrey slid out the driver's side behind him since a mountain of snow sat outside her door.

Trees hid the building from view, so they walked around the barricades and down the partially-cleared driveway until they reached the edge of the parking lot. Aubrey gasped and Chris whispered, "Whoa."

The front part of the building, which housed the skate shop and snack bar, was still intact. But the two-story section behind it had completely collapsed. Roof, walls, everything. It was a heap of tangled wires, mangled beams, and broken glass.

"Our ice is under there," Aubrey said quietly.

Chris slid his arm around her shoulders, and they stood in silence for a minute, staring at the wreckage. The lot was so quiet, and she imagined how loud the cracking of wood and glass must've been when the snow had crashed through the roof.

"I forgot my favorite sneakers in my locker," Chris said. "I was gonna come and get 'em today."

"I think you'll need to get a new pair," she said, still gaping at the scene.

They both got quiet again. She looked back and forth from the untouched front exterior to the area that looked like it had been hit with a bomb.

"Twelve years here." She shook her head as she thought back to her early days as an ice dancer. "I was such a little brat when I first came here to train."

"You?" Chris spat out a puff of air.

"Hard to believe, I know."

Chris let his arm drop, and he shoved his hands into his jacket. "I skated longer in Delaware, but it feels like I've been at this rink forever. It sucks we won't be able to finish out our careers here."

Even though Aubrey was leaning toward retiring at the end of the season, she felt a pang of dread over the impending end of her career. Sure, she and Nick would still have the Ice Champions tour next summer and maybe a few other shows in the future, but for the most part, she'd be out of the skating world. The only world she'd known since she competed in her first event at age seven.

It wasn't time to say goodbye yet, though. There was still the matter of winning an Olympic medal, and she wasn't going to let a snowstorm white-out her plans.

*Boston, here we come.*

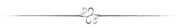

I LISTENED FOR THE click of the front door shutting and then trained my eyes on Sergei. "Why are you so opposed to this?"

"If we can find something reasonably priced, why not consider it?" he countered.

He hadn't answered my question, but I had a reply for his. "We're leaving tomorrow and won't be back for a week. We don't really have time to hunt for an apartment."

"I'll start now." He jumped up and dropped onto the sofa, opening his laptop on the coffee table.

A long sigh escaped my lips. When Sergei became fixated on an idea, it was hard to slow him down, but I wasn't going to let him run away with this.

"If we want our dream house on the water, we're going to need every last penny we can save. I just don't want to throw away money we don't have to."

Sergei pulled his attention away from the computer. "We have a good amount saved already."

"It's not just the money. Think about the convenience. My parents' house is five minutes from the rink. We don't know in what part of the city we'll be able to find an apartment. Or what the place will be like. With my parents it'll be nice and quiet and easy to go to sleep early and get up early. No noisy neighbors, no driving around looking for a spot to park, no traffic jams."

Sergei sat back and raked his fingers through hair. Spreading his arm over the top of the big chenille pillows, he said, "Do you remember the weekend last summer we stayed at their house for the Red Sox-Yankees game? Your mom got aggravated when I didn't clean her blender good enough. And every time we left the house, she asked where we were going and when we'd be back. The only person allowed to ask me that is you."

"I'll talk to her and ask her to give us room to breathe." I slid over to the couch and settled into the crook of Sergei's shoulder. "We'll have the whole upstairs to ourselves, and it can be like our own little apartment. We can escape up there and have total privacy."

I rubbed my hand across his firm stomach and gave him my best wide-eyed, hopeful look. His forehead crinkled as he appeared to ponder my argument for a long minute. Finally, he said, "Laura does make a killer breakfast."

"I guarantee she will get up extra early to make baked pancetta and egg frittatas for you. You know her favorite thing in the world to do is cook for guests."

Sergei curled his arm around me. "If that's where you'll be most comfortable, then I'll do it for you."

"Thank you." I reached up and kissed him tenderly.

"But if your mom makes one crack about where I'm going, what I'm eating… how I do my laundry… I won't be responsible for what I might say."

# CHAPTER THREE

AUBREY SIPPED HER SPARKLING WATER AND scanned the hotel ballroom. The Japanese Skating Union knew how to put on first-class skating events, and they'd outdone themselves for the opening reception of the Grand Prix Final. The skaters, coaches, and officials had been served an elaborate meal of sushi and seafood, and each large round table in the room was decorated with lavish cherry blossom centerpieces. Surrounding the centerpiece on her table were four small American flags.

"The German team needs a major fashion makeover," Nick said next to her, his gaze focused on a couple two tables to their left. "Sarah's boots are too casual for that dress, and Kristian's jacket is ten times too big. I just want to get him to a tailor pronto."

Aubrey shook her head in amusement and checked out her partner's own appearance. His black suit fit his lean physique perfectly, and his emerald tie brought out the green flecks in his hazel eyes. Just the right amount of gel spiked his charcoal-colored hair. His suit could be Armani, but she knew it wasn't. Nick had a knack for making clothes look expensive.

"Your next career should be stylist to the skaters," she said.

He paused with his lips on the edge of his wine glass. "I would *own* that job."

He totally would. She'd skated with him for twelve years and had been trying to keep up with him fashion-wise just as long. When they'd teamed up as twelve-year-olds, she'd crushed hard on him until she saw how excited he was over their sparkly costumes. She'd realized then that ship was never going to sail.

"Should we go mingle?" she asked. Most of the other members of the American delegation, including Em and Chris, had started making the rounds. And if she was moving around the room, she could avoid Damien Wakefield more easily.

"My *Project Runway* commentary isn't entertaining enough for you?" Nick asked.

"I don't want to be accused of being anti-social." She pushed back her chair and stood. "Do I have anything in my teeth?" She gave Nick a wide-mouthed grin.

He stood beside her, less than a head taller since she wore four-inch heels. His eyes squinted as he examined her face and then swept down over her strapless, royal blue silk dress.

"You look magnificently gorgeous as always."

He held out his arm, and she smiled and hooked hers around it.

They made their way to the group of Japanese skaters, and Nick whipped out his small digital camera, insisting they pose for photos with each athlete. As Aubrey vigorously nodded thanks to the reigning ladies' world champion, she spotted Damien heading in their direction. His long strides would have him in her face in about five seconds.

She gripped Nick's elbow and turned him away from the crowd. "Walk. *Now.*"

He gave her a quizzical look. "What's up with—"

"Aubrey!" Damien came up alongside and then circled in front of her. His dark eyes did a quick head-to-toe appraisal of her as he opened his arms. "You weren't going to say hello?"

He pulled her into a hug, and a whiff of his sweet cologne brought her back to the night she wished had never happened. She lightly pushed on his jacket to regain her personal space.

"Lots of people to see," she said crisply.

Damien turned to Nick and slapped his arm. "How's it goin'?"

Nick gave him a smirk. "Peachy."

"We need to catch up to Em and Chris, so…" Aubrey tried to step around Damien, but he blocked her. He wasn't a big, muscular guy, but his confident posture made him just as imposing.

"Anytime you wanna hang out this weekend, I'm game," he said, his gaze wandering to her chest before reconnecting with her eyes.

Her face burned, and she took a deep breath. Fighting to keep her voice quiet, she said, "I told you that's never going to happen again, so get out of my face."

She brushed past him without any opposition that time. Nick fell in step with her and leaned his head close to hers. "Tell me again how much tequila you had that night?"

"If you hadn't left me in the bar to go to sleep at such an early hour, you would've been there to stop me from making the dumbest mistake of my life."

"How was I supposed to know you were going to hook up with that jerk? You can't stand him."

"Well, after six tequila shots, I guess his cockiness somehow became appealing." She looked anxiously at a nearby group of coaches. "Can we not talk about this anymore?"

Nick was the only person who knew about the unfortunate incident at the Grand Prix event in Paris four weeks ago, and the only reason he did was he'd caught her doing the walk of shame the next morning.

"I'm taking it to the grave." He pretended to zip his lips.

She snuck a look back at Damien. What were the odds *he* would take it to the grave? He'd probably already blabbed to the whole Canadian team.

Em and Chris walked up, and Em noticed where Aubrey's attention had been. "Did you see what Damien said in an interview today? It was ridiculous even for him."

Chris fiddled with the knot of his burgundy tie. "I don't know why you're surprised by anything that punk says."

"Because he's reached an all-time high in delusion. He said he and Maddy are the favorites here, and they're setting a 'new artistic standard' in the sport." Em mimicked him with a snooty voice. "Seriously? First of all, we've beaten them at Worlds the last two years, so I think that makes *us* the favorites, and second, what's so artistically special about skating to *Swan Lake*? It's only been done a gazillion times before."

Aubrey pretended to scrutinize her candy-apple-red-painted nails. Em would be appalled if she knew she'd hooked up with Damien. Even with the alcohol excuse.

"He's just going to look like a fool when you guys win again," Nick said.

"We *have* to win. I cannot sit next to him at the press conference and listen to him gloat." Em scrunched her face in disgust.

"What's worse?" Nick asked. "Him being a public jerk or Maddy, who acts all sweet with the media but is a total witch to everyone else?"

"I can put up with Maddy," Chris said. "She just flirts with me, and I ignore her."

"She's not a witch to the guys," Em said. "Only the girls. She hardly talks to us and when she does, it's to say something ugly. She and Damien really are perfect for each other. They both think they're all that."

Aubrey shifted from one heel to another. She wanted to get out of this conversation. Just hearing a certain name made her stomach turn as if she was downing the tequila all over again.

"Let's go get some more pictures for your MySpace." She looped her arm through Nick's to urge him along. "People might start leaving soon."

Nick saluted Em and Chris and followed her toward the French delegation. "Is Damien the reason you hid out in your room the past two days? Or did you really not feel well?"

"I didn't feel well because I knew I was going to see him," she muttered.

Nick stopped and faced her. "And now you have seen him, and he got his little innuendo in, and you told him where to shove it. I think he got the message."

Over Nick's shoulder she caught a glimpse of Damien staring at her. He winked, and she quickly turned her head. Shooting him down once wasn't going to be enough. Not with his ego. He was going to keep making comments and giving her those stupid knowing looks.

She was never going to drink another drop of alcohol again.

I ROLLED MY SKATE bag through the revolving glass door and entered the packed hotel lobby. Japanese skating fans were among the most enthusiastic in the world, and large groups of them occupied the lobby at all hours, waiting to take photos or give us gifts. They treated us like rock stars. It was unlike anything we experienced in the U.S.

"Emily! Chris!" voices exclaimed from multiple directions.

Females of all ages descended upon us, offering us congratulations on winning the short program earlier that evening. I still wore my small gold medal since we'd hurried from the backstage ceremony to the shuttle bus.

"We take photo?" one lady asked as she held up her camera.

"Sure," Chris and I answered at the same time.

"Em, I'll take your bag upstairs." Sergei reached for the handle.

The lady frantically waved her hand at him. "You get in photo, too."

"No, no, they're the stars."

I curled my arm around Sergei's waist and nudged him to my side. "Get in here. You deserve the love."

He chuckled, and the three of us smiled through an endless stream of camera flashes. Between the bright bursts of light, I saw Damien and Maddy enter the mayhem, and the fans that had gotten their mementos of us drifted over to them.

After the last flash popped, we moved through the crowd, collecting gifts and doing our best to converse with everyone who approached us. With my arms full of gift bags and flowers, I stuck my pinky out to press the elevator button, and Chris and Sergei broke through the masses just as the doors opened.

Sergei rolled my bag inside and pulled a folded packet of green papers from his coat pocket. "I was looking at the protocols on the bus. You only got level two on the footwork."

Ah, the protocols, the tell-all document of our scores in the new Code of Points system. The paper showed both our technical and presentation marks, now called "Program Component Scores" or PCS for short. It gave the nitty-gritty detail of each element we performed — the difficulty levels the technical panel determined we achieved and the grades of execution awarded by the judges. Since the scoring system had been instituted two years ago, we'd had to become mathematicians to choreograph our programs.

I leaned toward Sergei and studied the lines of numbers

as he flipped between our page and Maddy and Damien's. Only one point separated our total scores.

"Their PCS are higher than ours?" I narrowed my eyes. "We had more than a point higher than them at Worlds."

Sergei licked his thumb and paged to the third-place team. "As much as the system has changed, the judges still play the same games."

The elevator dinged for our floor, and we exited into the hallway. Modern light fixtures guided our way down the quiet, spotless corridor.

Sergei stopped in front of Chris's door and folded the protocols in half. "We need to talk strategy for tomorrow."

Chris fumbled with his gifts as he extracted his room key from his back pocket. He slid the card into the lock and pushed open the door with his shoulder. "Come in before I drop all this."

He piled his loot on the desk while I set mine on the king-sized bed. I'd hung out in Chris's room at competitions many times, so the mess surrounding us didn't faze me, but it always amused me. The open boxes of PowerBars spilling onto the TV cabinet, the clothes thrown over the chair and ottoman, the half-empty water bottles all over the nightstand and the desk... it was as if the maid hadn't visited in a week.

Sergei pushed aside the jeans and T-shirts on the ottoman to clear a space to sit. He bent forward slightly and rested his elbows on his knees as he looked up at Chris and me. "I think we should put in the quad Salchow."

I sat on the bed, and Chris dropped down beside me. "We've been completing it about what... seventy percent in practice?" he asked.

"I don't know if it's worth the risk," I said.

I'd landed the four-revolution throw jump on two shaky feet at the Grand Prix event in China, but I'd splatted on it at Skate America. No pair had ever done it cleanly in competition. The top Chinese team was the only other couple attempting it.

"Even if you fall, with the crazy way the system is, you'd still earn enough points to make it worthwhile," Sergei said.

I pulled my legs up onto the bed to curl them under me. "A fall disrupts the program, though. I just think it might be better to leave it out and focus on skating clean."

"I don't know, Em." Chris scratched his hand through his thick hair. "I'm with Sergei on this. We need to show we're not afraid to take the risk when we're facing our toughest competition. Let them know they have to step it up to match us."

"Exactly." Sergei pointed at Chris. "It's all about setting the tone right now. If you land it or even just come close, then when you face them at the Olympics, they'll feel that extra pressure. They'll know they need to be perfect to have a chance to beat you."

Everything they said made sense, but we didn't have as much room for error in the free skate as I'd expected. I stared at the diamond pattern on the carpet. "I thought we weren't going to do the Sal here unless we had a bigger lead after the short."

"You're getting more consistent every day." Sergei's encouraging voice lifted my head. "You've only fallen three times this whole week of practice. I want you to do it again in competition so you'll get even more comfortable with it."

"The way I see it is go hard or go home," Chris said. "Maddy and Damien's scores are creeping up on ours. We can't sit back and let them pass us. We have to put it all out there."

I was clearly outnumbered. Sergei never made decisions about our skating without careful deliberation, so I had to believe he was making the right call. I just couldn't shake the thought that this one element might cost us a victory, and I hated losing. Especially to Maddy and Damien.

Sergei stood and leaned against the desk in front of me.

"Do you feel good about it, Em?"

I looked back and forth from him to Chris. They were both watching me with expectation in their eyes. I was the one who had to spin four times in the air and land on a thin piece of metal, so my confidence was key. Any self-doubt needed to be squashed now if we were going to make history.

I slowly raised my hand toward Chris for a high-five. "Go hard or go home."

# CHAPTER FOUR

A STEADY HUM OF NOISE BUZZED around Aubrey as she paced backstage, but she was totally tuned into thoughts of her upcoming skate. Only a few minutes remained before she and Nick had to take the ice for their free dance. Sitting in third place after the original dance, they were right where they'd hoped they'd be — in position to claim their second consecutive Grand Prix Final medal.

"Hey, soon-to-be roomie," Chris said as he came out of the skaters' lounge. He squeezed her shoulder. "Good luck out there."

She inhaled and exhaled a long breath. "Thanks."

"You guys are gonna kick ice. No question."

She smiled and patted the front of his navy Team USA jacket. "That's the plan."

She turned to pick up her water bottle from the chair behind her and found herself caught in Damien's gaze. His eyes wouldn't let go as he sauntered across the corridor.

Aubrey whipped around and faced Chris. "You and Em need to kick some *major* ice tonight."

Chris's brown eyes darkened as he shot a glare toward

Damien. "That is most definitely the plan."

Nick emerged from the locker room, where he'd gone to do one last hair check. He and Chris tapped knuckles and exchanged good luck wishes before he followed Aubrey toward the ice entrance. Their coaches Peter and Natalia waited with encouraging smiles.

"Can you hold this?" Aubrey handed Natalia her water bottle and removed her warm-up jacket, revealing her glittering purple dress.

Natalia swapped the bottle for the jacket and draped it over her arm, continuing to give Aubrey a quiet smile. Peter and Natalia were demanding but not cruel like their former coach Viktor. When Viktor had been banned from coaching after trying to force himself on both Emily and her, Peter and Natalia had moved from California to take his place. They'd shown Nick and her that coaches could be both strict and nurturing.

"It's time," Peter said, letting Nick and Aubrey go ahead of him to the ice.

They stepped out into the arena, and the bright lights hit them. Aubrey's pulse rate ramped up a few more notches. There wasn't an empty seat in the building, and the crowd was on its feet for the German team currently in fourth place.

*The pressure is on.*

Nick rolled his shoulders under his blousy purple shirt and then did a few knee bends and quick bounces on his skate guards. His antsy behavior had made her nervous when they were kids, but over the years she'd become more than used to it.

The Germans exited the ice, and Aubrey and Nick hopped on hand-in-hand. As they circled the rink to keep their legs warm, the announcer rattled off the scores, a series of numbers Aubrey could barely decipher. That was one of the good things about the new scoring system. Hearing the marks of other teams now wasn't nearly as intimidating as the days when "6.0!" was bellowed through the arena.

Nick guided her over to their coaches at the boards, and Natalia patted their hands. "Aubrey, you are beautiful flower. Nicholas, you are powerful stem. You present her beauty to the world."

Aubrey smiled and let Natalia's poetic words seep into her mind. *Beauty, power, strength.* Those were the keys to a successful free dance.

She and Nick glided to center ice, where he bent on one knee and she draped herself forward over his back. When the third beat of Beethoven's Seventh Symphony sounded, Nick rose, lifting Aubrey with him. They took their time settling into the music before they approached the first difficult element — the combination lift.

*Beauty, power, strength,* she reminded herself.

Nick picked her up, and she set one skate on his thigh as he glided in a straight line down the ice. Aubrey stood tall and focused on extending down to her fingertips, striking a statuesque pose. She felt like she was the mast of a ship. Dropping into Nick's arms, she closed her eyes as he whirled her in circles, swirling the cold air around her in a chilly blur.

Nick set her down, and she tossed her head back for both dramatic effect and to whip her long hair out of her face. They transitioned into traditional ballroom hold and powered into the serpentine footwork sequence, the most physically demanding element. Every turn had to be crisp, every edge perfectly placed in order to attain the highest score possible.

Aubrey pushed deeper into the ice, trying to ignore the growing burn in her quad muscles. They were almost finished with the sequence, having traveled the full length of the rink. Soon they could take a quick breather with a choreographed rest.

The crowd applauded the footwork but turned quiet as the music slowed, and she and Nick relaxed along with the melody. They floated through the steps, and a rejuvenating shot of adrenaline boosted her energy. She felt strong, ready to tackle the rest of the program.

One by one they ticked off the remaining elements, eliciting louder applause upon each lift and twizzle. With only the final rotational lift to go, Aubrey pulled in a deep breath and stretched her left leg onto Nick's shoulder. He pressed her up into the air and started to spin with her in a full split position.

Nick grunted, and she felt his feet wobbling as they rotated at rapid speed. At any moment they might spin out of control, and she had visions of herself flying off into the audience. She clutched her arm tighter around his neck and squeezed her eyes shut.

*Hang on, Nick!*

He steadied himself while coming out of the rotation, and he set her down gently, although with less flair than he usually presented. She heard him exhale, and they quickly twirled into their ending pose, arms outstretched toward each other.

Nick's eyebrows rose with a we-just-averted-disaster look, and he grabbed her into a long hug.

"That was a little scary," she said above the crowd's cheers.

"Totally off balance," he said between catching his breath.

"I'm just glad I didn't end up in someone's lap."

They parted to take their bows while gifts poured onto the ice. Skating around the flowers and stuffed animals, they met Peter and Natalia at the ice door and exchanged hugs and double-cheek kisses.

"Good save on the lift." Peter nodded to Nick.

"No way was I going down," he said and sat on the white couch in the kiss and cry, where they'd wait for the scores.

Aubrey plucked a tissue from the box beside the couch and sat next to Nick. Peter and Natalia flanked them and immediately began analyzing the replay on the monitor. As

Aubrey blotted the perspiration on her forehead, she watched the slow-motion video of the final lift and realized just how close Nick had been to losing his footing.

The announcer came over the sound system, and the crowd hushed to hear the score. Again, the numbers meant little to her. She trained her eyes on the spot on the monitor where the placement would be shown. With the top two teams left to skate, she wanted to see the number one.

"… for a total score of one hundred and fifty point four four!" the enthusiastic Japanese announcer boomed. "They are currently in first place!"

"Yeah!" Nick cried and pulled her into an embrace.

She pumped her fist against his back. They were guaranteed a medal, which would boost their résumé ahead of their big showdown with Marley and Zach at nationals. Prior results weren't supposed to factor into the judges' marks, but everyone knew they did. She and Nick had proven they could stand on the podium with the best in the world. Now they just needed to back it up with great skates in St. Louis.

They exited backstage, and Em flew toward Aubrey with her arms open. "You were amazing!"

"It got a little dicey near the end," Aubrey said, returning her hug.

"I knew Nick would hold it together. He's a rock, just like Chris."

"That's right. Partners of the Year right here." Nick pointed to himself and Chris, who'd joined their celebration.

"The year?" Chris corrected him. "How about the century?"

Em let out a single laugh. "It's sad how little self-confidence you guys have."

The federation's media coordinator beckoned Aubrey and Nick toward the "mixed zone," the gathering area for the journalists, so Aubrey gave Em's hands a quick squeeze.

"You're gonna kill it tonight. I'll be out there screaming

like mad for you."

"And then we'll party it up," Nick added as they backed away. "Drinks on me!"

THREE HOURS LATER, CHRIS and I wore our game faces as we prepared to take the ice for our six-minute warm-up. Well, Chris wore his version of a game face, which was always an inexplicably calm smile. In our seven years together, he'd helped me become less manic before a performance, but I still hadn't figured out how to achieve his level of serenity.

"From the United States — Emily Butler and Christopher Grayden!"

We shot off across the ice, stroking in tandem behind Maddy and Damien. Every time I heard my maiden name used, I questioned why I let our agent Kristin talk me into keeping it for professional purposes. My legal surname was Petrov, but Kristin thought I should use Butler for an "All-American" image. I just kept reminding myself how much our endorsement money was helping my dream house fund.

With our legs sufficiently warm, we set up for the side-by-side triple Lutzes, and I narrowed my thoughts to envision the perfect jump. Chris and I glided backward and simultaneously jabbed into the ice with our right toepicks, vaulting ourselves into the air. I spun three times and landed on one foot, wincing as my knee throbbed from the impact.

Chris had also completed his jump cleanly, and he smiled and reached for my hand. "Ready for the throw?"

My stomach danced with anxiousness. I'd landed the quad Salchow twice at practice that morning, but I'd also crashed once on my right knee, which tomorrow would be the same color as my black velvet dress.

*Think positively. You can do this.*

The Canadians and the Chinese team were on the

opposite end of the rink, so Chris and I ramped up speed and executed an easy throw double Salchow to get comfortable with the timing. As we skated past Sergei at the boards, he nodded and smiled, and I sped up the pep talk in my head. *Sergei believes in you. Chris believes in you. Trust in yourself.*

We threaded through the traffic of the other two pairs, and Chris set his hands on my hips, preparing for the take-off of the throw. In one quick motion, I swung my right leg forward and around, and Chris propelled me upward. The crowd became a blur as I pulled my arms tight to my chest and did four revolutions. I sensed the ground coming too fast, too soon, and my heart pounded in my ears. My crossed feet hitting the ice confirmed my fear. I couldn't stand up straight.

My rear end slammed into the ice, and I slid toward the boards, hitting the wooden barrier with a loud thud. Pain vibrated through my ribs and down my spine.

Chris bent over me and offered his hands. "You okay?"

He pulled me up, and I went to rub my back but saw Maddy and Damien eyeing me as they skated past us. I stood up straighter.

"Yeah, I just need a minute."

We skated slowly along the boards until we reached Sergei. He handed me my water bottle and leaned toward me. His eyes didn't blink as he stared into mine. "Are you alright?"

I took a quick drink and nodded. All eyes in the audience were on me, and I wasn't going to show them any sign of pain. Chris brushed a patch of ice from my filmy skirt, and I checked my stockings for any more evidence of the crash. After patting a bit of water from my thighs, I did a series of squats and stretches to shake off the ache in my back.

Chris glanced up at the clock on the scoreboard. "Should we run through one or two of the lifts?"

"No, just take the last minute to cool down," Sergei said. "You had a great practice this morning."

The faces in the crowd gave me concerned looks as I stroked around the rink. When the clock ticked down to zero, I scooted off the ice and snapped my skate guards over my blades before heading backstage. Sergei draped my team jacket over my shoulders and looped his arm around me.

"How's your back?"

"It's feeling better."

The right side of my ribs screamed a different response, but I knew my body, and I'd skated through worse falls. I could get through a four-minute program.

Time dragged at an agonizing rate as we waited for our turn to skate. I paced back and forth in a straight line between Sergei and Chris, blocking out their idle chatter. Our choreography ran through my mind, and I tried to channel the emotion of each move. Sergei and I had created the program together one night at the rink when we'd had the ice all to ourselves. We'd played the entire thirty-seven minutes of Rachmaninov's Piano Concerto No. 2 and just skated around, feeling where the music took us, finding the right stanzas to explore. Every second of the program had meaning to me, and I wanted to perform it perfectly every time Chris and I skated.

Our team leader motioned to Sergei, so he ushered Chris and me rinkside. I faced away from the ice so I wouldn't see how Maddy and Damien were skating, but I couldn't shut out the loud cheers. The more I heard, the more jittery my legs became.

Chris stepped in front of me and grasped both of my hands. "We're gonna nail this."

I bobbed my head up and down, focusing on Chris's warm hands instead of the deafening applause surrounding us. *We can do this. We WILL do this.*

A minute later, we shed our skate guards and took the ice. Adrenaline dulled my back pain, and I zoomed around the rink, ears on alert for the Canadians' marks. I'd studied all the numbers, and I knew our top score for the season. Would

Maddy and Damien top it?

The announcer read the free skate score and then gave their combined total with the short program. My neck tensed. Two points higher than our season's best. We were going to have to land the quad to win.

I slowed my pace as Chris skated to my side. We stopped before Sergei, and he gave us a confident smile.

"You've improved this program at every competition, and you're ready to take it another step right here, right now."

Chris and I both took deep breaths, and Sergei locked eyes with each of us. "Show them your determination. Show them your hearts."

I gazed at him for a long moment, connecting with his confidence, and then I put my hand in Chris's. Our names were called, and the audience erupted with a long ovation. As the final skaters, we had the marquee position — the chance to close out the event with a bang. And hopefully not me banging into the wall again.

*No doubting yourself! You rule the ice tonight!*

Chris stood behind me and wrapped his arms around me for our opening pose. I covered his arms with mine, gripping the silky material of his white shirt. The first notes resonated through the arena, but we didn't move. Our stillness plus the intense piano set the mood we wanted.

Then we began.

We gained speed with just a few strokes, charging into our first element, the triple twist. Chris tossed me above his head, and I spun in a tight coil before falling into his strong catch. Continuing forward, we followed the rise of the music and hit our side-by-side triple Lutzes right on the highest note. The audience roared with approval, and we soared through the next few elements.

Soon the music would transition to the adagio movement of the concerto. But first we had to do the quad. As we made long, sweeping crossovers together, setting up for the throw, I played one image on a constant loop in my mind — my body flying through the air and landing with a perfect ride-out and a big smile.

*See it, believe it, achieve it!*

Chris pressed my hips and launched me up and away from him. I had so much air under me I felt like I'd exploded out of his hands. My four rotations were crisp and fast, and I loosened my legs, preparing for the landing. One foot met the ice, just like in my imagination, and a surge of excitement jolted through me.

*I've got it! We did it!*

I spread my arms wide to hold my balance, and I looked up at Chris skating toward me. His grin couldn't be any bigger. The knowledgeable Japanese fans realized they'd just witnessed history, and I could barely hear Chris above their noise.

"Stay focused," he said.

I wanted to jump up and down in celebration, but I had to compose myself. The slow section of the music would be a good time to do that. We paused at center ice and looked into each other's eyes, holding the moment as the tempo changed. It was my favorite part of the program, where I could get lost in the emotion of the music and the lyrical choreography and not have to think about the jumps.

But the rest didn't last long. We knocked out the side-by-side spins with decent unison and then sailed toward our jump combination. With identical movement, we picked into the ice for the triple toe loop. Up, down, and then up again we jumped into the easy double toe to complete the combination.

I smiled at Chris, and we quickly transitioned into the lasso lift. He swung me up over his head, and as I stretched my core muscles to stay upright, my sore ribs pulsed in response. I kept smiling, not letting the pain distract me. *Only one minute left!*

Adrenaline took over again and carried me through our

remaining elements. In the final seconds, we completed the death spiral and the crowd began to applaud, sensing the end. Their ovation drowned out the quiet piano. Chris slowly dipped me backward as if we were dancing, and we held the pose as the music faded away.

Everyone in the stands leapt to their feet, showering us with applause and gifts. I threw my arms around Chris's neck, and he hugged me so tightly my feet came off the ice.

"History, baby!" he cried.

I laughed and kissed his cheek. We separated to bow to the fans but then hugged each other again as we skated in Sergei's direction. He was clapping and beaming at us, and I couldn't wait to jump into his arms.

Sergei embraced me before I could step through the ice door. He placed one hand on the small of my back and the other over my curly up-do. I pressed my face to his neck, staining his white collar with my deep red lipstick.

"Best quad you've ever done," he said close to my ear. "You were amazing."

I pulled my head back to see his smiling face. His lips were so tantalizingly close, and I was so hyped up with excitement that it physically hurt not to kiss him. We'd agreed no PDA beyond hugs when we were in our coach and student roles, so I restrained myself and took a step backward.

Sergei and Chris hugged and then joined me in the colorful kiss and cry, decorated with both real flowers and large floral images on the backdrop. On the monitor, our quad throw kept repeating in slow motion from multiple angles. I peered at the small screen, watching my blade hit the ice over and over.

"They're taking a long time for the score," I said with a worried glance at Sergei. "Do you think they're checking if I got the full rotation?"

"You got it." Chris pointed at the video. "I can see it right there."

I fidgeted with the cross pendant on my silver chain. The judges had been very strict lately about devaluing under-rotated jumps, and they were probably being extra observant since this jump would go into the record books.

Chris put his arm around me, and we stared at the monitor, willing the marks to show. Every second that passed made me twitch more with anxiety.

A brief announcement in Japanese lifted my head. Then we heard in English, "The score please for Emily Butler and Christopher Grayden."

I clutched Sergei's forearm and he covered my hand with his. The announcer continued, "The technical score is seventy-one point two four. The program component score is sixty-three point three two. The total segment score for the free skate is one hundred and thirty-four point five six."

I let out a tiny squeak. Our number was higher than Maddy and Damien's! We'd gotten credit for the quad!

The total score with the short program was read, and the announcer belted, "They are in first place!"

Chris smothered me against his chest, and we rocked back and forth with giddiness. Standing to acknowledge the crowd, we turned in circles and waved to all corners of the arena. Sergei embraced each of us again and stood with his arms across our shoulders.

"This was a great skate," he said. "It's exactly where you should be at this point in the season."

Chris nodded. "We can get even better from here. Onward and upward to nationals."

"But not before we celebrate!" I said.

Sergei grinned. "Yes, you definitely deserve to enjoy this."

We moved backstage, where the Chinese team and our fellow American pair Candice and Shawn congratulated us with hugs. Maddy and Damien were in the mixed zone, and we didn't come face-to-face with them until later when they entered the media room for the press conference.

They sat in the two folding chairs beside me on the podium, and Maddy didn't utter a word. She'd untied her hair knot, and her long brown hair swept over one shoulder. Her red fleece jacket was zipped all the way up to her chin.

Damien pushed his chair further back from the long table and stretched out his legs. He turned his head slightly in my direction.

"Nice quad," he said nonchalantly, as if we'd done one of the easiest elements in the sport.

Maddy sat just inches from him, so I knew she'd heard him speak, but she continued to look anywhere but at Chris at me.

"Thanks," I said.

The bronze medalists, the Chinese pair, took the two spots to our left, and a writer from IceNet called out the first question, the usual one asking how we all felt about our performances. Chris answered for us and then slid the microphone across the table to Damien and Maddy. Damien brought it toward his mouth and cleared his throat.

"We're really happy with our skate tonight. We focus on performing a complete program, giving attention to every detail and not just one element. It's about more than the jumps."

I fixed my eyes on the table and bit my lip, fighting to keep the annoyance from showing on my face. Damien's comment was an obvious jab at us, though not an accurate one. Our program wasn't just about the quad. Sergei and I had poured our whole hearts into the choreography, and we'd made the steps and transitions more intricate than ever.

While Damien rambled, I snuck a peek at the protocols lying on the table. The scores had the potential to be so close that our Olympic dream could come down to a hundredth of a point. Losing gold by one vote in 2002 had been devastating. I couldn't imagine the pain of losing again... and by a decimal.

I really needed to stop thinking about those things.

# CHAPTER FIVE

I WEAVED THROUGH THE CROWDED HOTEL lobby and looked for Chris. Aubrey and Nick were on their way downstairs so we could head to the nightclub across the street and start our celebration. I'd left Sergei in the restaurant schmoozing with the Swiss and Italian judges. The social games we had to play were sadly as important as the performances we gave on the ice.

Chris waved from near the front entrance, and I strode past a few gawking fans gathered on the matching blue sofas. They'd secured all their desired photos and autographs and were now just people-watching.

"The bellman said it's 80's night at the club," Chris said. "This has the potential to be epic."

I laughed and looked down at my bright red blouse and black jeans. "Should I have worn my leg warmers? Caked on some blue eye shadow?"

"Is Sergei coming or is he stuck with the old folks?"

"He said he'll meet us there... hopefully not three hours from now."

Chris shot his arm up, and I turned to see Aubrey and

Nick approaching from the elevators. Aubrey's black mini-dress and five-inch heels showed off her long, tanned legs, and Nick's crisp button-down shirt and pants matched her outfit. They would easily win Most Fashionable Team if such an award existed.

Aubrey checked her phone and then dropped it into her tiny red purse. "Are we ready? Where's Sergei?"

"He's coming later," I said.

Chris pushed open the double glass doors. "Let's roll."

The cold night air blasted over me, and I hugged my arms to my chest. My silky blouse didn't offer much protection. We hustled across the busy street and hurried inside the club, handing over the necessary yen for the cover charge.

The techno beat of an Erasure song vibrated the room, and I blinked a few times to let my eyes adjust to the colorful spinning lights. Some of the patrons packed in around us had come dressed for the occasion. *Miami Vice*-inspired white jackets and pastel T-shirts and Madonna-like lace gloves and giant hair bows were the most popular get-ups.

I spotted a couple of vacant stools at the bar and quickly grabbed Aubrey's hand. We hopped onto the tall seats, and within a few minutes the four of us held drinks, ready to toast.

Nick raised his glass of bourbon and Coke. "To another successful event for Team Cape Cod."

An image of our destroyed rink popped into my head, and I looked down at my drink. We had a lot to do to get ready for the move to Boston. And we'd only have a few days to get settled at our new rink before Christmas and—

"Em," Chris interrupted my thoughts, and I looked up. He, Aubrey, and Nick were waiting for me to raise my wine glass.

I joined them, and we tapped our drinks together. Aubrey was in the middle of her first sip when "P.Y.T." blared through the speakers, and she immediately jumped from her stool.

FIGHTING FOR THE EDGE

"This is my favorite Michael Jackson song! Let's go dance."

Chris took a long drink of his beer and turned to me. "You coming, Em?"

"I think I'll take it easy. My knee's still pretty sore."

"You want me to hang with you until Sergei gets here?"

"No, go ahead." I waved him toward the dance floor. "I'll enjoy my wine and start making my packing list for Boston."

Chris followed Aubrey and Nick into the tight mass of dancing bodies, and I turned to face the bar. Sliding my phone out of my jeans pocket, I scrolled to the notepad application and began typing the items I needed to bring to Mom's house. I didn't lift my head until I heard a nasally voice next to me order a cosmopolitan. Maddy was positioned against the bar, watching the bartender and completely ignoring my existence. I didn't want to make it any easier for her.

"How's it going?" I chirped in a peppy tone over the music.

She slowly shifted her brown eyes and gave me a sideways glance. "Drinking alone?"

I took a sip of wine. "Sergei's on his way."

The bartender placed Maddy's drink in front of her, and she gave the young man a dazzling smile. When she turned back to me, it was gone.

"I've always been curious," she said. "How it works being married to your coach. Is he... demanding at home, too?"

The tone of her question made our relationship sound salacious. I took a longer sip and set my eyes firmly on hers.

"Rink and home are two separate places. There's equal give and take between Sergei and me in our marriage."

Her mouth curved into a little smile as she seemed to ponder my response. "I'd gladly take whatever he's giving."

I stared at her, unsure whether to laugh or toss my red wine in her face. "That's my husband you're talking about."

"You should take it as a compliment."

She picked up her drink and walked away, her waif-like frame taking her across the room to Damien and two other Canadian skaters.

*Note to self — just let her ignore you from now on.*

A hand slipped around my waist, and I jumped but then quickly smiled at the hint of familiar spicy cologne. I leaned back against Sergei's starchy oxford shirt, and he angled his head down next to mine.

"What is such a breathtakingly beautiful woman doing alone in a bar?"

"You'll have to take that up with my husband. He's kept me waiting."

He pressed his lips to my hair and kissed his way down to my ear. "He promises to make it up to you... all night long."

A warm current of electricity streaked down my spine. I swiveled my stool to face Sergei. "This day just keeps getting better."

"You were really special out there tonight. You should definitely enjoy this victory."

"Oh, I'm enjoying it." I grinned. "You know how much I love winning."

He nudged one leg between my knees, bringing our bodies closer. I tilted my chin up, and he brushed a long curl away from my face.

"Winning is very sexy," he said.

"Yes, it is." I nodded slowly and fingered one of the buttons on his shirt. "You know what would be *really* sexy? Winning an Olympic gold medal."

He chuckled. "It always comes back to the Olympics."

"I know, I know. I shouldn't obsess. But it's getting so close that I can't stop thinking about it. And lately I've been thinking about all the freak things that could happen in the next eight weeks."

"Like what?" Sergei arched an eyebrow, seeming afraid to humor me.

"Like... I could step off a curb wrong and break my ankle. Just walking down the street and BAM! Olympics are over."

"I could carry you everywhere," he said with a smile.

"That sounds very appealing. Or I could get one of those motorized scooters old people use. A Hoveround!"

He rubbed both my shoulders and then cupped his hands under my chin. "Em, you can't live in fear that something terrible is going to happen. You'll drive yourself insane."

"More insane than I already am?" I asked with a laugh.

"I want this dream to become reality for you. I want it even more than I did for myself. But whatever happens in Torino, it's not going to define you. What will define you is how fearless you've been, how hard you've worked, how much you've inspired young skaters."

There was so much love and sureness in his eyes. I reached up and caressed his stubbly cheek, and as I touched my mouth to his, I let my palm trail down his chest. His warmth always gave me such comfort, and being in his arms made me feel totally at peace. I might need to take up permanent residence there the next eight weeks.

"What would I do without you?" I murmured against his lips.

He kissed me tenderly. "You'll never have to find out."

I wound my arms around his neck, and he rested his forehead against mine. "You were right, though," he said, breaking into a slow smile. "Winning an Olympic gold medal would be incredibly sexy."

I laughed and kissed him again.

AUBREY DOWNED THE LAST drops of her wine and slid the glass

onto a nearby table. She'd talked Nick and Chris into staying on the dance floor through a string of songs because she wasn't going anywhere near the bar. She didn't want her celebration tainted by Damien's suggestive looks and comments.

"Another drink?" Nick asked.

She thought about her previous intention to stay away from alcohol forever. A couple of glasses of wine wouldn't hurt, though, and she had more backup this time to make sure she didn't do anything stupid.

"If you're buying," she said.

"Of course, my lady. You good, Chris?"

Chris gave his beer bottle a slight shake to assess the contents. "Yeah, I'm set."

Nick shimmied through the crowd, and Chris moved closer to Aubrey. "See that table of girls over there?" He jerked his chin toward a group of three Japanese women dressed in cut-up sweatshirts and neon-colored leggings. "They've been checking me out since we started dancing. Should I go over and test my player skills?"

"No, no." She stepped in front of him as a blockade. "Rule number one — no hookups in foreign countries. Trust me, it's a bad idea. And rule number two — no hooking up with fangirls. I saw that group at the hotel getting autographs. You'll end up being discussed on some internet message board tomorrow."

Chris looked back and forth between her and the table of admirers. "Those are valid points. But I need to practice my game."

"We'll go clubbing as soon as we get settled in Boston." The music became louder, and she raised her voice, "Why don't you practice on me right now?"

"On *you*?"

"What? Am I not hot enough for you?"

He swept a long look over her. "No, you're plenty hot

enough."

His smiling eyes shone at her in a way she'd never seen from him. It made her a little tingly... something she'd definitely *never* felt around him before.

She cleared her throat. "So, give me your best line."

He laughed and tugged on the collar of his black crew-neck sweater. "I don't really have any lines. I've never tried to pick up a random girl."

"Then just imagine you see someone at a club — me in this case — and you're attracted to her and want to meet her. What do you say when you walk up to her?"

"I'd probably introduce myself and ask if she'd like to dance."

"That's good. Keep it simple. So you get her on the dance floor." Aubrey twirled around. "How close do you dance with her? You don't wanna be bumping and grinding right off the bat."

He laughed again. "I'll keep it respectable yet irresistible."

"Show me. Let's see your moves."

"You've seen me dance a million times, including five minutes ago."

"I haven't seen your I'm-dancing-with-a-girl-I-just-picked-up moves." She wiggled as much as she could in her tight dress. "Come on, show me what ya' got."

He grinned and pushed up his sleeves. "Okay, Boss. You want it, you got it."

"Bust a Move" had just begun playing, and Chris danced along to the hip-hop rhythm as he closed the space between Aubrey and himself. He set his hands lightly on her hips, and she felt the tingle again. It had been over a month since she'd gone on a date, so she was probably just excited to have the attention. Or maybe it was the wine making her giddy.

Their bodies moved together in time to the music, drifting closer and generating more heat with each beat. Aubrey wrapped her fingers around Chris's biceps, and he tensed, his fingertips putting more pressure on her hips. She clutched him harder and fought the urge to roam her hands over all his other tight muscles.

In her stiletto heels she wasn't much shorter than Chris, so she had a prime view of his smile, which never left his face. She couldn't stop smiling either. She hadn't felt this kind of energy in a long time. Or possibly ever.

Chris leaned toward her ear. "Do I pass?"

His warm breath puffed against her cheek, causing her to shiver. *Oh, yeah. With flying colors.* He pulled back to face her, and she looked up at his big grin. *Get a grip. It's just silly, nice-guy Chris. This is only a game.*

"I give you a B-plus," she said nonchalantly.

"Man, you are tough."

"I don't hand out A's easily."

The DJ queued up "The Right Stuff," and Chris backed up and pointed to the air. "I'll earn my A with this."

He jerked his shoulders up and down and shuffled his feet, mimicking the dance style of New Kids on the Block. Aubrey burst into laughter at his perfect imitation.

"I sang this at my fifth grade talent show," Chris said.

"Are you serious?"

"My mom has the VHS tape to prove it. Me and four of my buddies lip synched to this song and had all the girls screaming. It was the shining moment of my middle school career."

He continued to dance and then started singing along, belting out the words as if he was on stage. Aubrey couldn't control her laughter. Now, *this* was the goofy Chris she knew. She had no idea what kind of spell he'd put her under while they'd danced.

Nick returned with Aubrey's drink and eyed Chris with amusement. "I didn't know I was missing a show."

"You arrived just in time." She took the glass from him

and sipped between giggles. All the laughing had brought on the need for a restroom trip, but she didn't want to chance running into Damien on her way there. She didn't think she could wait any longer, though.

"Can you watch my drink?" She handed Nick her wine. "I'm gonna run to the ladies' room."

She raced to the restroom door on the far wall, staying behind the crowd as much as she could. On her return trip, she took a cautious step back into the club and kept her head down as she walked quickly toward the dance floor. Not far past the bar, a body blocked her path, and the pungent sweet cologne made her curse inwardly.

"In a hurry?" Damien asked.

She lifted her head and crossed her arms over her chest. "Yes, my drink is getting warm."

"I can get you a new one. How 'bout a tequila shot?" He gave her a wicked grin.

"How about you never speak to me again?"

"Have one drink with me. I guarantee you'll want more."

She let out a sharp laugh. "I don't know why you're pushing so hard. You don't need me or any girl. You're so in love with yourself that you can get your thrills just looking in the mirror."

Damien licked his lips and slid closer. "But it's much more fun getting my thrills with you. And I remember you enjoying quite a few of them the night we were together."

He squeezed her waist, and she slapped his hand away. "Don't touch me."

"Come on, I know you remember. You couldn't get enough." He pulled her against him and slid his hands down to her bottom.

She shoved his chest and broke free. "I said don't touch me!"

Chris rushed up to her side and shot a death stare at Damien. "What's your problem?"

"What are you — the white knight? Where's your horse?" Damien snickered.

"You're a punk." Chris got in his face, and they stood nose to nose. "I'm not gonna let you harass my friends."

"Oh yeah? What are you gonna do about it?"

"I'm gonna shut your mouth."

Chris cocked his arm back, and Aubrey gasped, but Sergei burst forward and grabbed Chris before he could throw the punch. He pulled him away from Damien and pushed him toward the bar. Aubrey hurried after them, and Em joined her.

"What are you doing?" Sergei barked at Chris. "Don't be stupid."

"He saw me arguing with Damien," Aubrey said.

"That jerk was asking for it," Chris spat.

"No matter how much of a jerk he is, you're not going to fight him," Sergei gave Chris an intent look. "Or anyone else. That's not the kind of headlines we need right now."

Em turned to Aubrey. "What were you arguing about?"

"He was just…" She fumbled with her reply, knowing she couldn't reveal the root of the confrontation. "He wanted me to have a drink with him, and he wouldn't leave me alone."

"Ugh. He's such a tool," Em said.

"Stay away from him." Sergei poked his finger to Chris's chest. "Understand?"

Chris stood with his hands on his hips, still fuming. After a long pause, he muttered, "Yeah."

Sergei slowly stepped away from him and put his arm around Em. As they passed Aubrey, he said, "Keep an eye on him."

Aubrey gave Chris a little smile, and his posture relaxed a bit. "I know you can handle yourself," he said. "I just saw the way he grabbed you, and you looked upset."

"I appreciate the backup. And even though it would've been a bad situation all around, I really wish you would've clocked him."

Chris's jaw unclenched as he laughed. "You and me both."

He rubbed his fist, and Aubrey replayed the scene in her mind — Chris's muscular physique wound tight, his usually warm brown eyes burning hot, the veins on his forearms popping. He wore intensity *very* well.

*What is going on with me tonight?* Chris wasn't her type, and she shouldn't be attracted to her good friend's ex anyway. That was too weird. Plus, they would soon be roommates, and she didn't need any unavoidable distractions. Not with nationals and the Olympics coming up.

Nick snuck up beside her and held out her abandoned drink. "Did you guys move the party over here?"

She took the glass from him. "Not quite. I'm guessing you didn't see what happened?"

"I got corralled by some fans. What'd I miss?"

She and Chris exchanged glances, and she linked her arm through Nick's. "I'll tell you later. I just want to get back to dancing."

The three of them returned to the most crowded area of the club, and Aubrey stayed nearer to Nick as they all danced as a group. There would be no more touching Chris. Not until she got over this mini-crush or whatever it was. Things would go back to normal once they got home.

Chris smiled at her, and she remembered the feel of his strong hands on her hips. Those hands would feel good other places, too…

There had to be something in the air in the club. No other explanation.

# CHAPTER SIX

"HONEY, I'M HOME!" CHRIS SANG AS he walked through the front door.

Aubrey laughed and stepped over the suitcase she'd just plunked down in the living room of their new apartment. "I was about to check out the rest of the place."

Chris dropped his large duffel bag onto the sandy brown carpet. "The location is awesome. Close to the T, lots of places to eat—"

"And most importantly, a Starbucks on the corner," Aubrey added.

Chris looked around the small living room, and his eyes settled on the television hanging on the painted brick wall.

"A forty-two inch plasma! Sweet."

"Can you really tell how big it is just looking at it?"

"A man knows the size of his TV."

She stifled a snort. "I could make a crude comment, but I'm going to be polite this time. Since we're new roomies and all."

"Well, that's no fun."

"Don't worry. You'll get your fill during our stay here."

She turned and surveyed the black leather couch and glass coffee table that sat across from the TV. Above the couch hung a large print of the Boston skyline at night. It was the only decoration on any of the white walls.

"This place has a definite masculine feel." She touched one of the red accent pillows on the sofa.

"Did you bring your smelly candles? That would make it less manly."

She laughed. "I didn't. I'll have to pick some up."

Chris spread his hands out wide. "You know what else we're missing? A Christmas tree."

She hadn't put up a tree in her apartment on the Cape, so she hadn't planned to get one in Boston, especially with the holiday just a few days away.

"I'm not a big Christmas person," she said. "And then we'd have to get ornaments and lights…"

"We can get some cheap stuff and make it the tackiest tree ever. How can you turn down that kind of fun?"

He gave her a grin that made it impossible not to smile and agree with anything he said. There was something so infectious in the brightness on his face.

"Okay, but let's go find our bedrooms first. Then we can have tree fun."

She grabbed the handle of her rolling bag and heaved the big suitcase up the first step of the narrow staircase. It hit the second step with a thud.

"Whoa, let me help you." Chris removed his jacket and tossed it onto his duffel bag. "That thing must weigh fifty pounds."

"I got it." She slung her purse strap around her neck and pulled hard on the bag, dragging it one more step. It felt like it weighed *one hundred* pounds.

Chris picked up the bottom end of the suitcase, his muscles stretching his gray T-shirt. "It'll be much easier this way. Just don't let go of your end."

Aubrey tore her gaze away from Chris's tanned arms and resumed walking backward up the stairs. She thought she'd put that strange night at the club behind her, but now she was remembering the high she'd felt while dancing with him. Their bodies had been so in synch, as if there was a magnetic charge guiding them. She turned to look behind her to see where she was going and also to not see Chris's face. His easy smile and those dimples weren't helping her forget.

They reached the top of the stairs, where two open doorways faced each other across the small landing. Chris set the bag on its wheels and poked his head into the room on the right. "This one's a loft."

Aubrey peeked in beside him. The ceiling sloped down over the bed, which took up most of the tiny room. The wall behind the bed was only half of one as the rest of the space was an opening that overlooked the living room below.

"You're way too tall for this room," she said. "You can barely stand up straight in here."

Chris went over to check out the other bedroom. "This one's bigger, but you should take it. You probably have more stuff than I do."

"You can't take the loft. You're gonna whack your head every time you get out of bed."

"I'm not sticking you in the munchkin room. I have better manners than that."

Those darn dimples appeared again. And she couldn't help smiling in return once more. "If you insist. Your mama would be proud."

She rolled her suitcase into the larger bedroom, which wasn't exactly spacious, but at least she could stand upright. Her cell phone sang the muffled tune of "Girls Just Wanna Have Fun" inside her purse, and she wondered if Chris could hear it. He'd recognize Marley's ringtone. She plucked the phone from between her wallet and a packet of tissues and pressed it to her ear.

"Hey, Mar."

"Hey, what are you up to?"

"Just moving into the new place in Boston."

"I thought you were waiting until after Christmas."

"I was, but it's supposed to snow this week, so I didn't feel like driving back and forth in it. We start skating at the new rink tomorrow."

"Did Chris move in yet?" Marley asked.

Aubrey peered over the half-wall in her bedroom that matched the one in the loft. Chris had gone downstairs and was headed toward the front door. She sat on the double bed and tucked one leg underneath her.

"Yeah, he just got here, too."

"Are you doing anything fun for your first night in the city?"

"He wants to get a Christmas tree for the apartment."

"That doesn't surprise me. He loves everything about the holidays. His constant humming of 'Jingle Bells' will drive you nuts." Marley laughed but sounded somewhat wistful.

"Do you miss him?"

Marley didn't answer at first, and a strange feeling settled in Aubrey's stomach. "We were together so long..." Marley finally said, and after another pause she added, "I made the right choice for my career. I needed to put skating first, and it's paying off."

It sure was. Until the current season, Marley and Zach had been firmly ranked behind Aubrey and Nick, but that fall they'd won gold and silver at their two Grand Prix events, just as Aubrey and Nick had. The gap that had previously existed between the two teams was gone.

"Nationals is going to be intense," Aubrey said.

"I know. I just want us all to skate our best."

Aubrey knew Marley meant it because that's the type of person she was. It's why she had to keep all her focus on Nick and herself, concentrate on their skating and nothing else. She couldn't think about the fact that she needed to defeat one of her best friends to win the national title.

The front door slammed, and Aubrey looked over the wall to see Chris carrying two boxes through the living room.

"I should get back to unpacking. I still have to unload the rest of my car."

"Have fun tree shopping."

Aubrey thought she heard the melancholy tone again. She ended the call and went out to the stairs but had to wait for Chris to reach the top before she could move any further. There wasn't enough room for both of them plus the wide boxes in Chris's arms.

He aimed for his room and didn't ask her about the call, so either he didn't hear the ring or he really was finally moving on from Marley. *And that matters because...?*

She quickly jogged down the stairs and made her way outside, zipping her fleece jacket closed. She'd found a spot for her Jeep right across Beacon Street, but she knew that wouldn't always be the case. Street parking in the busy neighborhood was going to be a royal pain.

She began hauling her belongings inside the brownstone, and Chris ran back out to help her carry the piles of clothes and boxes of shoes and accessories. They had to make seven trips before they emptied the Jeep.

"You do realize you didn't move to China." Chris laughed at the stack of boxes filling Aubrey's room. "It's only an hour and a half to the Cape if you forgot something."

"I'd rather have it all with me so I don't need to keep running back there."

"We can unpack later. Let's go get the tree." He slapped his hands together.

"Alright, alright. Keep your pants on."

Chris coughed. "I could make a crude comment, but I'll refrain in favor of politeness."

She laughed. "Touché."

Chris called Aunt Debbie as he and Aubrey climbed into his truck, and she rattled off directions to a tree lot in nearby Allston. Debbie was Em's family, but Aubrey had known her so long that she called her aunt, too. Aunt Debbie and Uncle Joe owned the Beacon Street apartment, and they'd told Chris and herself to call them anytime they needed help. Of course, Chris considered finding a Christmas tree a dire situation.

They followed the easy directions and found themselves in a large lot with row after row of lush firs. Up and down each row they wandered, passing up what looked like perfectly fine trees to her. She bundled her knit scarf tighter around her neck and huddled her chin against it.

"What's wrong with all these?" she asked as Chris led her past another batch of vibrant green firs.

"I'll know the right one when I see it."

They'd reached the back of the lot, which appeared to be the Island of Misfit Trees. Some were turning brown and losing needles, and some seemed to have stopped growing at an early age.

Chris pointed to a small one straight ahead. "That's it!"

Aubrey stared at the sad tree dwarfed by the other ones around it. "That one? It looks like the Charlie Brown tree."

"Exactly. That's what makes it awesome."

"I don't know if it can even hold ornaments. The branches look tragically anemic."

"You have to believe in Christmas magic."

She wasn't familiar with Christmas magic. Only Christmas lies and misery.

"Let's get this baby home." Chris signaled to one of the lot's employees.

With the misfit tree in the back of his truck, they stopped at the first drugstore they saw and descended upon the aisle of holiday decorations. Aubrey folded her arms and tapped her foot as Chris deliberated between a set of *Looney Tunes* ornaments and one with *Star Wars* characters.

All the shimmering tinsel and trinkets on the shelves were obnoxiously bright, just like the decorations outside her parents' house would be. Shiny and pretty to mask the unhappiness inside. Her neck grew tense just thinking about spending the holiday there.

"We should get both of these." Chris showed her the two boxes of ornaments. "What's better than Princess Leia hanging out with Yosemite Sam?"

He was such a goofball. *That's right. Focus on the goofiness and forget the hotness.*

Chris grabbed a pack of silver tinsel and a string of old-school colored lights and tossed them into his basket. She followed him quietly, noticing he indeed had begun to hum "Jingle Bells." She thought about mentioning her call with Marley but remained silent. No reason to snap Chris out of his cheerful mood. He was liable to get all wistful on her, too.

When they returned to the apartment, Chris set up the tree between the two skinny windows in the living room. Aunt Debbie had given Aubrey a stack of take-out menus for area restaurants when she'd picked up the apartment keys, so she found one for a Chinese place and called in an order. An hour later, she and Chris sat on the living room carpet, eating from the take-out cartons and wrapping the tree with the tinsel and lights.

"So, what's your beef with Christmas?" Chris asked. "Since I've known you, you've never been much into the holiday spirit."

She poked at her vegetable dumplings and avoided eye contact with him. "It's just too overblown. And the holidays with my family aren't the most pleasant experience."

"You said your parents don't get along so well?"

"They're not June and Ward Cleaver, let's put it that way. Although they look the part when they're out in the social scene."

"My parents used to be like that. They'd barely talk to

each other at home, but then they'd go to all these events my dad had to attend for the hospital board, and they'd look like the perfect Dr. and Mrs. Grayden. When I was in high school, my mom was close to leaving my dad because he was such a workaholic, but they went to a marriage counselor and it actually helped them."

"I cannot see my dad talking to a counselor. He's too tight to pay for something like that anyway." She opened her bottle of water and took a sip. "They're just going to keep bickering until they're old and gray and can't hear each other anymore."

Chris bent his leg and rested his elbow on his knee. His eyebrows drew together as he chewed slowly. "If you had the option of not spending Christmas with your family, would you take it?"

"How would I have that option?"

"It would require bending the truth a little... telling them you have to practice on Christmas day and you'd rather stay in Boston and not drive to Orleans just for Christmas Eve."

"Hmm..." She nibbled on one end of her chopsticks.

"And we could go skating at Frog Pond so you wouldn't actually be lying. I'll pretend to coach you. I can do a mean Russian accent." He grinned.

Her lips twitched upward, and she tapped them with the chopstick. "It's a very interesting idea."

"We'll go to Em's family dinner, and the next day we can feast on the leftovers you know Mrs. Debbie's gonna give us. And we can watch the *Christmas Story* marathon on TV all day."

She gasped. "Don't tell me you love that movie, too?"

"Uh, yeah. Who doesn't?"

"Em hates it, so she would never watch it with me. It's the one Christmas movie I love."

"Then you have to stay in Boston so we can watch it on repeat for twelve hours straight."

She bit her lip. "My mom won't be happy."

"But *you* won't be happy if you go home, and you deserve to have a fun holiday."

The sincere warmth in his eyes reached out to her like a virtual hug, one she didn't want to leave. She realized she was staring at him, so she dropped her gaze to her food.

"I'll call my mom later." She looked back up at Chris and smiled. "Staying here definitely sounds like a much better plan."

He whooped and jumped up. "This calls for some celebration music."

"You're not putting on Christmas carols, are you?" She moaned as he went over to his laptop on the coffee table.

"I'm gonna melt the Scrooge out of you, just you wait." He clicked on the mouse a few times, and "Jingle Bell Rock" started playing. With his fingers snapping, he returned to sitting across from her.

"My ears are bleeding," she said.

"This is a classic. You just have to embrace the cheesiness of it." He sorted through the ornaments spread over the carpet and picked up two of them. "Tweety Bird and Chewbacca. Now that would be a fascinating encounter."

She laughed and shook her head. Maybe Christmas didn't have to be completely horrible.

"MOM, YOU DON'T HAVE to cook for us every night," I said while turning on my parents' dishwasher. "We can make our own meals."

"I like having us all at the table together. It's good family time I don't get often enough with you."

She was already pulling out the guilt card, and Sergei and I had only been in Boston a few hours. When we'd returned from Tokyo the day before, I'd had a long talk with her, making sure she'd give us space to breathe. But she had a tendency of falling back into old habits, such as smothering me.

"I just don't want to feel obligated to be here for dinner at a certain time every night," I said. "We have our own schedule, and you promised to respect it."

"I will, I will. I just love seeing your face around here again." Mom touched her hand to my cheek.

"I echo that," Dad said as he entered the kitchen from the den. He kissed the top of my head on his way to the refrigerator.

I sat on the stool next to the island and listened to Mom and Dad discussing the projects they wanted to tackle while on winter break. They didn't have to return to teaching at Boston University until after nationals.

While Mom prattled on about organizing the mess in the garage, Dad gave her a patient ear, quietly sipping from his cup of water. They'd always had such a solid, steady relationship, treating each other as equal partners. It was exactly how I hoped Sergei and I would be after thirty years of marriage.

Sergei came in from the dining room with his cell phone to his ear. "Okay, I'll see you tomorrow. Drive safe."

"What time is Elena dropping off Liza?" I asked as he snapped his phone shut.

"Around noon. She'll meet us at the rink."

"She could bring her here," Mom said. "Jim and I will be home."

Sergei leaned against the counter. "You know Liza — she wants to skate as soon as she gets here. After four hours in the car, she'll be ready to jump on the ice."

"It'll be fun having a little girl in the house again for Christmas. Emily used to wake us up at five in the morning to open gifts." Mom smiled and rubbed my shoulder.

"Liza doesn't believe in Santa Claus anymore, but she's still excited about the gifts," Sergei said. "She's been trying to guess for weeks what we're giving her."

"Does she like pancakes?" Mom asked. "I'll be making my traditional pancakes and pancetta breakfast on Christmas morning."

I glanced at Sergei and then looked reluctantly at Mom. "Umm… we're not going to be here for breakfast. We're driving back to the Cape after dinner on Christmas Eve."

"You're driving back that late? Just to spend one night there?"

"We want to wake up Christmas morning in our house. We have our tree there and all Liza's presents…"

Mom's mouth wrinkled downward. "Oh. Well, I just assumed you'd be here."

"They'll be here Christmas Eve," Dad said.

Mom only sighed and made a quiet humming noise as she set about wiping the tile island with a dishrag. I could sense more of her guilt trips coming, so I hopped off the stool and turned to Sergei.

"Why don't we go finish unpacking?"

We retreated to our bedroom upstairs, the room I'd slept in for eighteen years. Sleeping in my old bed, skating at my old rink… it was like going back in time to my teenaged self. Except I had a very handsome companion with me now.

Since the master bedroom and both Mom's and Dad's offices were downstairs, Sergei and I had the second floor to ourselves. Mom had already freshened up the guest room down the hall for Liza, adding a pink bean bag chair, a CD player, and a small TV she'd borrowed from Aunt Debbie. Our new digs were more than comfortable, but it still wasn't the same as being in our own home.

After we transferred the contents of our suitcases to the walk-in closet and large oak dresser, I took a shower in the attached bathroom and then curled up on the window seat in the bedroom with my paperback of *The Good Earth*. The cushioned window seat had been my favorite spot in my room growing up. It was where I'd done all my reading and my daydreaming.

Sergei came out of the bathroom, shirtless and wearing his blue checkered pajama pants, and I smiled behind my book. In my daydreams, I couldn't have conjured up a better husband. Sergei gave me everything I needed, both physically and emotionally. And he wasn't too bad to look at. I laughed to myself. That was possibly the understatement of all time.

He sat on the queen-sized bed and stretched his long legs over the ivory comforter. Resting one arm behind his head, he turned to look at me. "You're so far away. I'm used to you reading in bed next to me."

"I was just enjoying my old spot. When we buy a house, I want a little nook like this."

"Maybe we can find one with a nook big enough for two."

I smiled. "That sounds nice."

I stood and padded across the carpet to flip off the light. Pushing aside the comforter, I climbed onto the bed and cuddled against Sergei's side.

"Better?" I asked.

"Much."

He leaned over me and kissed me gently, then longer and fuller with each kiss that followed. His mouth lowered to my throat, and I looked over his shoulder. Through the darkness, I could see the shadowy outline of the vanity set where I'd learned to put on makeup and the shelves that used to hold my stuffed animals. It was all a little bizarre, being in this room like this.

"This feels weird," I said.

Sergei lifted his head. "Me kissing you feels weird?"

"It's the room, not you."

"We've stayed here before."

"I know, but we've never..."

Sergei put his weight on his elbow. "Your parents are far

away downstairs. It's totally private up here. Remember that was one of your selling points?" He tickled my stomach.

I giggled and grabbed his wrist. "I think I'm experiencing some delayed teenage awkwardness of having a boy in my room since I never did that when I was actually a teenager."

"Then you definitely need to go through your rebellious phase now," Sergei said with a slow grin.

He kissed the tender spot below my ear, and his lips trailed down my neck while his hand skimmed along my thigh, nudging up my nightshirt. I pressed my fingertips into his back, feeling the resistance of his tight muscles. The longer he touched me the easier it was to forget where we were — which room, which house… which planet.

Then a knock sounded on the door.

I stiffened and tore my mouth away from Sergei's. He dipped his head onto my shoulder.

"You've got to be kidding me," he mumbled.

"Yes?" I called toward the door. My heart was now racing for a different reason.

"I forgot to bring up these extra towels for you earlier," Mom said.

I smashed my hand to my forehead. Couldn't her hospitality have waited until morning?

Sergei groaned as I slipped out from the warm cover of his body. I straightened my nightshirt and opened the door just enough to see into the hallway.

"Thanks," I said, taking the stack of fluffy towels from Mom.

Her eyes darted over me. "I didn't realize you'd be in bed this early."

"We have to be at the rink early tomorrow."

My mussed-up hair and swollen lips surely revealed I hadn't been sleeping, but that wasn't anyone's business except Sergei's and mine.

Mom continued to peer at me with her chin tilted slightly

upward. "Mm… well, get some rest then."

I shut the door and placed the towels on the chair in the corner of the room. Back under the comforter with Sergei, I sighed and gave him a kiss.

He pulled me closer and smiled. "Almost getting caught in the act by your mom… you're already embracing your inner teenaged bad girl."

# CHAPTER SEVEN

AUBREY CLIMBED ONTO THE BLEACHERS AT the Skating Club of Boston and looked down at the crowded rink. With the added skaters from the Cape, over twenty people occupied the ice for the morning practice sessions, jumping and spinning and miraculously avoiding collisions. Em and Chris skated through the crowd hand-in-hand as Barber's *Adagio for Strings* soared through the airy building, and a number of skaters cleared space and idled near the boards to watch their short program run-through.

Chris pressed Em up into the air, and his blades moved over the ice with swift, secure turns. Aubrey found her gaze staying on Chris as he set Em down gently and they twizzled into their circular footwork. Chris used his whole body to express every note of the passionate music. In his tight black T-shirt and pants, his long body lines showed with each movement. He was in complete control even while flying across the ice and taking Em into his arms. Aubrey had never held any desire to skate pairs, but she suddenly felt a little envious of her best friend.

She pulled her skates from their bag and put them on

while watching the end of the run-through. After the music ended and Em cooled down, she hopped off the ice and joined Aubrey on the bleachers.

"How was your first night at Casa Butler?" Aubrey asked.

Em slipped her bright blue guards over her blades. "Well, other than my mom almost interrupting Sergei and me having sex, it was pretty uneventful."

"Oh, no she didn't." Her shoulders shook with laughter.

"Yep, she sure did. The incident didn't exactly help my argument to Sergei that living with my parents was the best option."

"You can tell him you wouldn't have had any more privacy if you were living with me and Chris. Both of the bedrooms are open to the living room, so there's no hiding anything in our apartment."

"It's a good thing neither of you are dating anyone. That would be awkward." Em snickered. "I hope Chris won't be bringing home any random girls when he's out being a swinging single."

Aubrey stopped laughing and looked to where Chris stood with Sergei along the boards. She'd agreed to go clubbing with him to help him meet women, but that didn't sound like such a fun idea anymore. What if he did bring someone back to their apartment? The thought made her squirm more than it should.

She bent to tighten her skate laces and decided to change the subject. "Is it okay if I come with Chris to your Christmas Eve dinner? I'm staying here for the holiday."

"Of course. You're always welcome." Em gave her a concerned look. "How come you're not going home? Have things gotten worse between your parents?"

"I don't know." She sat up straight and combed her hair back from her face. "I haven't been there much lately, and I'd rather not find out. When I told Chris I wasn't looking forward to spending Christmas with my family, he insisted I stay in Boston. He even made up a story for me to tell my mom."

"Uh-oh." Em smiled. "You're already under his spell."

"Wh-what?" she stammered. How could Em know she'd been having all those crazy new thoughts about Chris? Was she that transparent?

"His power of persuasion. All his friends fall victim to it. How many things has he talked me into doing?"

"Oh… yeah." She exhaled. "He can be very convincing."

"Are you guys coming to church with us before dinner?"

"Chris didn't mention church. All he talked about was the abundance of food."

Em laughed. "Figures that's the most important part of the evening to him. He's right, though. There will be a ridiculous amount of food, so you might want to skip lunch."

"Who's skipping lunch?" Nick asked as he dropped onto the row below them.

"*You* should." She stuck her tongue out as she patted his stomach. "You're looking a little paunchy."

"Am I really?" He looked down and squeezed his narrow waist. "I knew I shouldn't have had those powdered donuts this morning."

"I was kidding. You're skinnier than most girls."

Em left to talk to an adult skater she knew from her old neighborhood, and Chris soon filled her spot on the bleachers. Aubrey wondered if he remembered her promise to go out to the clubs that night. She hadn't mentioned it since they'd left Tokyo. It was the last thing she felt like doing, but she was starting to think it might be just what she needed to douse her attraction to Chris. If he became occupied with another girl, he wouldn't be hanging out with her, flashing that adorable smile and making her feel all warm and fuzzy inside.

"Do you wanna check out the Boston singles market tonight?" she blurted out before she could stop herself.

"I know some places where you'd be very popular." Nick

let out a big laugh and hit Chris on the leg.

"While your clubs do provide the best dance music, they don't exactly have what we're looking for in the dating prospects department," Aubrey said.

Chris pulled up the hem of his pants and untied the laces on his boot. "Maybe we can do it another time. I'd rather stay in and veg out tonight."

She blinked with shock. That wasn't the response she'd expected. Chris had been so gung-ho about going out when they'd discussed it before the Final and again in Tokyo. She thought he'd be all over her suggestion. Mixed with her surprise and confusion was an undeniable sense of relief, which she didn't want to admit was the strongest emotion of them all.

"I'm always up for some vegging out," she said. "Unless you plan on playing more Christmas music. I don't know how many more versions of 'Silver Bells' I can take."

"You know you're secretly starting to love it. I saw you bobbing your head last night during 'Here Comes Santa Claus.'"

"I had a muscle tic," she said, trying to keep a straight face.

"*Right.* I told you — there will be no Scrooge left when I'm done with you." He grinned and tugged off his skate. "You might as well not fight it."

Oh, man. She was in so much trouble.

I ZIPPED MY SKATE bag and glanced at the huge clock on the far wall of the rink. Elena would be arriving soon with Liza. Sergei and I had last seen Liza a few weeks earlier at the U.S. Junior Figure Skating Championships where she'd won the bronze medal in the juvenile girls event. She'd been ecstatic since it was her first trip to junior nationals, but whenever I'd talked to her on the phone over the last two weeks, she hadn't been her usual chatty self.

Liza appeared at the front of the rink at ten minutes past noon, bundled in her pink puffer jacket and purple beret. Right behind her was Elena in one of her many long fur coats. When the two of them stood together, there was no mistaking they were mother and daughter. They shared the same glossy raven hair, high cheekbones, and porcelain complexion. But Liza's most striking feature came from Sergei — her big, beautiful blue eyes. And they were full of anxiousness as she scanned the flurry of skaters both on and off the ice.

"Hey, kiddo!" I jogged over and swallowed Liza in a hug. "I'm so happy to see you."

She squeezed her arms around my waist and clung to me. "I thought Christmas would never get here."

I peeked up at Elena with furrowed brows, but her eyes were fixed on Liza.

"Where's my dad?" Liza asked as she finally broke away from our hug.

I turned toward the ice, where Sergei had been teaching Courtney and Mark, one of his other teams. He'd spotted Liza and was securing his guards over his blades. Liza ran to him, and he crouched to embrace her. Her petite size was another feature she got from Elena.

"Is she okay?" I asked Elena. "She's been kinda quiet lately when I've talked to her."

Elena smoothed her short bob as she watched Sergei beam at Liza. "She have problem at the rink," she said in her thick Russian accent. "Some girls are jealous she won medal at nationals, and they say nasty things."

My heart sank. Liza was one of the sweetest kids I'd ever known. How could anyone pick on her?

"That's awful," I said. "Kids can be so cruel sometimes."

Sergei walked behind Liza with his hands on her shoulders as they came toward us. I loved seeing how big

Sergei's smile always got around his daughter. She had him wrapped around all ten fingers.

"Thanks for driving her up here," Sergei said to Elena. "It's been crazy today getting everyone settled into our new schedule."

"Drive is good," Elena said. "We listen to audio book."

"Oh yeah? Which book?" Sergei asked Liza.

"*Harry Potter and the Chamber of Secrets*. I read it already, but it sounds really cool on CD."

Sometimes when the four of us were together, I took a moment to appreciate how normal our arrangement was. After all the drama we'd gone through in the beginning — Sergei running into Elena in Russia after ten years apart, learning Liza was his daughter, then almost losing her when Elena tried to manipulate the situation — I thanked God for the amicable relationships we all had with each other.

The cell phone in Elena's hand chirped, and she smiled as she read the text. "George ask if we make it safe to Boston."

Elena's boyfriend of six months was a divorced father of two and an investment banker in New York City. One of the moms at Liza's rink had set them up. Sergei had been concerned about the impact on Liza, but from everything we'd seen, George treated both Elena and Liza like queens.

"Tell him Merry Christmas from us," I said.

"I will," she said, still smiling as she put the phone in her coat pocket. She brought Liza into her arms and pressed her cheek to the top of Liza's head. "You have fun and you call me any hour. I love you."

"I love you, too," Liza mumbled into the gray fur.

Elena slowly released her and then motioned behind her to the large red suitcase and matching tote bag. "These all her things."

"Thanks." Sergei reached for the suitcase. "Have a safe trip back."

After one more hug and kisses to both Liza's cheeks,

Elena departed and Sergei turned to me. "Can you show Liza around while I finish up with Court and Mark?"

We wheeled her bags next to the bleachers, and I took Liza through the locker room and the gym before heading upstairs to the lounge. It overlooked the ice just like the lounge at the rink on the Cape did. *Or at least it used to*, I thought sadly.

Liza stopped to look at the display case containing mementos from the club's storied history. Her eyes traveled from the trophies to the medals to the black and white photos of girls in long skating dresses.

"Are you sure it's okay for me to skate here?" she asked. "The ice looked pretty crowded."

"Of course. Everyone's been super nice about making space for us."

"I wish I could stay here longer than ten days. I miss nice people."

She started for the stairs, and I followed her down to the rink. Moving beside her, I angled my head to look at her. "Your mom said some kids have been giving you a hard time?"

Liza stared at the concrete floor and picked at the chipped pink polish on her thumbnail. "They said I only won a medal because the judges know my dad is a big shot coach and my stepmom is the world champion."

My heart fell again. "That is absolutely not true. You earned that medal by skating your best. It didn't matter who your parents are."

"Some of the girls won't talk to me anymore. They're like, 'You probably think you're too good to hang out with us now.' But I never said that! The only person I showed my medal to was Hope because she slept over one night."

I put my arm around her, and we walked to the first set of bleachers. We sat hip-to-hip, and I brushed her long hair behind her shoulder. With two parents who were once junior world pair champions, Liza was going to have enough heavy expectations placed on her as she advanced in the sport. I hated seeing her already burdened by Sergei and Elena's success... and mine, too.

"Sweetie, I want you to be proud of what you accomplished. You've worked so hard, and you deserve all the recognition you've received. Don't let those kids affect how you see yourself. Because not only are you an awesome skater, you're a pretty awesome person."

A little smile tugged on her mouth. "I still wish I could stay here longer and then go to St. Louis with you for nationals."

"I wish you could, too, but you'll be missing school for the Olympics, so we can't let you skip any more days." I bumped her knee with mine. "I bet by the time you go back to New York after the holidays, the kids at the rink will be cool again. They'll have found something new to talk about."

She scrunched her face, not looking convinced. "I hope you're right."

I rubbed her shoulder and rose from the bench. "I have to run home and get lunch before I pass out. Your dad will be done soon, so why don't you stretch and get ready for your lesson with him?"

I gathered my jacket and skate bag and made the short drive to my parents' house. After my most grueling practice in over a week, my stomach was begging for sustenance. I'd made turkey burgers earlier in the week and had frozen them, so I popped one into the stainless steel microwave and started gathering the lettuce, pickles and mustard. Mom breezed into the kitchen and stood across the island from me.

"How was your first day back at the old club?"

"Good. I saw a few familiar faces."

She stayed quiet as I painted my wheat bun with the mustard. When I turned to take the burger out of the microwave, she said, "Can I ask you something?"

*Oh, no.* When coming from my mother, that question only meant bad things.

I plopped the burger onto my bun. "Sure."

"Are you still on the pill?"

My head shot up. "Excuse me?"

"I saw a box of condoms in your nightstand, so I was wondering if you had an issue with the pill."

"What were you doing in my nightstand?"

"I was checking to make sure I'd put a flashlight in there. You know I like to keep them around the house in case we lose power."

"You could've asked me to check before you went through our stuff."

"You just moved in. I didn't think there was any big private stuff in there."

I pinched the bridge of my nose and took deep breaths. "From now on, can you please ask if you need something in our room?"

Mom gave a quick nod and tapped her fingers on the island. "So, you didn't answer my question."

"Oh my goodness! Yes, I'm still on the pill. We like to be extra careful, okay?"

"Because of what happened with Elena?"

"That's a big reason, yes. I mean, Sergei adores Liza and can't imagine not having her in his life, but Elena's pregnancy cost them their chance at the Olympics. It's obviously made him much more cautious."

"Well… I'm glad to hear he's taking that extra step to protect you."

I cringed inwardly at the total uncomfortableness of the conversation. I picked up my burger and held it just shy of my mouth. "Can we please change the subject?"

# CHAPTER EIGHT

AUBREY FLUFFED HER LONG HAIR OVER her shoulders and stepped up to the dresser mirror. She'd chosen a sleeveless black cocktail dress for the Christmas Eve dinner, and she was pleased with the look. The hemline fell right at her knees, and the ruching on the neckline scooped just low enough to be both sexy and classy. She leaned closer to the mirror and widened her emerald green eyes, making sure there were no flaws in her makeup.

Chris's footsteps pounded up the stairs, and he bellowed, "Ho, ho—"

He stopped in the doorway of Aubrey's bedroom, his mouth suspended open and his eyes darting over her. Up, down, and back again they traveled until they met her face, which was growing warmer by the second.

"You look really... that's a nice dress," Chris stumbled over his words while sneaking another peek downward.

"Thanks." She smiled.

The strange awkwardness in the air made it feel like they were going on a first date or something. And what a hot date Chris would make. He was wearing black slacks, a pink button-down shirt, and a white tie decorated with tiny candy canes. She'd always had a weakness for dark-haired guys in pink shirts. *Curse him!*

The silence was way too unnerving, so Aubrey blurted out, "Cute tie."

That seemed to break Chris out of his daze. He chuckled and smoothed his fingers over the candy canes. "Ah, so you like my Christmas-themed tie. Interesting development. And here I thought you were wearing black to express your disdain for the holiday."

"That was actually not a factor in my choice of attire. I'm wearing festive shoes in case you didn't notice." She extended one leg outward to show off her leopard print heels.

He took a quick look and a long swallow. "I did… notice."

She set her heel back on the carpet and swiftly picked up her red coat from the bed. "Should we get going?"

Since Aunt Debbie and Uncle Joe lived just a few blocks from the apartment, they set off on foot toward Commonwealth Avenue. Chris held the bottle of Prosecco they were bringing as a gift, while Aubrey kept her hands buried in her coat pockets. The frosty air burned her cheeks, and she picked up her pace.

They stepped off the curb to cross Marlborough Street, and her shoe skidded on the icy pavement. Her heart rate jumped as she wobbled and spread her arms, barely keeping her balance.

Chris held out his elbow. "Want something to hold onto?"

She was about to decline in order to assert her self-sufficiency, but with more slushy concrete ahead, she realized that wouldn't be the brightest decision.

She clutched Chris's arm, and as they continued walking he said, "You know, I had a selfish motive for getting you to come with me to this dinner."

Curiosity wrinkled her forehead. "Besides your quest to make me love Christmas?"

"Yes, although that is very important to me." He pointed one gloved finger at her. "The thing is, I didn't wanna go to the party by myself."

"Mr. Social Butterfly? I've never seen you have trouble talking to anyone at a party."

"Talking wouldn't be the problem. I just felt like everyone would be looking at me and thinking, 'There's poor Chris, all alone on Christmas.' I didn't wanna be that pitiful guy."

She viewed his profile in the soft light from the street lamps. His insecurity about certain things continued to surprise her, but it was refreshing that he wasn't afraid to admit it.

"You wouldn't have been pitiful," she said. "Though Em's mom probably would've given you her favorite worried look and insisted you spend all of tomorrow at their house."

"Having her feed me all day doesn't sound half bad, but I'm much more stoked about our plans." He smiled.

They turned onto Commonwealth, and white lights twinkling in the trees guided their way down the avenue. As they passed one stately brownstone after another, Aubrey noticed each one had an ornate wreath hung on its front door.

The large first-floor windows of Aunt Debbie's house glowed with an orange hue, sending out a warm invitation to come inside. Aubrey took the steps up to the red door while maintaining her grip on Chris's elbow, and when they reached the top Chris pressed the bell.

Uncle Joe opened the door. "Merry Christmas!"

Aubrey stepped inside and hugged him, unable to fully wrap her arms around the burly man. "Thanks so much for including us."

"You're both family," he said.

Aunt Debbie swooped into the foyer for more hugs. "Your timing is perfect. We just got back from mass."

Chris handed her the Prosecco and met Em at the wide archway between the foyer and the family room. "The heathens are here!"

Em laughed. "I lit a candle at church for your souls."

"We need more than one candle." Aubrey slid off her coat. "We need a bonfire."

The family room was packed with people, all of whom Aubrey had met before. She slowly made her way through the room, chatting with Em's aunts, uncles, and cousins. With the fireplace crackling, the statuesque tree smelling of pine, and carols playing low on the stereo, she felt like she was in one of those scenes on a Christmas card. And it was actually kind of nice.

Uncle Joe called everyone into the dining room, and they all found places at the long cherry wood table. Em had said Aunt Debbie put in two extra leafs to fit everyone. Aubrey sat between Em and Bri, Em's twenty-year-old cousin, and Chris sat across from her, but the two of them didn't talk much during dinner. Em's Aunt Gayle was on Chris's left, and she treated him to a constant stream of chatter.

Aubrey listened to the myriad of conversations happening around the table, and they were all lively and upbeat. It was so different from the mood at her family's holiday table. Usually her dad's attention stayed on the TV while her mom spilled neighborhood gossip and her brother and sister-in-law yammered on about their law careers. The meals seemed to last hours.

She savored every bite of the vegetable lasagna and wished she could sample the other mouth-watering pasta dishes, but she had to stay in peak shape for nationals. One day soon she'd be able to eat without constantly counting calories.

After everyone helped clear the table, they began trickling back into the family room. Aubrey and Chris paused in the doorway from the dining room, and Aunt Debbie grinned and pointed above their heads.

"Gotcha," she said.

They both looked up. A small bundle of mistletoe hung from the frame.

"You have to kiss," Liza said with a giggle.

Chris wouldn't really kiss her, would he? *He'll probably give me a tiny peck. No biggie.*

Then why was her heart racing?

"I'm ready." Chris closed his eyes and puckered his lips like a fish.

Of course he would make a joke out of it.

"You're such a doofus," she said and started to walk away, but he grabbed her waist.

"Hey, you have to obey tradition. I'll be serious, I promise."

The dimples disappeared, and Chris angled toward her. She drew in a breath, but then he leaned slightly left, placing a sweet kiss on her cheek. His lips were soft and warm. Not only was Scrooge melting, but some other parts of her were as well.

Chris smiled at her, and she quickly shuffled into the family room. "A serious moment from Christopher Grayden," she said, hoping the exaggerated shock on her face would cover up any possible blushing. "I didn't think it was possible."

Em perched on the arm of a nearby easy chair. "It's a rare occurrence, but it does happen."

"I'm going to be serious the rest of the night," Chris said.

Em laughed. "You won't last five minutes."

"It's time for gifts!" Bri said, crouching next to the pile of presents spilling out from under the tree.

Aubrey sat on the piano bench so she wouldn't be in the way of the mass gift exchange. She, Em, Chris, and Sergei had done their own rowdy exchange with their group of friends at the rink that morning. Chris dropped down beside her on the bench and stared into the distance.

"What is the purpose of life?" he said in a monotone voice. "What does it all mean?"

Aubrey groaned. "I'd like the jokes back, please."

"Okay, but just remember you asked for it."

Aunt Debbie walked over with two small gift bags and presented them. "These are for you two."

"You got us presents?" Aubrey looked at her wide-eyed.

"Everyone has to have something to open. House rule."

"Thank you," Chris said. "This is really, really nice."

Aunt Debbie retreated to the big sectional sofa, and Aubrey reached inside her bag and under the red tissue paper. Her fingers closed in on metal, and she pulled out a shiny silver necklace.

"It's beautiful. It will go with everything." She looked over at Aunt Debbie. "Thank you so much."

Chris ripped the tissue from his bag and smiled at the Baltimore Orioles cap he produced. "Thanks, Mrs. Debbie."

"Em said you could use a new one."

Em looked up from tearing the wrapping paper on a large box. "I told her you've been wearing the same ratty cap since I met you."

"And it's been through some good times," Chris said.

Aubrey placed her necklace back in the bag and sat quietly observing the "oohs" and "aahs" from the group as they opened their presents. There were also a number of laughs over the gag gifts in the pile. It was how Christmas should be among family — cozy and festive. But she could never be around her dad during the holidays and feel festive. He'd ruined it all.

Chris rose from the bench and straightened his tie. "About ready to head home?"

Even though they'd lived in the apartment less than a week, it strangely didn't feel weird thinking of it as home.

She stood with her gift bag. "Yeah, I'm beat." The holiday had been a non-factor during lessons that morning. Peter and

Natalia hadn't shown any lenience, working Nick and her as hard as any day of the year.

She and Chris made the rounds, bidding everyone goodnight and thanking Aunt Debbie and Uncle Joe once more for including them. The night had grown even colder, and they walked briskly to the apartment with Aubrey holding onto Chris again for security. They were just inside their front door when her phone blared with "Mamma Mia."

"Hi, Mom," she answered while shrugging out of her coat.

"How was your dinner?"

"It was fun."

Chris turned on the TV and pointed at *A Christmas Story* playing on the screen. Little Ralphie was being booted down the slide by Santa Claus.

"It has begun," Chris whispered.

She smiled and sat on the slippery leather couch, kicking off her heels. In the background of the phone line, she heard her dad and her smile faded. He was obviously too busy to get on the line and talk to his daughter on Christmas.

"I really wish you would've come home, even if it was only for a few hours," her mom said. "It's not the same without you here."

Aubrey rested her head on her hand. "It was just easier to stay here. There's a lot going on."

"You hardly ever come home anymore, and you know how much I miss you."

The sadness in her mom's voice pierced her heart, and she squeezed her eyes shut. Maybe she should've sucked it up and gone to visit her family. Her mom wasn't the main reason she wanted to stay away. But she did tolerate her dad's crap, and that made her partly responsible for the mess that was their marriage. A mess Aubrey couldn't stand to be around.

"It's just hard…" Aubrey's voice croaked with tears. Ugh, she hated crying. She'd done enough of it all those

Christmases ago when she'd discovered her seemingly perfect family life was a lie.

She looked up and caught Chris watching her with concern, and she dipped her head. He set the remote control on the coffee table and went into the kitchen.

Her mom sniffled. "So, I guess we won't see you until nationals?"

"Probably not. We have a lot of work to do the next two weeks."

"Well, call me and let me know how you're doing."

Aubrey cleared her throat. "I will."

"I hope you have a good day tomorrow. Don't work too hard."

Guilt swam in her stomach, knowing she'd be doing a lot more playing than working. "I'll talk to you soon," she said and ended the call.

She leaned back and closed her eyes again, taking slow breaths. She wasn't going to let her mom make her feel guilty for keeping her distance. It made her too angry to go home and see how unhappy her parents were with each other but refusing to change their situation.

"Are you okay?" Chris's voice sprung open her eyes.

He'd loosened his tie and opened the top button of his shirt. In one hand he held a bottle of beer. He joined her on the couch, and she sat up straighter.

"Yeah." She nodded quickly. "Just my mom… you know, she wishes I was there and all."

He continued to watch her with the little bend of concern between his eyebrows. "I feel like there's more to the issues with your family than you've said. Just seeing how upset you looked when you were talking to your mom."

She stared at her phone, wiping the tiniest specks of dust from its screen. She hadn't told anyone what had happened. Not even Em. It had made her so sad and angry that she'd just wanted to bury it.

"If you wanna talk about it…" Chris paused. "I just want you to know I'd be glad to listen."

She looked into his eyes. There was something in them that gave her a feeling of total trust. She did want to talk, to finally let it all out. So she put the phone aside and began.

"When I was in high school, I used to help out at my dad's office after school sometimes. I thought it was cool to see all the building plans and to watch neighborhoods and shopping centers created from scratch, and it was fun because I got to see my dad more since he was always at work."

She shifted on the sofa so she was angled more toward Chris. "The Christmas I was sixteen, I found a black velvet box and a card in my dad's desk. Inside the box was the most gorgeous diamond bracelet I'd ever seen. I knew I shouldn't, but I opened the card, and my dad had written this really romantic note, mushier than anything I'd ever heard him say to my mom. And I thought, that's so awesome he's giving her this amazing gift and telling her all these wonderful things. She's going to absolutely love it."

"Well, Christmas morning came, and I watched excitedly as my mom opened her gift bag. But the velvet box wasn't in there. It was a gift card to a spa, and there was no card either. And stupid me thought my dad might be waiting to give her the bracelet when they were alone. But the day ended and it never happened."

Chris put his beer on the table and spread his arm across the back of the sofa, bridging the space between Aubrey and himself. He remained quiet, and she continued, "Two days later I went to my dad's office to work, and I saw the bracelet. On the arm of his twenty-six year old secretary." She let out a bitter laugh. "How cliché can you get — the boss getting it on with his secretary. I couldn't believe it. I think I was in denial at first, and then I was ready to run to my mom and tell her everything. But I couldn't do it. I have no problem speaking my mind to anyone, but every time I tried to tell her, I just couldn't find the words."

"I don't know if I could've done it either," Chris said.

"After a while I started to suspect she might know, and she just chose not to do anything about it. I think she's settled with her comfortable life and being the wife of an important businessman in the community and all the social crap that comes with it, and she doesn't wanna give that up. And my dad has his comfortable life with a wife who does everything for him. It makes me so mad because they're so clearly unhappy together, but they just continue to pretend to everyone on the outside that their marriage is wonderful."

"Do you think your dad is still cheating on her?"

"We went to Hawaii a few years ago, which I thought was my dad's attempt to put family first, but I was sorely mistaken. He either played golf or worked on his computer the whole time, and I heard him on the phone late one night talking to someone." She shook her head in disgust. "And it wasn't a business associate."

Chris sighed hard. "I'm sorry."

"I don't think he'll ever change," she said.

"I see now why Christmas brings up bad memories."

She ran her thumb along the hem of her dress. "It was such a long time ago, but I'll never forget what he said in that card. It made me sick to think of him with that woman, telling her those things he should only be saying to my mom. I think about it every time I see him at Christmas and he gives my mom some other meaningless gift that he put no thought into whatsoever."

"That really sucks," Chris said.

She pushed her fingers through her hair, tugging it away from her face. "That's a great way to sum up the situation."

They sat in silence for a few moments until Chris said, "Maybe this year will be the start of only wonderful Christmas memories."

She couldn't help but smile a little. "You think you're that good, huh?"

"Oh, I know I'm that good. We'll have so much fun tomorrow that from now on, it'll be all you can remember." He tapped her shoulder.

Her smile widened because she believed that could actually happen. She felt better just from talking to Chris, and she'd always thought talking about it would dredge up the hurt and make her feel worse.

"Baby steps," she said. "We have many years of yucky Christmases to erase."

"I'm all over it," he said with confidence. "It shall be done."

Aubrey slowly stood and curled her toes into the thick carpet. "I'm gonna get some sleep then. To prepare for this epic day tomorrow."

Chris stood as well and stuck his hands in his pockets. He looked down at her with a thoughtful gaze. "I know I joke around a lot, but… you really shouldn't have to think about all that junk with your dad. I just wanna see you happy."

A surge of emotion swelled in her chest, and before she knew it she was hugging him. He took a moment to react and then circled his arms around her waist, enclosing her in his warm embrace. She bit her lip to stop the tears, but inside she was still a jumble of emotion. Being in Chris's arms felt so comforting but also so exhilarating. Way more exhilarating than any hug between friends should feel.

She backed away. "Sorry, I didn't mean to get all needy."

"It's okay." His eyes shined with a smile. "I have plenty of hugs to spare."

*I'd better get out of here before I do something else impulsive.*

"Well, have a good night." She picked up her shoes and her phone and walked toward the stairs. "Wake me if you hear Santa."

Chris slapped his hands together. "There's the Christmas spirit!"

# CHAPTER NINE

I AIMED MY DIGITAL CAMERA AT Liza and snapped as she tore into her final present of the morning. Opened boxes of clothes and games surrounded her on our living room carpet. She squealed upon revealing the set of paperback mysteries, and I clicked the camera again. She looked too cute in her pink snowflake pajamas and big fuzzy slippers.

Sergei took a small box from under the tree and slid it in front of me. "Em, there's one more for you."

He'd already given me a number of gifts, so I wasn't expecting more. I crawled over to the tree and picked up another small box.

"There's one more for you, too." I smiled and handed it to him.

"Open yours first," he said.

I put down my camera and shook the box, giving Sergei a curious grin. "It's very light."

My fingers ripped away the gold paper and found a plain white box. I opened it and saw a postcard from Monte Carlo with a photo of majestic buildings rising above the sparkling blue Mediterranean Sea. Picking up the card, I flipped it over and read the back — *Sting, July 4, 2006, the Sporting Club, table 370.*

"Are we going to the Sting concert in Monte Carlo?" I shrieked.

"It's during your break from the Ice Champions tour. We're going for three days." Sergei grinned.

I continued to gape at the postcard. Seeing our favorite artist in one of the most beautiful cities in the world? Best gift ever!

"I can't believe you did this." I threw my arms around Sergei and then pressed my mouth to his.

"Monte Carlo's by France, right?" Liza asked.

Sergei's lips left mine. "Yes, it is."

"Cool." Liza stood and gathered up an armful of boxes. "I'm going to go try on my new outfits."

She hurried up the stairs to her room, and I gave Sergei another kiss. "This trip must be really expensive. Should we be spending—"

He placed his finger to my lips. "I've got it covered. After all the years of hard work you've put in, you deserve something special to celebrate the end of your career."

"It's beyond special." I touched his stubbly cheek. "Thank you."

He took my hand and kissed my palm. "I get to spend three days on the Riviera with my gorgeous wife, so it's a pretty great gift for me, too."

I smiled. "And you still have another present to open."

He shredded the wrapping paper and peered at the blank DVD case, turning it over and back around.

"You have to put it on to see what it is." I winked.

He eyed me with amused curiosity as he inserted the disc into the DVD player below the TV. I got up and moved to the sofa, and Sergei sat beside me, snuggling me against him. I laid my head on his soft T-shirt and watched the black screen come to life.

Sergei and I stood on the ice at our rink. His hair was shaved close to his head, making him look even younger than he was, and I wore my Skating Club of Boston fleece jacket. Sergei was holding my wrist in demonstration, and I was nodding with vigor.

"Oh wow." He squinted at the TV. "Is this our first lesson?"

I grinned. "Remember Aubrey's mom videotaped parts of our lessons so my parents could see how they were going? My mom thought she'd lost the tape, but she found it when she was cleaning her office. I had it transferred to DVD."

Sergei's eyes stayed glued to the screen as the video showed us doing back crossovers together around the rink. I laughed and pointed at the TV. "I look so terrified!"

"I was so nice to you. Why were you terrified?"

"I told you before, you made me nervous because you were so stinkin' hot." I squeezed his thigh.

He let out a loud laugh. "Is the black eye you gave me on here?"

"No, she unfortunately didn't get that on tape. But we do have the day I couldn't do a death spiral to save my life. Your voice isn't audible on the video, but you can see yourself talking me off the ledge."

"Oh, yeah, I remember that. I think it's the biggest meltdown I've ever seen you have."

We watched more of the footage, alternately laughing and cringing at the collisions we endured. Every one of our lessons ended with smiles, though.

"This is really awesome, Em," Sergei said.

"We can show it to our kids someday," I said.

He kissed the top of my head and gently rubbed my stomach. "Maybe next Christmas we'll have a little one on the way."

"So soon?" My head popped up.

"We've talked about starting a family after you retire."

"I know, but I thought we'd wait a little while so I can get settled into coaching and we can find a house and everything."

Sergei nodded slowly but didn't say anything. He didn't have to because the disappointment in his eyes said it all.

"I'm not talking years," I assured him. "I might not be pregnant next Christmas, but maybe we can start trying then."

He tucked my hair behind my ear. "I'm not going to lie... I'll be ready the minute you take off your skates for the last time, but I won't push. I don't want you to feel rushed."

"I've just been skating for so long that I feel like it's going to take some time for me to get used to a new identity, and I need to do that before I add being a mom to the mix."

"You're already a mom." He tapped the tip of my nose. "And a great one."

"Liza's easy. A baby is a whole different story."

He touched his lips to my hair again and held me quietly. When he finally spoke, he said, "I missed so much with Liza that I guess I'm just excited I can see it all this time. I want to be there for everything... from the first ultrasound to the delivery and everything after that. Changing diapers and reading bedtime stories..."

"You're going to be an amazing dad." I looked up at him. "And I'm not just saying that because I'm ridiculously in love with you."

He smiled and kissed me, and I cozied deeper into his arms. So much was going to change soon — new career, new home, new goals. For seventeen years I'd been a skater, and it was going to take more than a few weeks to adjust to losing that role. I'd had no chance to prepare for being a mom to Liza, and I wanted it to be different with our child. Sergei might disagree, but for me, more time was never a bad thing.

AUBREY'S EYES FLUTTERED OPEN, and she heard the shower

downstairs running. She turned over in bed and the sight of a big stuffed snowman next to her startled her. A sticky note stuck to the snowman's hand read — *Squeeze me.*

She gave the furry hand a squeeze, and "Have a Holly Jolly Christmas" burst forth. She laughed to herself and listened to the song play. It had been a long time since she'd awoken happy on Christmas.

She climbed out of bed and combed her fingers through her hair. With the snowman under her arm, she descended the stairs and turned into the living room, running smack into Chris's bare chest.

"Oh!" they both exclaimed.

She instinctively reached out, and her hand landed on his waist. She realized then he was only wearing a towel. His skin was still wet and warm from the shower.

Oh, how she wanted to lean into him.

*No, no, no.*

She snatched her hand away and took a step backward.

"I didn't know you'd be up this early." Chris gave her a sheepish look and clutched the knot in his towel. "I didn't wake you?"

"No, no." She shook her head more energetically than necessary. She needed to do something to distract her from the drops of moisture glistening on Chris's chest. One had dripped downward and was snaking between his perfect six pack. It was about to disappear into the towel, which hugged his hips incredibly low. Good thing he was holding onto it. Or not so good...

"You met Frosty?" he asked.

"What?" She saw he was looking at the snowman. "Oh! Yeah, he was a great surprise to wake up to. I'm not usually a stuffed animal kinda girl, but he's extremely cute."

He smiled and rubbed his hand through his damp hair. "So, I'm getting you to like all kinds of new things — Christmas, stuffed animals... what's next?"

*The silly guy who dated my best friend for four years?*

She looked down and played with the snowman's red scarf. "Don't get too full of yourself."

"I'm sure you'll keep me in line," he said.

A slight pause hung in the air, and she didn't dare look up. Chris cleared his throat. "I'm gonna get dressed. The movie's about to start again if you wanna kick off the marathon."

"Do I smell coffee?"

"Yep, it's ready to pour."

He circled around her to take the stairs, and she hugged the snowman to her chest as she walked to the kitchen. This attraction to Chris would fade soon, right? She'd never stayed interested in any one guy too long, so it was only logical. This surely was nothing more than just another meaningless fascination.

*Except there was that moment last night when you poured your heart out to him. You connected with him.*

She fixed a cup of coffee and hurried to the living room. Ralphie and his quest for a BB gun would get her mind off annoying and persistent thoughts.

Chris came down shortly after she got settled under a blanket on the couch. Over the next few hours, they quoted the movie together and counted the number of times someone told Ralphie he was going to shoot his eye out. Uncle Joe's leftover pesto pasta served as lunch, and they didn't turn off the TV until late afternoon when they departed for Frog Pond.

They didn't have to walk far to reach the outdoor rink at Boston Common. A number of people filled the ice, and Aubrey knew she'd have to dodge many of them if she wanted to skate at even half-speed. She and Chris laced up their boots and joined the crowd, starting off with casual strokes around the ice.

"Think I could get some of these people to clear out so I can run through my original dance?" She laughed.

"Can I run it with you? I know some of the samba section from watching you practice it every day. I can shake my moneymaker." Chris shook his shoulders and his hips.

She laughed harder. "I don't know. Nick's set a high standard to live up to. He's one-quarter Latin, so he really thinks he's Ricky Martin in our program."

"Well, I'll put my white-bread dancing up to his one-quarter Latin any day."

"Let's go then!"

They found a pocket of space, and she refreshed Chris on some of the samba moves. When he took her hand and they skated together in dance hold, she found herself grinning wildly again like when they'd danced at the club. Their bodies weren't pressed together as they'd been in Tokyo, but she still felt that undeniable connection, something that made it seem so natural to be that close to him.

While singing the words to Ricky Martin's "Por Arriba, Por Abajo," she and Chris broke apart to dance side-by-side, and the people skating around them stopped to watch. They cheered them on with applause and catcalls as they shimmied their way through the choreography. A loud ovation broke out when they finished, and Chris grabbed Aubrey's hand to lead her into a bow.

He took off his black beanie and unzipped his jacket. "I have too many layers on for all this booty shaking."

His thick hair looked adorably rumpled. Aubrey shoved her hands in her coat pockets, refraining from reaching up and running her fingers through the dark locks.

"I think I've done enough practicing." She pulled out her hands to make air quotes around the last word.

"This is your day, so whatever you wanna do is fine with me," Chris said.

They left the ice to change back into their non-skating boots, and Aubrey was zipping her skate bag when a snowball hit her back. She turned to see Chris a few feet behind her wearing a mischievous grin.

"Sneak attack, huh?" She popped up from the bench and slung her bag over her shoulder. "You'd better run."

She scooped up two handfuls of snow, and Chris raced behind a tree. He came out firing with two snowballs of his own, which missed her as she ducked and ran. She sprinted toward a much wider tree and molded one big ball of ice. Chris's approaching footsteps on the crunchy snow told her he was closing in on her, so she jumped out from behind the trunk and hurled the snowball at him. It whacked him in the face, and she let out a strangled gasp.

"Holy…" His hand flew to his left eye, and he bent over at the waist.

"Oh crap! I am *so* sorry!"

He dropped his hand and slowly stood up straight while rapidly blinking. "I think I can still see."

"You're bleeding." She touched the small cut on his cheek.

"I don't care about blood. I'm just glad I'm not blind. You coulda took my eye out!"

After watching six hours of Ralphie being warned about shooting his eye out, Aubrey couldn't stop her laughter from bursting forth. "Did you hear what you just said?"

Chris quickly went from being appalled to howling along with her, the two of them practically in tears they were in such hysterics. When they finally regained normal breathing, they started walking home along Beacon Street. The redness on Chris's cheek and around his eye seemed to be getting darker.

"I really am sorry," she said. "I guess I should've looked where I was aiming."

"You should think about softball as your next Olympic career. That's quite an arm you've got."

When they reached the apartment, Aubrey went into the bathroom for the first aid kid she'd seen in the closet. She rummaged through it and carried the antiseptic, ointment, and a Band-Aid into the living room.

"Are you gonna tend to my wound?" Chris asked. "You did put it there."

He pointed to his cheek with a pout, and she laughed. "Go wash your face and then I'll fix you up."

He returned a few minutes later, and she directed him to sit in one of the chairs in the small eating area next to the kitchen. As she wiped the tiny freckles on his cheek with the antiseptic, her pulse began to speed up. He was so close and staring at her so intently. *Say something... anything. It's too quiet.*

"Em would've killed me if you had to wear an eye patch," she said. "It doesn't exactly go with your programs."

"I could totally rock an eye patch."

She giggled as she envisioned Chris wearing one and trying to do his and Em's serious classical choreography. "You could've changed your program to *Pirates of the Caribbean*. It would've been amazing."

"That's so twisted." He laughed. "But I love it."

His gaze lingered on her again, turning more serious the longer their eyes stayed connected. Was she imagining it or was he giving her the I-want-to-kiss-you look?

She fumbled with the ointment and Band-Aid, nervously applying them to the cut, and she felt like kicking herself. What was her problem? She broke guys' hearts on a regular basis, and now she was a fluttery mess from touching some guy's face?

"Thanks." Chris smiled. "You're the best nurse I've ever had."

She turned to clean up the table, and the answer to her question became very clear.

Chris wasn't just some guy.

He was so much more.

# CHAPTER TEN

AUBREY SHOOK THE BAG OF MICROWAVE popcorn and carried it into the living room. Only the glow of the television and the colored bulbs on the Christmas tree lit her way. Even though a couple of days had passed since the holiday, Chris still insisted on lighting the tree every night.

He sat on one end of the couch with the remote control pointed at the TV. Aubrey poured the popcorn into the two bowls on the coffee table and then huddled under a blanket on the other end of the sofa. Chris liked to watch TV in the dark, which would be fine if she wasn't battling the constant urge to snuggle with him. He looked so cuddly in his faded red Olympics T-shirt and gray sweatpants.

She picked up one of the bowls and wrapped the blanket tighter around her body. The fleece would have to be a sufficient cuddle substitute.

"So, what are our movie choices?" she asked.

Chris flipped through the On Demand menu. "How about *The Notebook*?"

"Are you serious?"

"It's a good story," he said defensively. "And Rachel

McAdams is hot."

"So is Ryan Gosling, but it's not enough to make me sit through that schmaltz."

"Then you haven't seen it yet?"

She tossed a piece of popcorn into her mouth. "Em tried to talk me into going to see it when it was in the theater, but I refused."

"You've gotta see it." He set the other bowl in his lap. "It's quality schmaltz."

"You may have gotten me to like Christmas and stuffed snowmen, but sappy movies are an entirely different story."

He grinned. "Now I really want you to like it."

His gorgeous grin got her every time, but she wouldn't let him know the effect he had on her. She let out an exaggerated sigh. "I guess I can give it a try. But if the sap becomes unbearable, I'm totally stealing the remote."

"I'll take that deal." He placed the remote between them on the couch. "You have to give it thirty minutes, though."

"Can I set a timer?" She laughed.

"Ye of little faith."

He selected the movie and put a handful of popcorn into his mouth. The opening credits and accompanying romantic score began to play, and Aubrey turned to Chris.

"Even the music is sappy," she said.

Chris threw a piece of popcorn at her, and she laughed as it landed on her blanket. The action started on the screen, so she put her attention on the movie. As the love story unfolded, she found herself drawn into it and enjoying the passion between Allie and Noah. They were so intensely crazy about each other. While they were locked in a smoldering kiss, she snuck a peek at Chris and caught him looking back at her. He quickly averted his eyes toward the TV, and she did the same.

She waited for him to make a joke about her not taking the remote yet, but it didn't happen. When she stole another look at him, his focus was firmly on the TV.

Her heart pitter-pattered way too quickly for just movie-watching. There'd been an intensity in Chris's eyes... similar to how he'd looked at her when she'd patched up his face. She couldn't have imagined it twice, could she?

She returned to munching on her popcorn and immersed herself in the drama on the screen, keeping her eyes glued to the movie. Allie and Noah lost touch, and Allie got engaged to another man, a great guy named Lon, but as soon as Allie saw Noah again, they gave in to their old feelings. Aubrey didn't dare look at Chris as Allie and Noah shared a passionate love scene, tearing their clothes off and tumbling onto the bed. She'd watched plenty of love scenes with guy friends before and hadn't felt any awkwardness, but a tense energy hung in the space between Chris and her. She felt like she was holding her breath the entire time.

When the action finally transitioned to the morning after, she shifted under her blanket. She'd been frozen the past ten minutes. Chris came to life, too, and set his empty bowl on the coffee table. As Aubrey watched Allie and Noah lie in bliss together, a realization came to her.

"Allie cheated on Lon," she said.

Chris sat back and nodded slowly. "Yeah, she sure did."

"I can't be in her corner anymore."

Chris scratched his jaw. "She should've gone home and talked to Lon and broken it off with him before she hooked up with Noah."

Aubrey glanced at the TV and then at Chris, studying him in the dim light. "Do you think you would've been able to stop yourself if you were in that situation?"

"I know I would've," he said immediately. "There's no excuse for cheating. Even being reunited with the love of your life."

She'd normally think a guy was all talk if he said something like that, but she believed Chris really meant it. With all the angst she'd experienced because of her dad's cheating, hearing there was still an honest man out there gave her a warm feeling of hope. The same sensation she'd been feeling more and more around Chris.

"You think I'm full of it," he said.

She realized she'd been staring at him with who knew what kind of expression on her face. "No, not… not at all," she stammered.

She'd seen how many girls had flirted with him when Marley hadn't been around at competitions. He'd always been nice, but he'd never encouraged them.

"If I'm with someone, I'm all in." His eyes locked on hers. "I would never betray that person."

Her mouth grew drier, and she forced a swallow. "Sadly, I think you're a rare breed."

His lips curled just enough to show a hint of his dimples. "It's nice to be appreciated."

He really needed to stop. He needed to stop doing and saying things that made her want to kiss him until she couldn't breathe.

She peeled her eyes away from his smile and put them on the movie. "I do want to see how the rest of this plays out, although I have a good idea."

"The end is pretty depressing, so feel free to turn it off before then if you want."

"Uh-oh. That kinda confirms my suspicions." She slid the remote control across the leather cushion. "Let me know when I should change the channel."

She'd be happy to avoid any additional love scenes, too. *No more romantic movies,* she thought adamantly.

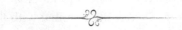

I STRETCHED MY LEG across the bleachers and massaged my right hip. I'd taken a couple of hard falls on the quad Salchow that morning at practice, but I'd also landed seven clean ones.

My success rate was getting higher every week. It couldn't happen at a better time with our departure for nationals coming in just eight days.

Aubrey climbed up to my spot in the top row and chugged from her large bottle of water. Beads of sweat shone on her face and neck, and her ponytail sagged onto her back.

"I saw you going hard in the gym," I said. "You looked like you were racing the Tour de France."

She pushed up the sleeves of her T-shirt and took another gulp of water. "I had a lot of energy to let out."

"You're going to need a nap before the party tonight. You have to be awake for midnight."

She groaned. "Nick is so ridiculous, insisting that I find someone to kiss. Just because I've happened to kiss someone at midnight the years we won gold at nationals doesn't mean there's a correlation between the two. He takes superstition to an all new level."

"It is pretty ridiculous. He said there'd be a lot of people at the party, though, so you shouldn't have any trouble finding a hot guy to help you out."

Aubrey stayed quiet and fiddled with the cap on her bottle, snapping it open and closed. She was more annoyed by Nick's demand than I'd expected. She'd never been bothered by kissing random guys on New Year's before.

"You're sure you and Sergei don't wanna come with us?" she asked.

"No, we're looking forward to our quiet evening alone. My parents said they won't be home until after midnight, and Liza will be at her sleepover. Sergei thought she should spend the evening with us, but she begged him so hard to go. Since she's been having trouble with her friends in New York, we thought it would be good for her to spend time with the new friend she made here."

"Poor kid." Aubrey frowned. "If I was at her rink, I'd have some words for those girls."

"Like you did for the ones who were bullying me when we first met at skating camp?" I laughed.

"Exactly. Except I wouldn't use scratching and hair-pulling as my main tactics this time."

She headed for the locker room, and I turned my attention to Courtney and Mark running their long program on the ice. I'd coached the pair with Sergei until the previous season when they'd moved up to senior level. They were Sergei's most promising young pair at only seventeen and nineteen years old, and they had a good chance to make the Olympic team. Since I'd coached them for four years and we'd formed a close bond, it would make the Olympics even more special if they were part of the team with me.

Chris stopped at the foot of the bleachers and called out, "Think fast."

He tossed one of the two bananas he was holding in my direction, and I caught it before it landed in my lap. "Ready to answer the same questions we've gotten fifteen hundred times?" he asked.

"Maybe this reporter will surprise us," I said and took the steps carefully down to him.

"I'll bet you twenty dollars we're asked how confident we feel about the quad."

I peeled my banana as we walked to the front office. "Umm… yeah, I'm not taking that bet."

We huddled around the phone in the office, where the staff had said we could do our newspaper interview. Piles of papers and binders covered the desk and filled the shelves lining the small room, making it feel even smaller.

Chris took a bite of his banana and looked at his watch. "We have a few minutes."

"So, will you be charming all the ladies at the party tonight?" I asked. "Finally getting back out there on the dating scene?"

He chewed slowly and took his time answering. "I don't

know. Life is good right now."

"Oh?"

"I'm just doing my own thing... hanging out with friends..." He kept his eyes on the desk instead of on me.

"You and Aubrey have been hanging out a lot."

"Well, we live together. It's convenient." He laughed, but it was sort of a nervous laugh.

"I know, but I'm surprised you're getting along so well." I watched his face closely. "I didn't think you had much in common."

He threw his banana peel into the trash can and pulled the phone closer to him. "Sometimes not having much in common makes things interesting."

He pressed the speaker button and dialed the reporter's number. As it began to ring, I continued to study him. The way he'd avoided looking at me during our conversation more than piqued my curiosity. It wasn't like Chris to be anything other than direct.

Something was definitely up between Aubrey and him. Which one of them could I pry the scoop from first?

# CHAPTER ELEVEN

"WELCOME TO THE SOIREE." NICK PUT his arms around Aubrey's and Chris's shoulders.

Aubrey couldn't see much of the décor with the throng of people packed into the living room and kitchen, but what she did see looked swanky — polished wood floors, fancy artwork on the walls, and an elaborate chandelier in the dining area. Nick's friend-of-a-friend must have a nice-paying job to afford such a huge apartment on Beacon Hill.

She took off her long black coat, and Nick let out a low whistle. "I have the hottest partner in the business. No doubt."

Her silver beaded mini-dress showed off plenty of leg. When she'd seen it on sale a few months earlier, she'd known it would be perfect for New Year's Eve because of its bling factor. Chris seemed to be wowed by it too, considering the ogling he'd done before they'd left their apartment.

"You're a doll." She kissed Nick's cheek and then wiped away her deep red lipstick stain.

"In that dress you'll have a line of guys waiting to kiss you at midnight." Nick took her coat and passed it to Chris. "Come with me. There are a few eligible bachelors you need to meet."

"I feel like you're pimping me out," she said.

Nick steered her away from Chris, and she turned to give him a little wave. He offered a weak smile.

The first guy Nick introduced her to turned her off right away. She could barely breathe from the cologne bath he'd taken. When he paused to sip from his beer, she excused herself to get a drink in the kitchen. She also took the opportunity to scope out the room for Chris. In her five-inch strappy heels, she didn't have to crane her neck to see over the crowd like she usually did.

She spotted Chris talking to a pretty brunette, and she took two steps forward to interrupt them before stopping and making a beeline for the kitchen.

*Leave him alone. Let him have his own fun.*

After being connected to him at the hip for the past week and a half, that was hard to do, but she stayed in the kitchen and surveyed the drink options. While she poured a glass of red wine, a super tall guy with curly blond hair smiled at her from across the narrow island.

"Hi, I'm Greg."

She finished pouring and smiled back. "I'm Aubrey."

"How do you know Hunter?"

*Who?* she thought, and then she remembered he was the party's host. "Oh, I don't. My friend Nick sorta knows him."

"So you haven't been here before, then?"

She took a sip of wine and shook her head. "It's a sweet apartment."

"There's a rooftop garden that has a great view of the fireworks. Hunter only lets a few people know about it so it doesn't get too crowded."

"And you're one of the special people who know?"

"Now you are, too." He winked and smiled.

She thought ahead to midnight and her task at hand. Greg was certainly kissable from a looks standpoint — cute,

JENNIFER COMEAUX

no overpowering cologne, nice set of teeth — but the wink reeked of cheesiness, and his eyes weren't giving her a genuine vibe. Plus the idea of kissing anyone except a certain dark-haired guy across the room didn't appeal to her at all.

"So what do you do, Aubrey?" Greg came around to her side of the island. "Let me guess — you're a model."

*Oh, goodness. The cheese is getting thicker.*

Not in the mood to go into her usual spiel about skating, she took a different approach. "I'm an interior designer."

She'd watched enough decorating shows to be able to wing it until she could lose him. The guy wasn't interested in her occupation anyway. That was apparent from the fact that his eyes were spending more time on her body than her face.

She asked him what he did for a living and emptied her glass while he rambled on about the pharmaceutical sales business. She couldn't help but think she'd much rather be home cozy under a blanket and watching TV with Chris. He'd gotten her hooked on reruns of *Seinfeld*, and she'd sucked him into her obsession with *House Hunters* on HGTV. Who knew being a nightly couch potato could be so much fun.

"Don't you think so?" Greg asked.

She'd completely zoned out and had no idea what he was talking about. "I'm uhh... I'm gonna go freshen my makeup. It was good talking to you."

Not her smoothest exit ever, but she didn't care. She looked at her watch. Another hour of empty conversation lay ahead. Maybe she could hang out in the bathroom for a while.

She took her time reapplying her lipstick and repositioning the bobby pins in her hair bun. Nick accosted her as soon as she reentered the living room, and he worked the two of them into a small circle of people. She eventually ended up in a one-on-one with the guy standing next to her, and Nick gave her a thumbs-up behind his back.

This guy got credit for not checking out her legs every two seconds, but she still wasn't feeling him. Her attention drifted to Chris and the brunette locked in deep discussion near the dining table. They must've really hit it off to talk that long. She took a long drink of her wine, but it couldn't wash away the bitter taste in her mouth.

As midnight neared, she decided her best option was to go up on the terrace where maybe Nick wouldn't find her. She could just tell him she'd kissed someone. There was no harm in lying about a dumb superstition.

When she saw Greg and a few others heading out, she threw on her coat and followed them. Greg had found himself a curvy redhead, so he wouldn't be bothering her. They took the elevator up to the top floor and exited through a door at the end of the long hallway.

Ice covered all the planters where she assumed flowers sprouted in the spring and summer. She stood in the corner of the terrace and checked her phone for any new messages. There was a text from Marley wishing her a fun night and saying she and Zach were at a party at their coach's house. It contained lots of exclamation points. At least someone was having a good time that evening.

She dropped the phone into her small black purse and stared out at the lights of Cambridge across the Charles River. Maybe the fireworks would put her in a better mood.

"There you are," she heard behind her.

She turned and saw Chris shrugging on his jacket. He was alone. Her mood felt slightly better already.

"How'd you know about this place?" she asked.

"The girl I was talking to, Megan. She told me about it."

Her spirits shifted downward again. "Is she on her way up?"

"I think she's coming with some friends. Her boyfriend called so she was talking to him. He's stuck in L.A. on business."

Spirits soaring back up! She felt like she was riding the Space Mountain of emotions.

Chris continued, "She's from Baltimore so we were talking about where we went to school and stuff. Turns out we know some of the same people."

"That's cool."

Chris looked around as he buttoned his jacket. "You're out here alone?"

She paused and lifted one eyebrow. "Uh-oh. You mean you don't see all the other people?" She gasped. "Am I a ghost whisperer?"

He laughed. "I meant you're not with anyone."

"Nope. But you can't tell Nick or I'll have to kill you."

He chewed on the inside of his bottom lip as he stared at her. "I've never been a superstitious guy, but do you really wanna tempt fate in an Olympic year?"

"Are you telling me I need to find someone to kiss in the next—" She looked at her watch. "Two minutes?'

"Well…" He glanced down at the ground and then up at her. "You could use *me*… since you let me use you at the club in Tokyo."

Her voice stuck in her throat, and she had to inhale and exhale an icy breath before she could reply. "Yeah… that would work."

"Ten! Nine! Eight!" the other partygoers shouted.

Her heart hammered against her chest. She had to play it cool. Chris was giving her a simple kiss. She couldn't get carried away and try to make out with him, which is what she wanted to do. So badly.

"Three! Two! One!"

Fireworks exploded in the distance, and Chris hugged her. "Happy New Year."

*Okay, hug first.* She wrapped her arms around his broad shoulders. "Happy New Year."

He held onto her but pulled his head back just enough so they faced each other. His eyes stared into hers as his warm breath fanned across her lips. She thought she might have a heart attack from the anticipation.

His hands pressed gently on the small of her back and then his mouth was on hers, so soft and careful. And quick. Too quick. Their lips divided, and she expected him to pull away, to leave it at that one kiss.

But he didn't.

His mouth lingered within a whisper of hers, daring her to lean forward. The fireworks boomed overhead, but they were nothing compared to the emotions exploding inside her — mostly desire but also a surprising amount of fear.

"Whoa! What is this?"

Aubrey looked behind Chris, and Nick stood there half-laughing, half-gaping at them. Chris let her go, and the cold air hit her with a sobering blast.

"Is something going on I should know about?" Nick's eyebrows danced up and down.

Aubrey exchanged glances with Chris and then put one hand on her hip. "You told me I had to kiss someone."

"Yeah, but I didn't think you'd have to resort to Chris." Nick held up his hand. "No offense intended. You know what I mean."

Chris didn't respond as he still looked a bit startled. Aubrey said, "Look, there was no one here I wanted to kiss, Chris offered to help me out, and I did what you wanted me to do, so… there it is."

Nick slowly bobbed his head, still eyeing them suspiciously. "There it is."

She hugged her arms to her chest and started toward the exit. "I'm gonna see if I can get a cab."

After a moment, Chris followed her. "I'll go with you."

They entered the warmth of the building and rode the elevator down to the lobby in silence. The awkwardness hung so thick in the air she almost choked on it. Why wasn't Chris cracking jokes like he usually did? Maybe if *she* made some kind of joke about the situation, all would return to normal.

But she couldn't think of anything to say because there was absolutely nothing funny about what had happened.

With no cabs in sight in the residential area, they walked a couple of blocks to Charles Street, where Chris flagged down a yellow taxi. Aubrey's phone rang with "Candy" as they climbed inside, and she breathed with relief. A call from Em would save her from more awkward silence.

"Happy New Year," she answered.

"Happy New Year," Em said. "I just wanted to call before I conk out again."

"Did you miss the countdown at midnight?"

"Almost. I fell asleep on the sofa at ten o'clock and just happened to wake up at quarter to twelve. I hope your night was more exciting. Did you find a hottie to kiss?"

She looked at Chris out of the corner of her eye. "I did."

"Sounds like it was a good night, then."

"Yeah, it was… interesting."

They finished with good night wishes, and she put away her phone as the taxi pulled up in front of the brownstone. She tried to give Chris money to split the fare, but he wouldn't take it. At least they were talking again.

Chris headed straight for the kitchen after he dropped his jacket onto the couch. Aubrey threw her coat next to his and lingered for a minute in the living room, but he didn't reappear so she went upstairs. She'd get comfy in her PJs and try to think of something witty to say for when she returned downstairs. Maybe Chris thought she was uncomfortable from their kiss and that's why he was being so quiet. Or maybe he regretted doing it.

Or… maybe he'd felt the same rush she had, and he didn't know what to do about it either.

She took off her heels and removed the pins from her hair. Reaching behind her, she tugged on the zipper of her dress, and it stuck not far from the neckline. She pulled harder, but it wouldn't budge. With her arms contorting every which way behind her back, she wrestled with the zipper, cursing as it refused to move. Asking Chris to help her get undressed wasn't the witty conversation starter she needed. But unless she cut herself out of the dress with a scissors, there was no alternative.

She went down to the living room, and Chris looked up from his laptop. He'd shed his sweater, leaving him in the white T-shirt he'd worn underneath. Music played softly on the computer, and when she moved closer she heard it was "Crush" by Dave Matthews Band.

"Can you help me?" she asked. "My zipper is stuck. I've been trying and trying, but I can't get it."

Chris sat frozen, one hand on the computer and the other gripping a bottle of water. Had he heard her?

"Sure," he finally said.

He set down the bottle and made his way behind her. She swept her hair over the front of one shoulder to get it out of Chris's way, and she stood as still as a statue as he leaned in close and fiddled with the zipper.

Each second Chris stood behind her made it harder to stay composed. The crisp, clean scent of his body wash teased her, reminding her of what could've happened on the rooftop if Nick hadn't interrupted.

He made a swift tug, and a zipping noise followed. She turned her head slightly, but Chris didn't move.

Then she felt it.

His fingertips touched her skin, so lightly they were like a feather brushing down her back. Goose bumps spread over every inch of her body. Chris bent his head and breathed in her hair, and a warm shiver rocked her body. She couldn't stop this. She didn't want to stop this.

She turned, and their eyes connected for a split moment before their lips crashed into each other. Chris's mouth opened hers, stealing her breath and making her dizzy. She grasped his waist and pressed against him, and he groaned low in his throat, deepening their kiss.

His hands cupped her face then threaded through her hair, tangling the silky strands. His touch felt so good, so right. She pushed up his T-shirt, dragging her fingernails across his back, and his mouth left hers for just an instant as he pulled the shirt over his head and tossed it onto the floor.

He returned for another breathtaking kiss, and she wrapped her arms around him, melting into the hardness of his muscles. She'd never felt so vulnerable, like she was losing all control of herself. She was at the total mercy of Chris's lips and his touch.

He unzipped her dress farther and slipped his hand inside, and the heat of his palm on her skin made her body ache even more for him. Her knees were about to give way. She was a few moments away from surrendering completely to him.

She had to stop this. Somehow.

There were too many risks, too many feelings, too many fears. She couldn't let herself be exposed.

Chris softly kissed her throat, and she fought within herself, summoning the strength to pull away from him.

"I can't…" she said breathlessly. "I can't do this."

And she ran up the stairs.

# CHAPTER TWELVE

AUBREY SHUT HER BEDROOM DOOR AND pressed her back against it. Her body was buzzing, her breaths coming in quick gasps. She could still feel Chris's hands on her skin, still taste his hot kisses.

Stumbling forward to the closet, she ripped off her dress and put on a T-shirt and flannel pajama pants. She needed something to help her feel normal again if that was even possible. Her emotions were so out of whack she couldn't make any sense of them.

She collapsed onto the bed and lay on the blanket, gazing at the low ceiling. She'd made out with a lot of guys, gone further with a few, but there'd always been a part of her she'd kept emotionally closed off to them. No one had ever come close to breaking through and reaching it... until now.

And that terrified her.

Besides that not-so-little issue, there was the Marley factor.

A light knock on the door shot her up into a sitting position. She stared at the door for a minute before she took a few calming breaths and walked slowly toward it, opening it even more deliberately.

Chris had put his shirt back on… thank goodness. He rested one hand against the door frame, and his eyes crinkled with concern.

"Are you okay?" he asked. "I didn't mean for things to get so… intense."

"Yeah, it's… it's okay." She rubbed her arms, though she didn't know why because she wasn't cold. "We just shouldn't… you know, because of Marley."

"We broke up months ago."

"But you were together a long time."

Chris took his hand off the frame. "Can I come in so we can talk?"

She glanced behind her at the only seating option — the bed. *Not a good idea.*

"Let's go downstairs," she said.

They sat on the sofa, and she pushed aside their coats and wrapped herself in the fleece blanket that was folded under them. Again, not feeling cold but needing something as a comforting shield.

Chris watched her bundle herself into a cocoon before he began, "I've had more fun the past couple of weeks than I've had in a really, really long time. And it's because of you."

Even wrapped in the blanket, she felt goose bumps prickle the back of her neck. "I've had a lot of fun, too, but if you want more than that, I can't…" *Why am I having so much trouble getting the words out?*

Chris's eyes darted over her face, so she looked away at the laptop on the coffee table. She didn't recognize the rock song playing, but the singer was wailing about love gone wrong.

Chris tapped his fingers lightly on his jeans. "Why don't we just keep having fun? Keep doing what we've been doing?"

"Including what we were doing a few minutes ago?" She

FIGHTING FOR THE EDGE

swung her eyes over to him.

"Is that a trick question?" he asked.

Laughter snuck up on her, and she couldn't contain it. It felt wonderful after all the crazy emotions she'd experienced that night.

"How do you always make me laugh even when I'm being serious?" she asked.

"I was being serious, too," he said with a little smile. "Depending on how I answer your question, I could get in a lot of trouble."

"How's that?"

"If I say I'm cool with keeping things platonic, your feelings might be hurt, even though I'm trying to be a gentleman. And if I say I want to pick up where we left off a few minutes ago, you might think I'm just another guy with a one-track mind."

"So which is it?"

He paused and gave her a long look. "Both."

She smiled. "Very smooth. And you claim you have no game."

"My game is very much a work-in-progress." He shifted so his whole body was facing her. "Bottom line is — I wanna hang out with you. That's all."

She loosened the blanket so she could angle more toward him, too. "I just want to make sure you don't have any expectations because I know you're usually all about relationships and romance—"

He pshawed. "I'm Mr. Casual now, remember? I am firmly anti-romance."

"Oh, you are?" She laughed.

"Yes, I am." He nodded and then his face lit up with an apparent idea. "I can prove it to you. I'll take you out this week for the most unromantic evening you've ever experienced."

"Where are you taking me — the city garbage dump?"

He let out a loud laugh. "I said unromantic, not disgusting."

She lifted one eyebrow. "This sounds like a date."

"A casual date. Between two people with no expectations. Just having fun."

It seemed harmless enough. She was so happy to have joking Chris back, and keeping things light meant she didn't have to face her fears and all those other confusing emotions. How could she say no?

"I'm in."

He grinned. "Excellent."

So, Chris really was just looking to have fun, and he had no deeper feelings. She thought she'd felt something more from him. In the moment before he'd kissed her on the rooftop, she'd seen a look in his eyes that felt... *real*. But she must've been mistaken. She should be happy, right?

I SLOWLY LIFTED MY eyelids and read the digital clock on the nightstand. Why did I feel so tired after nine hours of sleep? Pangs of hunger turned my stomach, telling me I needed to get up.

The sound of rhythmic breathing came from the side of the bed, so I rolled over and saw Sergei in his gray gym shorts doing push-ups on the carpet. The muscles in his bare back and shoulders rippled with each thrust of his arms. I quietly watched his workout for a few minutes, enjoying the rise and fall of his tight backside.

"I can't think of a better way to start the New Year," I said. "Can I get this view every morning?"

Sergei stopped and sat back on his knees. "I can give you an even better one."

In an instant he was on top of the bed and hovering over me, his arms outstretched as they'd been on the carpet. He bent to kiss my neck, and the moisture on his chest dampened my nightgown.

I squealed. "You're all sweaty."

"Come take a shower with me."

I was ready to jump out of bed with him, but my stomach growled again. "Can I get breakfast first? I'm starving."

He smiled and cupped my hip, running his hand up along my ribcage. My stomach responded with a very different and much more pleasant sensation.

"Yes, feed this beautiful body," he said. "And then it's all mine."

"Always," I whispered.

While he went into the walk-in closet, I got up and put on my robe. I opened the bedroom door and was at the top of the stairs when the smell of cabbage assaulted my nose. The rolling contents of my stomach rose to my throat, and I hurried to the bedroom with my hand over my mouth.

I opened and slammed the door shut and swallowed hard, trying to push down the sickening sensation. Sergei came out of the closet and gaped at me.

"What's wrong?"

I crept to the bed and took my paperback from the nightstand to fan myself. "I don't feel so good."

"You were fine a minute ago." Sergei sat beside me and combed my hair from my face.

"My stomach felt weird when I woke up, and I thought I was just hungry, but when I smelled my mom's cabbage cooking, I almost hurled."

"You look forward to eating that every New Year's Day."

"I know. The smell has never bothered me."

"I hope you don't have some kind of bug."

"I got the flu shot," I said, still fanning.

"That doesn't protect you from everything. Why don't you lie down and I'll get you some crackers and soda."

I settled back against the pillows and closed my eyes.

When Sergei returned, Mom's voice carried behind him.

"Sweetie, you're sick?" She came over to the bed and put her hand on my forehead. The cabbage odor had travelled with her, and I started sweating again.

"The smell," I said, clamping my hand over my nose and scooting to the other side of the bed.

"You must be feeling really bad if it bothers you that much," she said.

"Can you give her some space?" Sergei stood tall over my petite mother.

She looked at me with knitted brows and then went toward the door. "I can make you some soup or mashed potatoes later. Something light."

"Thank you, that would be good." Sergei herded her out the door.

I got comfortable again, and Sergei put the can of ginger ale on the nightstand and handed me the box of crackers. "Try to eat a few."

I dug into the box and took a nibble on one of the saltines. "You can go take your shower. I'll be okay."

"You sure?" He rubbed my leg.

I nodded as I chewed slowly. And I did feel better the more I ate. By the time Sergei finished showering, my stomach had settled. I got dressed and made my second attempt to go downstairs, but as soon as the cabbage smell hit me again, I had to do another about-face.

Sergei followed me into the bedroom. "You feel sick again?"

"It's almost making me gag."

He stroked my hair and then my back. "We'll just take it easy up here then."

We watched TV, or rather Sergei watched and I dozed in and out, until lunchtime. He brought me a bowl of mashed potatoes Mom had whipped up, and I insisted he go down and enjoy the holiday spread she'd prepared.

I felt fine after eating the entire bowl of potatoes, so I told Sergei not to worry about leaving me. He had to pick up Liza from her sleepover, and she wanted to skate for an hour or two since she was going back to New York the next day. He kissed my forehead on his way out, and I curled up on the window seat with my book.

I read for a while but then started thinking about my stomach issues. I hadn't gotten my period yet that month, but I was often late due to the stress and strain I put on my body every day. Maybe I had some hormonal thing going on that had made me feel sick.

I got up and looked in my purse for my calendar. Flipping to December, I counted the days. My finger froze on the page.

Eight days late already? It didn't seem like it had been that long. I counted again.

Still eight.

My heart began to thump with worried beats. That was *really* late. *But I'm on the pill, and we always use extra protection.*

Except...

My eyes zeroed in on Friday, December ninth, the night of the nor'easter. The night we'd played strip poker and there'd been a lot of wine and a lot of intense passion. But not a lot of caution.

*No, it's too improbable. It was just one night. And I'm ON THE PILL.*

I went to my laptop on the desk and clicked on the search engine. My fingers shook while typing — *odds of getting pregnant while on birth control pill.*

Millions of hits popped up. I clicked on a string of them and read.

*Pill is ninety-nine percent effective when used properly.*

*If taken correctly, chance of getting pregnant is less than one percent per year.*

I read on an on, and every site spouted the same statistics.

I rubbed my temples as I thought about the past month and whether I'd done anything that could've made the pill ineffective. Nothing came to me. Could I possibly be in that miniscule percentage?

Sergei opened the door, and I quickly closed the web browser. "You're back early."

"We were at the rink and Liza went to use the restroom, and when she came out she said she didn't feel good and wanted to come home. She might have a bug, too. She barely said two words in the car."

A wave of relief washed over me. If Liza was sick, there was a good chance I had the same thing. I knew the odds of me being pregnant were too small.

"I'll go check on her," I said.

I knocked on Liza's door and peeked inside when she didn't answer. She was lying on the bed with her back to me, facing the window. I sat on the bed and touched her shoulder.

"Hey, sweetie, you're not feeling good?"

She was hugging one of the pillows, and she curled her arms tighter around it. "I think I got my period," she mumbled.

*Oh, man.* I wasn't ready for that talk yet. If we should even have that talk. I didn't know what Elena had told her, if anything.

"Has your mom talked to you about it?" I asked.

"Not really. Hope got hers already so she tells me all about it."

Being educated by another eleven-year-old... not the best scenario.

"I'll go to my room and get you some supplies, okay?" I said. "I'll be right back."

When I stepped into the hall, an unfortunate realization hit me. Liza wasn't sick, so maybe I wasn't either. The percentages flashed through my mind.

I continued forward to my bedroom, and Sergei looked

up when I entered. "I wonder if Liza has what you have," he said.

*I WISH I had what she has.*

"She doesn't have a bug," I said. "She got her first period."

Sergei's mouth hung open as he seemed to be digesting the news. "Oh. Is she okay?"

"I think so. I came to get some stuff for her." I motioned to the bathroom.

He rubbed the back of his neck. "Should I go talk to her?"

"Give her a little time. Even though you're an incredibly cool dad, it's probably still mortifying for her to think about discussing it with you."

"You're probably right." His hand moved from his neck to his face. "I don't even know what to say."

"It's best not to say too much. I'll never forget when I got mine at the rink and I had to call my dad to pick me up. I just wanted to crawl into a hole."

I returned to Liza with the personal items she needed, and she slowly opened up with questions, the same I remembered having when I'd been her age.

"Is my body gonna change really quickly?" she asked. "I've heard some of the girls at the rink say it can mess up your jumps."

"You'll start feeling some changes, but everyone goes through it at a different rate. If something starts to feel off, be sure to talk to your coach and she can help you. And your dad can help, too. He's been through this with a lot of students."

She cringed. "I don't really wanna talk to him about this."

"It's embarrassing, I know." I smoothed her long ponytail. "But he's a great listener, so just know he's always there if you need him."

"My mom is going to make this into so much drama." She groaned.

*Elena and drama? Shocking!*

"Do you want me to call her and let her know what's going on or do you want to tell her when you get home?" I hoped she'd choose the latter.

She looked up at me with her big blue eyes. "Can you call?"

I could never say no to the kid when she gave me that wide-eyed gaze. She and Sergei had some magical powers in those magnificent baby blues.

Liza said she was tired, so I kissed her head and started for the door. As I was leaving, she asked, "Am I gonna get PMS?"

I laughed. "What do you know about PMS?"

"Hope says her big sister gets it and it makes her mean."

I shook my head. "You don't need to worry about that too much right now." I went over to the bed and gave her a tight squeeze. "And you're too sweet to ever be mean."

Sergei was gone from our room, so I took the quiet opportunity to call Elena. With bigger issues on my mind, I wasn't in the mood for her drama, so I hoped she wouldn't go all overbearing-mother on me.

After exchanging pleasantries, I told her the news, and she gasped. "So soon? I am much older when I have my first."

"Well, she's almost twelve. She's about the average age."

"Is she scared? Is her stomach hurting? I can leave now to get her." Rustling ensued in the background.

"She's fine. There's no reason to come get her early."

"She should be with her mother," she snapped.

I pinched the bridge of my nose. Elena was never going to stop playing that card. Most instances I didn't fight back because the headache wasn't worth it, but I couldn't hold my tongue this time.

"Sergei and I are her parents, too, and we're taking care of her just fine. I understand you want her with you, but she doesn't want this to be a big deal. So, we shouldn't smother her right now."

"I do not smother. I just want my daughter home."

*You don't know who you're talking to. I am an expert on smothering mothers.*

"She'll be home tomorrow," I said. "I'll tell her to call you tonight."

Having convinced Elena not to jump into her car, I tossed my phone onto the bed and stretched out on the comforter. My hands went to my abdomen, and I said a prayer that my body would return to normal very, very soon.

*Less than one percent.*

No way could I be pregnant. Nope. Not happening. Not now.

# CHAPTER THIRTEEN

"Work it!" Chris shouted as Aubrey and Nick samba danced their way past him in their third run-through of the day.

Aubrey flashed him a smile while her skates moved furiously across the ice, keeping time with the fast beat of the music.

Nick swung her up onto his shoulders, and she locked into a full laid-out position as he spun around and around for their rotational lift. After the final turn he deftly set her down, and they finished the program nose-to-nose, breathing heavily in synch.

"Best one yet," Nick said after a deep exhale.

They skated along the boards to cool down, and Aubrey wiped her forehead with the back of her hand. "I think the holiday yesterday recharged me. I slept until two in the afternoon."

"Was that because you and Chris were up late continuing your New Year's Eve celebration?" Nick asked with a knowing smile.

"What are you talking about?"

"When I saw you on the terrace, the sexual tension

between you two was so thick I needed an axe to cut through it. No way did you not go home and get busy."

The image of Chris ripping off his shirt popped into her head, and she took a long swallow. "We did not *get busy*. We're friends."

He hummed quietly as he gave her a sideways look. "I have a good sense for these things."

He also had a gossipy mouth, and she didn't want her private business circulating around the rink.

"I think your sense is on the fritz," she said and skated ahead of him.

With the end of the session near, she hopped off the ice and changed into sneakers for her workout in the gym. Em did the same next to her on the bleachers and then leaned in close.

"Can you come outside with me a minute?" she asked.

Em had been very quiet when she'd arrived at the rink that morning. All she'd said about her holiday was that she'd been sick. She still looked a little pale.

"What's up?" Aubrey asked as they walked out into the gray afternoon.

Em zipped her blue warm-up jacket up to her chin and glanced around the quiet parking lot. "Can I ask you a favor?"

"Sure." She watched Em continue to look around nervously. "What do you need?"

"I need you to buy a pregnancy test for me."

Aubrey's jaw stuck open. "A what?"

"A pregnancy test," Em said in a hushed voice.

"You think you're pregnant?"

"I'm over a week late. I'm on the pill, but it's not a hundred percent foolproof, and we usually use extra protection, but we didn't the night of the storm, and I'm scared to death that I'm somehow in the crazy less than one percent that can end up pregnant."

Em's frantic breath created icy puffs through the air. Aubrey stood motionless, trying to process the ramble of information she'd just received.

"Okay." She grasped Em's shoulders and took a moment to collect her thoughts. "We're not going to freak out because the odds are very slim, right?"

Em nodded slowly.

"We'll get the test, and this could all be a false alarm." She squeezed Em's shoulders before letting her go. "I just have one question. Why do you need me to buy it for you?"

"Because your face isn't on a Coca-Cola billboard on the Mass Pike. I don't want anyone that might recognize me to see me with the test."

"Good point."

"I don't want Sergei to know about this either unless I really am…" She pressed her hands to her face, and her eyes watered with distress.

Aubrey saw Em was close to breaking down, so she put her arms around her and tried to sound as optimistic as she could. "Remember — it's still very unlikely."

"I know, but I've been having symptoms."

Aubrey stepped back. "Do you want me to go get the test now? I can work out later."

"No, let's stick to our normal schedule and then we can go to my house."

They spent the next hour in the gym, where Aubrey watched Em from the bike across from hers. If Em had gotten pregnant the night of the storm, she'd be two months along at the Olympics. She wouldn't even be showing, but was it possible to compete at their level while in the early stages of pregnancy? There'd been professional skaters who'd performed in shows until they were three or four months along, but shows were nothing compared to the daily grind of competitive skating. If Em couldn't skate…

Aubrey's feet slowed on the pedals. She didn't want to even let that thought enter her mind.

When they left the rink, Aubrey made a quick stop at the

drugstore and then met Em at her parents' house. Her dad poked his head out of his office as they passed through the foyer.

"Happy New Year, Aubrey."

"Hey, Mr. Jim." Aubrey shoved the drugstore bag deeper into her purse. "Happy New Year."

"Em, are you feeling better today?" His blue eyes showed concern behind his glasses.

"I'm okay," Em said, avoiding his gaze and walking away. "We'll be upstairs."

As they climbed the steps, Aubrey said, "I assume your mom's not around? She can smell a problem a mile away."

"She and Aunt Deb went outlet mall shopping. She'll be gone all day."

They shut themselves in Em's bedroom, and Aubrey handed her the package. Em sank onto the window seat and stared at the rectangular box.

"I'm not ready to do it yet," she said. "Talk to me about something. Anything other than this."

Aubrey sat on the bed. "Umm…"

"Tell me about the New Year's party… about the hot guy you met."

*Should I get into the Chris situation right now?* She really wanted to talk about it, and the news could be big enough to distract Em from her troubles.

"Well… I didn't exactly meet him. I already knew him."

"Who was it?"

Aubrey felt a smile forming on her lips. "Chris."

"I knew it! I knew something was going on with you guys."

"How did you know?"

Em waved her hand. "That's not important. Tell me about the kiss."

Aubrey smiled bigger. She'd definitely succeeded in distracting Em, and she had no objections to reliving that night.

"It was Chris's idea to help me out since I hadn't found anyone to kiss and it was almost midnight." Aubrey brought her legs up onto the bed and crossed them. "So, he kissed me, and I think he would've done it again but Nick interrupted us."

"What happened after that?"

"Long story short, we went home and we ended up making out." Aubrey watched Em's eyes get bigger. "But that's as far as it went."

"That's still pretty huge."

"We're not dating or anything. Neither of us wants to get serious, and I wouldn't do that without talking to Marley."

"So, are you like friends with benefits?" Em's forehead wrinkled.

"No," Aubrey said emphatically. "At least not the kind of benefits that usually come with that arrangement. We're just hanging out and having fun. I don't wanna overanalyze this because things are good, you know? I just enjoy spending time with him."

Em studied her with a thoughtful gaze. "You like him a lot."

Aubrey looked down at the sandy-colored carpet. She wasn't prepared to think about the feelings she had for Chris much less discuss them.

"He's a really great guy," she said.

Em's cell phone rang, and she bit her lip as she looked at the screen. "Hey, love," she answered.

Aubrey looked around the room as Em listened to Sergei on the other end of the line. She'd spent a lot of nights there, singing karaoke with Em in their pajamas, giving each other manicures, and watching *The Breakfast Club* on the old VCR. She never dreamed she'd be in that room supporting her best friend while she took a pregnancy test.

"No, I don't need anything," Em said and paused. "Okay.

Love you."

She ended the call and stood with the test in hand. "He'll be home in an hour. I need to do this."

She marched to the bathroom and closed the door, and Aubrey went over to the antique vanity where she and Em used to do makeovers. It was weird seeing Sergei's cologne and his comb next to the mirror.

Em rushed out of the bathroom with the same intensity with which she'd gone inside. "It says to wait at least two minutes but not more than ten."

"Try to breathe. I know it's hard," Aubrey said.

She took a long inhale and exhale. "We didn't get to finish talking about you and Chris."

"You've got bigger things to deal with right now."

"I wanted to say something before Sergei called." Em's eyes softened from their anxious look. "Be careful, okay? I don't want either of you to get hurt. I love you guys."

Aubrey hugged her. No one would get hurt if they kept everything fun and games. She just had to make sure she stayed in control. She couldn't let herself get carried away like she did on New Year's.

Em slipped out of her embrace and took another deep breath. "It's time."

I PAUSED IN THE doorway of the bathroom and eyed the white stick on the sink. In a few seconds, my life would change with a simple plus or minus sign. It was a moment I'd thought Sergei and I would share together... in the future when we were actually planning a family.

*Maybe I should've waited for him to do this.*

I glanced at my panicked expression in the mirror. No, if it turned out negative, there was no need to put him through the worry, too.

I crept toward the sink, holding my breath. Keeping my eyes on the mirror, I folded my hands in prayer and waited until the last possible moment to look down at the stick.

Positive.

My heart pounded harder, so hard I started to gasp. I covered my face and peeked between my fingers, hoping the plus sign would miraculously change into a minus.

It didn't.

With my hands on my head, I slowly turned and walked into the bedroom. Aubrey's eyes widened.

"Em…"

"This can't be happening." My voice shook. "No, no, no."

"Oh, Em." Aubrey touched her mouth.

"I can't be pregnant! This can't be real!"

Aubrey grasped my waist and steered me to the bed. "Come sit down."

I sat and bent forward, letting the blood flow to my head. This had to be a bad dream, a wickedly cruel nightmare spawned from my months of pre-Olympic stress. I'd been so worried about a fluke accident happening and ruining my Olympic chances. Never, ever, ever did I think that accident would be a baby.

*I'm having a baby.*

Tears seared my throat, and I choked back a sob. Finding out I was pregnant, having Sergei's child, should be a wonderful thing, but instead I felt overwhelming fear and dread.

Aubrey rubbed my back. "Don't think the worst. There've been women who skated pregnant—"

"Not at the Olympics!" I cried as I sat up. "What if the doctor says it's too dangerous? What if he tells me to stop skating immediately?"

"You're in perfect physical shape, you train smart, you take care of yourself — those are all things in your favor."

Aubrey's words weren't calming my nerves. I just kept

thinking of more bad things.

"How am I going to tell Sergei? He's not going to believe this is happening again. It's like some horrible twist of fate."

"Your situation is nothing like what happened with Elena. You're married, and you were careful—"

"Not careful enough," I squeaked.

Aubrey circled her arms around me, and our heads rested together. "You'll find a way to get through this. You're one of the strongest people I've ever known."

I dabbed at my eyes, and we sat for a few minutes quietly holding onto each other. I needed to pull myself together before Sergei came home. This wasn't the kind of thing I wanted to blurt out as soon as he walked in the door.

Aubrey hugged me long and hard as she left. Alone and jittery, I threw away the pregnancy test, did a spontaneous scrubbing of the bathroom, and then showered and changed. As I sat at the vanity and put on my makeup, I scrutinized myself in the mirror, looking for anything different in my appearance. How long would it be until I started to put on weight, until my clothes, my costumes became tighter? Normal women didn't show until a few months into pregnancy, but I wasn't a normal-sized person. A few added pounds on me would be a huge deal.

I'd just finished applying my lip gloss when Sergei breezed in and kissed the top of my head.

"You look like you're ready to go out," he said, removing his heavy Team USA jacket.

I swiveled on the stool. "I was thinking we could go into the city, maybe take a walk and then grab dinner." We had to get out of that room. Telling Sergei the news was nerve-wracking enough. I couldn't do it in my childhood bedroom, where it would feel like I was a teenager who'd been knocked up by my boyfriend.

"You must have your appetite back." He went into the closet with his jacket. "I was worried when you looked a little shaky at breakfast this morning."

"Yeah, I'm feeling better." *Probably only until tomorrow morning.*

"Let's go wherever you want then. I'll get changed real quick."

"Have you heard from Liza?"

He reappeared with a dark pair of jeans and a sky blue sweater over his arm. "She called when I was in the car. They'd just gotten home."

"Good. I hope Elena doesn't hover over her too much. I told her to call me if she wants to talk more."

Sergei tugged his long-sleeved T-shirt over his head. "Thanks again for taking the lead on her uh... problem yesterday. If I'd had to deal with it on my own, she probably would've locked herself in her room."

One corner of my mouth curled upward. "You would've handled it fine, but I'm happy I could help."

After Sergei changed and we bundled up in our coats, we walked to the Coolidge Corner T stop. The night was cold, but it felt invigorating, giving me more energy. At least now I knew why I'd been so tired lately.

The train into Boston was busy with rush-hour riders, although not as packed as the Green Line heading outbound from the city. Sergei hugged my waist with one arm and held onto the railing with the other as we stood in the crowded car. Through the twenty-minute ride, I thought of all the responses I might get from Sergei upon hearing my news. Sure, he wanted kids soon, but not *now*. Not with the biggest moment of my career six weeks away.

We exited at Arlington Street, and I suggested we walk through the Public Garden. It was a peaceful escape from the noisy streets filled with people and traffic. Sergei and I joined our gloved hands, and we strolled along the snow-cleared path toward the frozen lagoon.

"I'm glad you wanted to spend tonight alone because I

need to talk to you about something," Sergei said.

I tilted my head up to him. "There's something I need to talk to you about, too."

"You can go first," he said.

My chest tightened, and I felt like my voice had disappeared. I touched his arm. "You... you go."

"Okay." He peered at me a moment and then said, "I've been asked by the Skating Club of Boston if I'd be interested in coaching here permanently."

I stopped walking. "They want you to move here?"

"Us. Want *us* to move here." Sergei took my other hand in his. "They know you'll be coaching with me once you retire."

"What about all your students? They'd have to move, too?"

"I'd have to talk to them. They could possibly commute, like most of them are doing now. Court's done with high school, so she and Mark might be able to move up here. There are a lot of things to think about, but the number one thing is whether this is something you'd want to do."

His eyes searched mine, looking for a response. But I had none. I couldn't wrap my head around all the changes that were suddenly knocking at my door. A baby, leaving our home, possibly losing my chance at the Olympics... it was too much. I pulled my scarf away from my neck, seeking more air.

I shook my head. "I can't think about this right now."

"I know you've got nationals on your mind and—"

"It's not nationals." My head moved back and forth with more vigor. "It's something else."

"Is it what you needed to talk to me about?"

I switched to nodding briskly. A few people passed us on the path, and I squeezed Sergei's hands and pulled him further under the trees. Our boots squished the slushy snow covering the grass.

"What is it, Em?" Sergei's thumbs stroked mine.

I stared up at him, the man I loved more every day we

spent together. My throat swelled with emotion, and I swallowed hard. This wasn't how this moment should feel. I should be jumping up and down, ecstatic to tell Sergei we're having a baby. I shouldn't be frightened and worried and in denial.

*Just say it. You have to face that this is real.*

I looked directly into his deep blue eyes. "I'm pregnant."

As expected, he said nothing. He uttered no sound, moved not one inch. He'd become one of the frozen statues that decorated the Garden.

When more than a minute passed with still no response, I pressed my hand to his chest. "Sergei?"

His lips parted, and he whispered, "How?"

"The pill didn't work."

He stared at me again. "You're pregnant."

"Yes," I croaked.

He placed his palm on my cheek, and the soft leather of his glove warmed my face. His caring touch brought out the tears I'd been holding back, and my chin began to tremble.

Sergei took me into his arms and held me tightly to his body as if he was shielding me from a storm. With his mouth pressed to the top of my knit cap, he mumbled, "How far along are you?"

"I think about five weeks."

"Have you been to the doctor?"

"No, I took a home test."

Silence set in again, and the faraway sounds of car horns and tires on wet pavement came into focus. Sergei remained quiet, but the caress of his fingers in my hair let me know he was still there with me in the moment. His head was probably spinning as much as mine had been since the second I saw the plus sign.

He leaned back and cradled my face in his hands. "We'll get you to the doctor tomorrow, and we'll find out what we need to do, what's best for you and the baby."

Tears leaked from my eyes. "I'm really scared."

Sergei wrapped me in another embrace. "Let's go home."

I nodded against his jacket. How had I thought I could go to dinner after this? It must've been a product of my denial of the situation. All I wanted to do was to curl up in Sergei's arms, to feel safe. And the way he held onto me, it felt like he never wanted to let me go.

# CHAPTER FOURTEEN

SERGEI STILL LOOKED DAZED WHEN WE reached my parents' house after our walk. We attempted to duck upstairs unseen, but Mom caught us as she came out of the kitchen.

"Dad said you were going out for dinner."

"We had a quick one," I said, which was partially true. I'd felt lightheaded walking back to the T, so Sergei had insisted I get a sandwich to eat on the ride home.

"Sergei, I heard from my friend Christy earlier," Mom said. "Her husband is on the board at SCOB, and she said you've been invited to coach there permanently?"

Was there nothing my mother didn't know? It was a miracle she hadn't figured out I was pregnant yet.

"I've been asked, yes, but Em and I haven't had time to fully discuss it yet."

"Well, I think it would be a great opportunity. There are so many more kids to teach here, the airport is closer for all the traveling you do... of course, you'd be closer to family, too—"

"There are a lot of things to consider," Sergei interrupted. "Which Em and I will do. Just the two of us."

Mom ignored his chilly tone and peered at me. "Sweetie,

your eyes are red."

I turned and started up the stairs. "The cold probably irritated my contacts. Have a good night."

Sergei trailed close behind as I went to our room. He took off his leather jacket and helped me out of my coat, and I spun to face him with my hand pressed to my forehead.

"I'm going to have to tell her soon that I'm pregnant because she *will* find out. When I was a kid, she could take one look at me and know I wasn't feeling well."

"I can predict exactly how that conversation will go." Sergei paced along the carpet. "She's going to bring up Elena and ask me how I could let this happen again. And she's right."

I stepped in front of him. "Don't say that. We're both responsible."

"But I should've protected you. I shouldn't have—"

"Stop." I placed my hands on his face. "Stop putting this all on yourself."

He brought me into his arms and held me tightly like he'd done in the Garden. "Whatever you need, I'm going to be here for you, every moment of every day. I will do whatever I have to do to protect you and the baby."

He couldn't protect me when I was on the ice, though. Only I could do that. And Chris.

My heart sank. Chris didn't deserve to be dragged down by my problems again. He'd supported me through the fiasco surrounding our first Olympics and the chaos when Elena and Liza had come into my life, but this could be the biggest complication of all.

Was I wrong to be thinking about skating? Even if I was super careful, I'd still be taking a risk every time I put on my skates. But how could I give up on my dream and let Chris down when we were so close? Of course, none of that would matter if the doctor told me to quit immediately.

We both piddled around the room in a haze for a while,

and I eventually found my way to the window seat, not to read but to look out at the clear, cold night. The clouds that had draped the sky earlier had drifted away, leaving the crescent moon in full view.

Sergei came over and rubbed my knee. "Can I sit with you?"

I scooted forward so he could sit behind me. He nestled me against his chest, and I leaned my head back on his shoulder.

"What are you thinking?" he asked.

What *wasn't* I thinking?

"There's just so much to do, so much I thought we'd have time to prepare for. We don't have our own house yet... I guess now we're not even sure what city we're going to live in..."

"We'll take it one step at a time." He kissed my temple. "We don't have to rush."

I returned to staring out the window as Sergei lightly stroked my arm. His hand moved down to my stomach, and his lips brushed over my hair.

"Em, do you realize what we did? How improbable it was?"

I looked up at him, and his eyes glistened. He wrapped his arms tighter around me. "We made a baby."

The love in his voice sent my emotions reeling. Sergei was already excited about the baby. I could hear it. I wanted to share in his joy, but it still didn't seem real to me. The only thing that felt real was the devastating fear that I'd lost my chance at my Olympic dream.

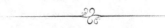

AUBREY FLIPPED THROUGH THE fashion magazine in her lap, not really seeing the pictures on the pages. Her mind was still at Em's house. She couldn't imagine how Em felt, knowing everything she'd worked for could be in jeopardy. Not to mention the fact that she was having a baby, something she knew Em wasn't ready for just yet.

The front door of the apartment opened, and Chris fumbled with multiple plastic bags as he pulled the key from the lock and kicked the door shut.

"You went grocery shopping?" Aubrey left the magazine on the couch and took two of the bags from Chris. "I would've gone with you to help."

"I was at Starbucks, so I figured I'd stop next door at DeLuca's and pick up a few things."

They carried the groceries into the galley kitchen, and Aubrey started pulling out items and setting them on the laminate countertop.

"You got my favorite chocolate milk." She smiled.

Chris took a green box out of his bag. "And the veggie burgers you like."

She smiled wider and continued unpacking until they'd put everything neatly away. She'd thought keeping the apartment tidy would be a chore living with a guy, but since the day they'd moved in Chris had gone out of his way to keep the place clean. Having seen the mess that was his apartment on the Cape, it made his efforts all the more impressive.

Chris pushed up the sleeves of his sweatshirt and leaned against the counter. "So, tonight. You ready to be wowed by my unromantic plans?"

After the emotional afternoon, Aubrey had thought about postponing their "date," but going out would be a good distraction. She couldn't tell Chris about Em's pregnancy because that was a conversation the two of them needed to have. Hopefully once Em got the good news from her doctor that she could continue to skate.

"What should I wear on this outing? My rattiest clothes?" She laughed. "I have some old sweats that would be perfect."

"It doesn't matter what you wear because you look amazing in anything." His eyes flashed over her. "But something nice and casual will work."

Aubrey took his suggestion and dressed in her favorite boot-cut jeans and a purple loose-fitting blouse that fell slightly off one shoulder. Adding the necklace from Aunt Debbie and a pair of big silver hoop earrings, and her nice casual outfit was complete.

Chris awaited her downstairs, all cleaned up in a bright red polo and jeans. She pumped him for information on his plans, but he remained mum. Once they donned jackets and gloves, Chris led her to the Arlington T stop, still with no hint of their ultimate destination, no matter how many questions she asked.

They rode the T through just a couple of stations before Chris motioned that they'd reached their stop. Aubrey knew the Haymarket station well because it was the one she and Em traveled to whenever they visited the North End, Boston's "Little Italy" and where Em's mom had grown up. Em loved the neighborhood, so she'd taken Aubrey there many times to enjoy the fantastic restaurants.

"Ooh, are we getting Italian food?" she asked.

"We shall see," Chris said dramatically, letting her step ahead of him on the escalator.

They passed a number of restaurants as they walked along the narrow streets, and every so often Chris would stop and look as if he was about to open the door to one of them, only to fake her out and turn around. When they paused in front of Regina Pizzeria, she said, "This better be the place because I'm about to gnaw my arm off."

"Lucky for your limbs, we've arrived." Chris smiled and opened the door. "After you."

The delectable aroma of baking pizza crust greeted them upon entering. They peeled off their coats and slid into a booth on the back wall of the cramped restaurant.

"See, it doesn't get any more unromantic than this," Chris said. "Tables crammed together, pizza boxes stacked up all over the place, paper napkins. No candlelight or fancy food in sight."

Aubrey laughed. "It's a great choice. I've been here with Em a few times."

Examination of the menu spurred a heated discussion over which toppings they should get on their pizza. Red peppers or jalapeno peppers? Cherry tomatoes or chopped tomatoes? Aubrey was adamant that onions not be anywhere on the pie while Chris tried to explain the benefit of their flavor. In the end Aubrey got her way, and she bit into her steaming slice with a hum of satisfaction.

"I swear," she said between bites. "The thing I'm most looking forward to after skating is being able to eat however much I want, whenever I want. I'll run five miles a day to stay in shape if I need to, but I will have that third slice of pizza or that monster dessert anytime I like."

"It's starting to sink in lately that the end is really near." Chris wiped his mouth with a napkin. "I mean, we'll have the tour this summer, but we only have two competitions left. It's just weird to think I'll be spending my days somewhere other than the rink soon."

"What are you most looking forward to after you're done?"

Chris took a drink from his large cup of water. "Being out of the cold. Before I start school, I almost want to get a job in construction or something so I can be outside most of the time."

A shirtless Chris pounding nails under the burning sun? Now there was a delicious image.

"You'd look pretty hot in a tool belt, swinging a hammer." Flirting was allowed on non-romantic dates, right?

Chris's smile gleamed. "You know, there's a tool kit under the kitchen sink at home. I could break something that would require a hammer to fix."

She laughed and sipped her water. "I like that idea."

"I think you're gonna like the next part of our evening then. I won't be swinging a hammer, but I will be swinging something."

"Are there indoor batting cages around here?"

"No, but you're thinking along the right track."

Aubrey squinted while in deep thought. "You have a piñata set up for us somewhere?"

Chris laughed. "Getting colder."

"You love giving people surprises, don't you?"

"I'm a big kid, I know."

She smiled and spun her straw around in her glass. "No, it's sweet."

Chris's leg bumped hers under the table, and they didn't move from each other for the rest of dinner. It was such a small gesture of affection, but it made her gooey inside. She would've been happy sitting there with Chris all night, talking and trying to one up him with her most embarrassing skating stories. Their laughter continued well after they left the restaurant.

"See if you can top this one," Chris said as they boarded the Green Line train. "When I was eleven, my partner and I were performing in our rink's spring show, and she accidentally kneed me in the groin. I stopped in the middle of the program, dropped to the ice, and started crying. All while holding the family jewels, so everyone could tell exactly what happened."

Aubrey's laughter filled the near-empty car. "Okay, you win," she gasped.

When the train rumbled into Kenmore Station a few minutes later, Chris jumped up. "This is us."

Fenway Park loomed ahead as they walked south from the station. Chris seemed to be leading her straight there.

"Did you rent out the ballpark so we could take batting

practice?" Aubrey asked. "That would be incredibly epic."

"Yes, it would. But reserving the entire ballpark just for the two of us could also be construed as a romantic overture, so I'm afraid that's not in the cards for us."

They continued along under the shadow of the Green Monster, and Chris pointed to the big brick building on the corner. "Have you been there before?"

She had been to the multi-level bar before, specifically to the bowling alley on the third floor.

"Aha! We're gonna swing bowling balls," she said.

"Close, but not quite."

They went inside and up to the second floor, and Chris bought them each a beer, again telling Aubrey to put away her wallet. They'd had the same discussion over the dinner bill. Chris had said since the evening was his idea, he wanted to take care of it.

Besides the bar, the sprawling second floor included a number of pool tables, video games, and ping-pong tables. Comfy-looking couches were situated in a separate area, and large TVs hung throughout the space. A small crowd had gathered to watch one of college football's bowl games.

"I know we're not playing pool because that would be a total cliché date move," Aubrey said.

"That's correct. The only reason guys wanna play pool with girls is to see you leaning over the table, looking sexy. Not that I wouldn't enjoy that... immensely."

His dimples deepened, and Aubrey wanted nothing more than to touch her lips to each one of them. From the glow in his eyes as he smiled at her, she didn't think he'd mind in the least.

"So..." Chris said. "How good are you at ping-pong?"

Aubrey put her coat and purse on a chair and spread her hands on the game table. "The question is not how good but how *great* am I at ping-pong. My brother and I had one of these in our garage growing up."

Chris whistled low. "That's some big talk. You prepared to back that up?"

"Bring it on."

They set up to play, but Aubrey halted right before she was about to serve. "I have to get my hair out of the way."

"Look out, she's getting serious." Chris held up both hands.

She couldn't find a rubber band in her purse, but she had a pen, which she slid through the bun she'd twisted.

"Did you just pin your hair up with an ink pen?" Chris asked. "You're like MacGyver."

She laughed and picked up her paddle. "Now I'm ready. Oh, you're not one of those guys that throws a game just to score points with a girl, are you?"

"No way. I will show you no mercy." Chris bounced back and forth on his side of the table like a boxer in the ring. "But if I happen to get distracted by your pretty smile, I'll just imagine my paddle is Damien Wakefield's face."

Aubrey's smile disappeared. If Chris knew she'd slept with Damien, he would be so disgusted. She felt sick enough herself every time she thought about it.

"Sorry, didn't mean to bring up that jerk," Chris said. "I'm sure you don't want to think about what he did to you."

"What he did to me?"

"At the club in Tokyo." Chris's grip on his paddle tightened. "Sergei should've let me punch him."

"Oh. Yeah, he deserved it." Aubrey stared at the tiny ball in her hand.

"Enough about him," Chris said. "Let's get this match started."

Aubrey pushed aside all unpleasant thoughts and focused on serving the little white ball. Chris won the first point with a smooth backhand and then the next two using wide-angle shots.

"I'm waiting to see that greatness you were talking

about." He twirled his paddle.

Aubrey shook out her shoulders. "I'm just getting warmed up."

Chris grinned and gave the ball a hard serve, and Aubrey smacked it past him, following with a fist pump.

"Brace yourself. You're about to be pummeled by the greatness."

They both wore their game faces as they whacked the ball back and forth, trading points and shouts of joy and despair. Their celebrations became more animated as the match went on, and when Aubrey smashed a winner for the deciding point, she broke into a long victory dance, highlighted by some of her samba moves.

Chris folded his arms and watched her with an appreciative smile. "Losing is worth getting this show."

She stopped in mid-shake. "You shouldn't be reaping any reward."

"Aw, come on. I need something to ease the pain of defeat." He put his hands on her hips and gently rocked them. "Give me a few more shimmies."

She clutched his hands and tried not to laugh. "Nope. No more."

He pulled her closer, and her urge to laugh faded away, supplanted by pulse-pounding desire. She held onto Chris's hands, not wanting them to leave her body.

"Can I ask you something?" he said.

*You can ask me anything.*

"Since you're more of an expert on these situations... on these non-romantic dates..." His eyes flickered down to her mouth. "Is kissing allowed?"

She licked her lips and decided to play with him. "It's highly discouraged."

Chris's face froze, and she looped her arms behind his neck. "But I believe there's an exception. For losers of ping-pong games."

Chris relaxed into a grin. He flexed his fingers against her hips and kissed her, as softly as he'd done on the rooftop but longer and with more sureness. She felt so light, like she was floating, drifting on a heavenly cloud.

Chris slowly broke away and gazed at her. "Should we head home?"

She held his gaze and nodded without a word.

As they waited on the platform for the T, Chris stood very close to her, keeping her heart rate at an elevated level. Would kissing on the train be obnoxious? She'd never been a fan of PDA, but there she was contemplating making out on public transportation.

When they boarded the train, Chris sat across the aisle from her even though she had an empty seat beside her. Only three other people occupied the car. Had he suddenly decided to back off?

He angled sideways so he was facing her. "If you're wondering why I'm not sitting next to you, it's because I really want to kiss you again, but not here."

Her floaty feeling returned, and Chris hadn't even touched her. She was going to have to work incredibly hard to stay grounded around him. But that light, body-buzzing sensation felt *so* good…

The walk from the T to the apartment seemed more like a mile than a few blocks. All she could think about was what awaited her once she and Chris were alone. The same energy of anticipation was coming from him, too, as he stayed relatively quiet during the walk. Their pace grew quicker and quicker the closer they got to Beacon Street.

The key clicked as Chris turned it in the lock, and as soon as they were inside and he shut the door, Aubrey pinned his back against the frosted glass. She couldn't wait any longer.

They dove into one kiss after another, stripping off their coats and stumbling their way onto the couch. Aubrey curled her fingers inside Chris's collar, and his pulse throbbed against her thumb. She was starting to feel out of control again, teetering on the edge of total abandon.

"I think we…" she began, catching her breath as Chris's mouth briefly left hers. "I think we should set some limits. We can't let things go too far again."

He tucked a long lock of hair behind her ear. "Do you wanna stop now?"

His face showed genuine care, truly deep concern. It was so new, so different from anything she'd ever experienced with a guy. She leaned in and softly kissed the spot on his cheek where his dimple would be, and he turned so their lips met. As their kisses became fuller and their bodies pressed harder, Chris's hand slipped under the back of her blouse.

"Is this okay?" he breathed against her lips.

She nodded and returned her mouth to his.

He caressed her back and moved slowly, sliding his palm over her waist and up her side so the tips of his fingers brushed the edge of her bra. She shivered and squeezed his thigh.

"Should I stop?" he asked.

She was soaring on a cloud again, and his voice barely registered. She shook her head and drew him closer.

He kissed her neck while his touch inched higher, making her burn even hotter. Every part of her cried out for more, but she'd have to say no.

She didn't need to as Chris didn't take things any further. Whenever his eyes met hers between kisses, she saw the same tender look in them, the one that hit her right in the heart. There was so much honesty in those warm brown eyes. This couldn't all just be meaningless fun to him.

What if he did feel as much for her as she did for him? Was she ready to open up, to put her heart out there for the taking? Nothing had ever scared her more.

# CHAPTER FIFTEEN

SERGEI SAT IN THE CHAIR NEXT to mine and took my hand, intertwining our fingers. Dr. Bachemin had said he'd be with us in a few minutes. He'd already examined me, and I was anxious to know if everything looked fine. I'd taken some hard falls on the quad the past month, not knowing I had a baby inside me to protect.

The doctor shut the door to the office and sat behind his desk, and I squeezed Sergei's hand. *Please let him say I'm okay and I can skate.*

"Thank you for fitting Emily in so quickly," Sergei said.

"Of course." Dr. Bachemin smiled, showing the deep lines around his eyes. "I know how unique your situation is and how important it is that you make a plan."

Dr. Bachemin had delivered all my cousins and me, so he was very familiar with my family and my skating accomplishments. I thoroughly trusted his advice. I just hoped it would be what I wanted to hear.

He looked at my chart on his desk and back up at me. "Both you and the baby appear healthy and strong. With the information you gave us, I've set your due date as September first."

*Due date.* I still couldn't believe Sergei and I would be parents in a mere eight months. Aside from the tiredness and the nausea when I had an empty stomach, I didn't feel pregnant. I'd always thought I would immediately feel some connection to the baby, but I didn't. It seemed more like an abstract thing we'd been discussing.

"We were worried," Sergei said. "Emily's been skating her normal routine up until the last few days, and she's fallen a number of times."

"Everything looks good. But a fall on the abdomen could damage the placenta, so it's obviously something you want to avoid from now on."

"I don't usually fall on my stomach," I said. "It's usually my backside."

"I'd like you to stay on your feet all the time, but I know that's not possible if you continue skating," Dr. Bachemin said.

I gripped the arm of the chair as hard as I was squeezing Sergei's hand. "Do you think it's okay for me to keep skating?"

"That decision is really up to you. Your body is accustomed to the exercise, and you're in great health. My biggest concerns are the physical trauma caused by falling, the mental stress I'm sure you experience before and during competitions, and overexertion, both physical and mental."

He had concerns, but he wasn't saying no way, no how. I felt lighter for the first time in days.

"I can ease up on my training." I glanced at Sergei and then at the doctor. "And I'm very consistent on my jumps, so falling isn't something I do much."

"Except on the quad," Sergei said.

"There's one element I have issues with," I explained.

"My suggestion would be that you not do that element any longer," Dr. Bachemin said.

"She won't be," Sergei said with no hesitation.

I was so happy I could skate that I hadn't thought about

specific jumps. It sounded like Sergei had, though.

"I'll make whatever adjustments necessary if it means I can compete," I said.

Dr. Bachemin stared at me as he clicked his pen on and off. "You know how you train better than I do, so if you think you can cut back and still do the things you need to do, then I'll trust you on that. But you have to be vigilant about not overworking yourself. I cannot stress that enough."

I nodded vigorously. "I'll be very careful."

We talked with the doctor a few more minutes before he had to leave for his last appointment of the day. When Sergei and I reached his SUV, I leaned back against the headrest and let out a slow breath.

"I have to go tell Chris now."

I hadn't practiced as hard the past two days, and I'd used my bruised hip and my "stomach bug" as an excuse. If only those were my real issue.

"I'm coming with you." Sergei started the car. "We all need to talk about how we're going to adjust your training. And if Chris gets angry, I don't want him upsetting you. He can take it out on me."

"You don't have to shield me from every tense situation the next eight months."

"The doctor said to keep your stress down. You're under enough with nationals next week. You don't need anything adding to that."

"Chris won't go ballistic. That's not who he is. He'll probably be too much in shock to speak."

Sergei turned on the heater, but he didn't put the car in drive. Instead, he reached out and touched my leg. "Em, are you sure this is what you want to do?"

"Telling Chris? He has to know."

"No, are you sure you want to keep skating?"

He didn't think it was a good idea. The doubt in his voice gave it away. But I couldn't imagine quitting and always wondering if I'd made the right choice. I couldn't let go of a lifetime of work that easily.

"I can't give up when I'm still physically able to do this," I said.

"But there are a lot of risks. Maybe we should think about this more before any decisions are made."

"There's nothing more to think about. You should understand better than anyone how I feel. If you'd had a chance to live out your dream, you would have."

"I do know how you feel, how badly you want this. That's why I think you might not realize the dangers of the situation."

"If Dr. Bachemin thinks I can do it, then that's all I need to know." I covered Sergei's hand with mine. "I promise I won't push myself. I just… I have to try to make it through the Olympics. If I don't, I'll live with that regret forever."

He lifted his palm to my cheek. "I just want to keep you and the baby safe."

"We will be. I will be *so* careful, and there's no steadier partner than Chris."

Sergei's eyes darted across my face. I could see the wheels turning in his mind.

"You'll have to trust me, to listen if I tell you to pull back or to stop doing something," he said. "We'll see how nationals goes first, and then we'll decide what to do from there."

He pulled the car out of the parking lot, and I mentally practiced my speech to Chris. I had to sound confident and sure that we could compete with no problems. Sergei might only be thinking about nationals, but I still had the Olympics firmly in my sights.

We found a tight parking spot a block from Aubrey and Chris's apartment, and Chris answered the door when Sergei rang the bell.

"Hey, are you escaping from your mom's house for a while?" he asked.

I took off my coat as I walked past him into the living room. "No, we have something we need to discuss."

"Is that Em?" Aubrey's voice called from above.

I craned my neck up to see her leaning over the opening in her bedroom wall.

"Hey," I said and gave her a subtle thumbs-up. She smiled.

"What's up?" Chris asked as he plopped down onto the leather easy chair. "You two look serious."

Sergei and I sat on the couch, and Aubrey's head disappeared into her room. I thought of the speech I'd prepared and launched into it before I became too jumpy.

"I have a physical issue that my doctor said I can skate with, but I won't be able to train at the same level," I said.

"Is it your hip? It's gotten worse?"

"It's not my hip." I paused and Sergei squeezed my knee. "I'm pregnant."

Chris's mouth fell open. "You're *what*?"

"I'm only five weeks along, so I should be able to make it through the Olympics." I leaned forward so I'd be closer, hoping my belief would spread to him. "Believe me, this was a huge shock to us, too. We obviously didn't want this to happen now. We thought we'd done everything to prevent it—"

"I don't need to know the details." Chris held up his hand and then raked it through his hair. "You're telling me you're gonna do the jumps, the throws... the *quad* while you're pregnant? Isn't that dangerous?"

"The quad is out," Sergei said.

"She could fall on the other throws, too. She could fall on a lot of things."

"We're so solid on everything other than the quad," I said. "I know we can get through the next six weeks with minimal mistakes."

Chris stared at the carpet for a long minute. "And the

doctor gave you the okay to do this."

"We just have to scale back our workload and—"

"You realize you're putting your baby's life in my hands."

He still wouldn't look at me, but I could hear his trepidation. And that wasn't something I heard from Chris often, if ever.

"I've trusted you with *my* life for seven years, and you've never let me down," I said. "This isn't any different."

"It *is* different." Chris bent over and held his head in his hands.

I didn't know if I should keep reassuring him or let him have a moment. I hated that I had to burden him with this. As a team, we always treated everything we did as a joint effort — we never placed blame on one another or took credit on our own — but this was entirely my problem that he unfortunately couldn't avoid.

"I told Em we'll see how nationals goes," Sergei said. "I don't want to think any further than that right now."

Chris sat up straight and finally looked at me. "Em, you're not doing this because of me, are you? If you didn't have a partner, would you keep skating?"

"I would," I said quickly, not needing any time to think about my response. "I have to see this through."

"I just don't want you to feel obligated because of me. I don't want that on my head if…" He looked down, and I knew what he didn't want to say. It was the scenario I couldn't allow myself to think about.

"Everything will be fine. It will." If I said it enough times, God would surely hear me.

Chris watched me closely, and I kept my eyes on his. We'd learned to read each other very well over the years, so I couldn't waver in my confidence even a tiny bit.

"So, how much do we have to scale back?" he asked.

We spent the next half hour outlining a plan of how many

hours we should train and how many run-throughs we should do the next few days before we'd leave for St. Louis. If anyone at the rink asked why we weren't practicing as much, we'd tell them we were protecting my hip from further injury. Chris didn't look convinced our plan would work, but he quietly agreed to go along with it.

I wanted to stay and talk more with Chris, to find out what he was thinking, but I realized he probably needed some time to digest everything. We'd always been open with each other about our feelings, so he would come to me when he was ready.

As Chris walked Sergei and me out, he reached for my arm and stepped in front of me. He didn't immediately speak as he seemed to be searching for the right words.

"I haven't said congratulations yet," he said. "I mean… you're having a baby."

He sounded as stunned as I still felt. I hugged him long and hard and wondered for the millionth time how I'd been so blessed to find such an amazing partner. From stories I'd heard from some other pair girls, their partners would've totally lit into them if they'd been in my predicament. And here was Chris congratulating me, regardless of how freaked out he probably was over the situation. He was truly a gem.

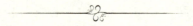

AUBREY CLICKED THE VOLUME button on the TV remote and looked up at Chris's bedroom. He'd been so quiet since Em and Sergei had left. They'd talked for just a minute, and he'd passed on dinner, opting to take cereal up to his room. She wanted to give him space, but she also wanted him to know she was there for him if he needed to talk.

She went upstairs and slowly pushed his half-open door. He was sprawled on his stomach on the bed, staring at his laptop. The empty cereal bowl sat on the carpet.

"Whatcha' doin?" She ducked under the sloped ceiling and sat on the bed.

"Searching for information on skaters who competed while pregnant."

She stretched out next to him and squinted at the message board on the laptop screen. "Any luck?"

"Not much. I only found stuff on some professional pair skaters who've done it. No one trying to win an Olympic gold medal." He shut the computer and slid it to the side of the bed. "Never in a million years did I think we'd be dealing with this. I thought of all people, Sergei wouldn't let this happen."

"Try to cut him a little slack. He waited two and a half years until the wedding night to get some action. If anyone deserves to have fun in their marriage and to not always worry about being extra careful, it's Em and Sergei."

Chris cringed and propped himself onto one elbow. "Em is like my sister. I prefer not to think about the fun they're having. Like I'm sure you don't wanna think about your brother's sex life."

"With the cold wench he's married to, there's probably not much to discuss," she said dryly.

Chris made a feeble attempt at a laugh, and Aubrey shifted onto her side so she was facing him. "Are you worried Em won't be able to compete at the Olympics?"

"I'm worried about protecting her. That's what's kinda freaking me out most about the whole thing."

"Well, don't tell Nick I said this, but... I think you're the strongest, most dependable partner in the world. I have total faith that you'll protect her."

"The thing is, I could be the strongest partner in the history of skating, but accidents happen. If we're in a lift and I hit a rut in the ice or I catch a toepick..." He shook his head. "I couldn't live with myself if I was responsible for Em losing her baby."

She put her hand on his forearm. "I know you're going to

do everything in your power to prevent any accidents from happening. That's all you can expect of yourself."

"I can't let this get into my head. If I'm not skating with a hundred percent confidence, then I'm putting both Em and me… and the baby at risk."

"You just have to pretend like nothing's changed. Keep the same mindset you've always had. Knowing how focused you are on the ice, you'll have absolutely no problem doing that."

He gazed at her with a soft glow in his eyes. "You give a pretty awesome pep talk."

She smiled. "I owed you after all you did to cheer me up at Christmas."

"You didn't have to say anything. Just being around you cheers me up."

He slowly leaned forward and pressed his mouth gently to hers. She couldn't count the number of times she'd been kissed, and none of them came close to comparing. There was so much feeling, so much warmth in the way Chris's lips caressed hers. When he broke away, she felt lost without the connection.

"I'm gonna miss you next week," he said.

Her forehead wrinkled. "Aren't we both going to St. Louis?"

"Yeah, but it won't be the same. I'm gonna miss your pre-coffee grumpy face in the morning and seeing you in your cute pajamas at night." He touched her hip and traced one of the yellow stars on her blue flannel pants.

She smiled as he outlined more stars down her thigh. "I'm gonna miss your crazy hair in the morning."

She mussed up tufts of his hair to mimic how he looked when he rolled out of bed every day. He was somehow both adorable and sexy as all get out. Curling her fingers into his thick locks, she watched his eyes grow hooded, his breathing become heavier.

His mouth found hers, and he angled over her as her back met the mattress. He braced his arms on either side of her so his body was close enough to share its heat but not near enough to crush her. She clenched his hair with one hand and felt her way down his chest with the other, slipping it under his shirt and over his hard abs.

Chris lowered his weight further, and their hips moved against each other in a daring rhythm. There was something dangerously intimate about being in his bed, but she didn't want to let go of that incredible rush.

He swept a line of kisses along her jaw and whispered hotly in her ear, "I'll remember the limits."

*Forget the limits*, she longed to say, but she had to do this right. For the first time in her life, she wanted more than the physical stuff, and there might be a chance she could have it.

Everywhere Chris kissed and touched her tingled, turning her into a live wire. The sparks between them threatened to start a fire that couldn't be doused. But Chris pulled back before the heat became unstoppably intense.

He moved to her side, but his eyes didn't leave her. She stared up at him and set her hand on his chest so she could feel the rise and fall as his breathing slowed.

"Would you stay here tonight?" he asked. "Sleep next to me?"

With any other guy, she'd question the intentions, but she had no doubt Chris was sincere. He really just wanted to have her close to him. She'd never received a more special invitation.

"I'm not going anywhere," she said.

He turned off the lamp beside the bed and spooned her against him, wrapping one arm around her. His hand slid between hers and the bed sheet, and he laced their fingers together, giving her an overwhelming sense of security.

She had to do whatever she could to hold onto him, to make things work between them because she couldn't imagine her life without him. The first thing she had to do was talk to Marley and make sure she was okay with her becoming more serious with Chris. But she'd have to find the right time, maybe when the dust settled after nationals.

Chris lifted his head to kiss her shoulder, and she squeezed his hand as he settled back behind her. All the confusing emotions she'd been battling, the fears she'd been afraid to face... she finally understood exactly what she was feeling.

She was in love.

# CHAPTER SIXTEEN

WHY, OH WHY, DID OUR FIRST practice at nationals have to be scheduled in the evening?

I circled slowly around the Savvis Center ice, trying to put mind over matter. The matter being the queasiness in my stomach because I hadn't been able to eat dinner yet. Only a few early arrivals to nationals week watched from the stands, including Mom and Dad, and Mom sharply observed every tentative stroke I took. I'd hoped to wait and tell her my news after the event so she wouldn't hover over me the entire week, but I suspected she was going to start asking questions soon.

Chris skated to my side and took my hand. "You're not gonna throw up on me, are you?"

"I think I'll be okay, but no more spins."

"We can do the footwork sequence."

I nodded and swallowed a couple of times, clearing the sour taste from my throat. "We have to practice at night again tomorrow. I want to kill whoever made this schedule."

We finished the forty-minute session by doing our footwork and our spiral sequence, two things that wouldn't make me dizzy. Skating over to Sergei behind the boards, I gave him a little smile but he looked too anxious to return it. He'd been wearing the same tense look every time I stepped onto the ice.

"You're usually one of the most relaxed coaches at these practices," I said, taking my warm-up jacket from him. "If you keep looking this nervous, people are going to notice."

Sergei's jaw relaxed and he sipped from his cup of coffee. "I might need to spike this with vodka from now on."

"There was a coach at my old rink who did that all the time," Chris said. "For different reasons I'm sure."

I zipped my jacket over my black body suit and exited the ice behind the three other teams in our practice group. A small group of spectators had gathered in the section of seats next to the skaters' entrance, and they held out their programs and other paraphernalia to be autographed. I needed to get food pronto, but I didn't want to blow past the fans who'd showed up to such a late practice.

"Hi." I smiled at the first young woman in line. "Thanks for coming out so late."

"I wouldn't miss it." She passed me her spiral-bound program and a pen. "I flew in today and I've been to all the practices."

"Where'd you fly in from?" I asked as I signed my name next to the black-and-white photo of Chris of me.

"New Orleans."

My head shot up. "Did you make it through Hurricane Katrina okay?"

"I was very lucky. Just some minimal damage to my house."

An older woman squeezed next to her along the railing separating us, and a powerful whiff of sweet, flowery perfume engulfed me. It turned my already weak stomach upside down, sending a surge of sourness into my throat.

I shoved the program and the pen at Chris. "I have to go."

With my hand clamped over my mouth, I rushed through the tunnel backstage and barely made it to the trash can. As I slowly lifted my head, one of the event volunteers handed me a wad of tissues, and I noticed a bevy of reporters and skaters eyeing me as they milled about.

Sergei rushed toward me and rubbed my back. "Are you okay?"

The volunteer was still standing next to me, so I had to play along. I thought quickly of something that would make me ill. "Yeah, my migraine's just really bad. I'll feel better after I eat."

I wiped my mouth as Sergei put his arm around me and steered me toward the locker room. "Maybe I should go back out there with Chris."

"No, we're going to dinner. Get your stuff and I'll go out and explain you aren't feeling well."

I did a quick change and met Sergei at the shuttle bus that would take us back to the Renaissance Hotel. It was, thankfully, a short ride through downtown St. Louis. Waiting just inside the entrance to the lobby were my parents, both of their brows furrowed in concern.

"Sweetie, we saw you run out of there when you were signing autographs. Did you get sick?" Mom asked.

"I just need to get something in my stomach. I couldn't eat much before practice."

Mom moved closer to me and lowered her voice. "I think there's more to it than that."

I was so busted. I'd tried to hide my nausea spells, but she'd caught me a couple of mornings nibbling on crackers, and I'd had to hide out in the bedroom one night when she sautéed mushrooms. The smell had been even more sickening than the cabbage odor.

"Can we talk after dinner?"

She agreed, and I sighed with relief when she said they'd already eaten. I didn't want her at the table scrutinizing every move I made.

Sergei and I headed for the hotel restaurant, and the hostess led us to the table next to Courtney and her mom Karen. We wouldn't be able to discuss any sensitive topics, which made me very happy. It seemed all we talked about lately was heavy stuff.

I touched Courtney's shoulder before sitting. "How was your practice?" She and Mark had been in the group before ours.

"Not great." She brushed her long curly blond hair over one shoulder. "My jumps are still back in Boston."

"First practice on a travel day doesn't count." Sergei sat across from me. "It's all about getting a feel for the ice."

"I definitely felt the ice. On my butt."

"I didn't have the best practice either," I said. "But the only thing that matters is how we skate on Wednesday and Friday."

"Are you doing the quad here, Em?" Mrs. Karen asked.

I glanced at Sergei. I'd been asked that question by every media outlet in our pre-nationals interviews, and I'd gotten used to reciting our lie, but when I had to tell it to someone I knew very well, I didn't feel quite as comfortable.

"We're not doing the quad at all anymore." I paused to place my order for a ginger ale and the club sandwich. "It's just not consistent enough."

It pained me every time I had to say that because the jump had become more than consistent enough before I'd found out I was pregnant. Now I'd never know if I could land it at the Olympics.

Mrs. Karen twirled her pasta around her fork. "I thought you looked good on it when I saw you before you moved to Boston. And the one you landed at the Final was perfect."

I looked at Sergei again, and he read my silent plea to take over our phony explanation.

"They were doing really well with it but still not at the

percentage we needed to justify the risk," he said.

"And Em has a hip injury, too," Courtney added.

Ah, yes. My hip. The other part of our lie.

"It's nothing serious." I focused on situating the linen napkin in my lap. "We just want to be cautious."

It was déjà vu, and I was back in 2002 when Sergei and I were keeping our relationship secret. I'd longed to tell Courtney the truth back then just as I wished I could now. But my condition needed to stay hidden because I couldn't chance that information falling into the wrong hands. If the media got wind of it, my pregnancy would be blown up into a huge story, and the judges might look at me differently. They weren't supposed to let anything other than the skating influence their marks, but we all knew that was a joke. If they knew I was pregnant, they might think I wasn't as strong or capable, and that perception would find its way into their scores.

My phone buzzed inside my purse, and I answered it when I saw Chris's name.

"How are you feeling?" he asked.

"Better. Food is on the way."

"I think you should eat every hour on Wednesday before the short program."

I laughed. "I'll be sure to have a good meal schedule in place."

"Sergei was super smooth covering for you with the fans. I had them telling me their personal migraine stories after that. Oh, and they all wanted me to send you their good wishes to feel better."

"That's really sweet." Migraines, hips... I hoped I didn't have to make up any more ailments before the week was over.

The waiter set down our dinner, so I told Chris I had to go. I cleaned my plate before Sergei could finish half of his grilled salmon.

"I get so hungry lately," I said quietly. Courtney and Mrs.

Karen had left, but other diners sat nearby.

"There's another person to feed now." Sergei smiled and spoke in the same low voice.

"That would be fine if spandex wasn't a necessary part of my wardrobe."

"We can watch your weight, but don't stress about eating. Your health is the most important thing."

I eyed the cheeseburger on the table to our left. I could seriously eat that whole thing, and I'd just scarfed down a sandwich and fries. How much food did a pregnant woman need?

I refrained from ordering dessert even though the white chocolate brownie was calling my name. Sergei and I went up to our room, and Mom and Dad came knocking shortly thereafter. Our tiny room felt even smaller with all four of us in it.

Mom stood in the narrow space between the TV and the king bed, and she set her eyes on me. "You're pregnant, aren't you?"

My neck tensed in anticipation of all the questions and concerns sure to come. "Yes."

"What happened to being extra careful?" She alternated her pinpoint stare from me to Sergei then back to me.

"I guess God has a wicked sense of humor," I said.

Dad reached out and embraced me, but Mom stayed back. He held my head between his hands as he looked at me. "Are you sure it's okay for you to skate?"

"Dr. Bachemin said I could. I've cut down on practicing."

"Emily, this is incredibly dangerous," Mom said. "Do you know how important the first trimester is? How many things can go wrong?"

This was exactly what I didn't want — a rehash of the potential dangers of my decision. I'd committed to skating, and second-guessing myself wouldn't help my confidence.

"I've already had this conversation a few times," I said.

"Well, I think you need to have it again," Mom replied.

"What she needs is to get some rest." Sergei moved behind me and massaged my neck. "We can continue this another time."

"Are you telling us to leave?" Mom snapped.

"It's been a long day," Sergei said.

Mom glared at him, but then her face softened when she turned to me. She took my hand and clasped it between both of hers. "I'm only saying these things because I'm worried about you. I can't believe my baby's having a baby."

Her voice wavered, and my throat tightened. I put my arms around her. "I'm okay. I'm doing everything the doctor suggested."

"Please be careful." She squeezed my shoulders before letting go.

Dad came behind her and kissed my cheek. "The timing might not be ideal, but this is a wonderful thing."

"Thanks, Dad." I hugged him, and he held me tightly.

He offered Sergei his hand, and Sergei shook it as Dad patted him on the back. "Thank you, Jim."

"Call me tomorrow, okay?" Mom looked back at me as she and Dad started for the door.

Once Sergei and I were alone, I dropped onto the bed and pulled off my sheepskin boots. "Well, this week's off to a great start. Throwing up at practice, my mom getting on my case…"

Sergei knelt before me and rested his forearms on either side of me. "What can I do to make it less stressful?"

I leaned forward and gave him a soft kiss. "Try not to have a panic attack every time I'm on the ice. Seeing you so anxious is making me extra nervous."

His mouth curled slightly upward. "I'll try."

"Thank you." I kissed him again.

He moved next to me on the bed and combed his fingers through my hair. "I just love you so much. I can't bear the thought of you getting hurt."

"Nothing bad is going to happen. Now that my mom knows, she'll be saying novenas morning, noon, and night. I'll have every saint in heaven watching over me." I tugged on his sweater, bringing him closer. "So all you need to worry about is relieving my stress."

Our lips reconnected, and I guided him over me as I fell back onto the blanket. The slow sweep of his tongue relaxed me into the bed, easing the tension from my body. If only I could bottle that feeling and take it with me onto the ice. I'd be the calmest, most stress-free skater in the world.

AUBREY OPENED HER ROOM door, expecting to see Marley, but instead she found a grinning Chris. He was wearing a green Cape Cod Baseball League T-shirt, and his hands were stuck in the pockets of his faded jeans.

"Hey, I can't hang right now," she said, hesitating. "Marley's coming over."

"This will only take a minute." He slipped inside and shut the door, backing her against it. "I just wanted to see you."

His lips brushed hers, making her squirm with anticipation. He followed by giving her just one tender kiss, but it brought every nerve in her body to attention. She'd experienced that feeling a lot lately — every day the past week in fact. Their nightly ritual of watching *Seinfeld* reruns had turned into a nightly make-out session. Huddled on the couch under a blanket with only the flickering light from the TV — it had been inevitable. Whenever they were in the same space, they had increasing trouble keeping their lips and their hands to themselves.

"You wanted to see me or you wanted to kiss me?" she asked with a smile.

"Is that another one of your trick questions?"

She laughed and hugged him, wishing she could tell him how lonely she'd been without him already, and they hadn't even been in St. Louis an entire day. *No big emotional revelations allowed.* She had to play it cool until she talked to Marley and until she knew exactly how Chris felt about her.

She and Chris had discussed anything and everything since they'd moved in together, but Marley was one topic Aubrey hadn't brought up. It was time to stop being afraid of it.

"Have you seen Marley yet?" she asked.

"I haven't. I'm sure I'll run into her soon, though."

She unwound her arms from his shoulders. "Do you think it'll be hard to see her?"

Chris appeared to ponder her question. "I think it'll be awkward at first but not hard. I realized once I stepped back and looked at our relationship that I was trying too hard to hold onto something that wasn't meant to be. I didn't wanna admit that things weren't great between us before she even left for Seattle."

"I always thought you guys were solid."

"I tried my hardest to convince myself we were because I didn't wanna lose that comfort, that stability we had together. But there was definitely something missing."

A spark of hope ignited inside her. If things hadn't been wonderful between them that meant Marley might be more accepting of Chris and her dating. And on another positive note, now she knew for sure Chris wasn't still hung up on Marley.

"Do you think she felt the same? That there was something missing?" she asked.

"I think she did but that she used moving away as the easier excuse to break up."

Aubrey toyed with her chunky purple bracelet. "She'll be here in a few minutes, so I don't know if you wanna stick around or…"

"I should probably head out. There'll be plenty of time this week for us to have our awkward reunion."

She walked him to the door, and he turned to her with his hand on the knob. "Watching *Seinfeld* won't be the same tonight." His gaze lowered to her mouth and then settled firmly on her eyes.

Warmth spread through her, and she took a slow step closer to him. Kissing his right dimple, she said, "Have sweet dreams."

He backed into the hallway, still smiling. "I know I will."

She closed the door and pressed her forehead to it. Her brain had been spinning with so many thoughts lately that she found it hard to stay focused, making her training for nationals quite a chore. All she could think about was how she wanted to spend every day and every night with Chris from now on. She never thought another person could bring her so much happiness, but whenever she was with him, even the coldest, grayest days seemed warm and sunny.

So this was what love felt like, what Em had been trying to explain for years. She got it now. Boy, did she get it.

A knock vibrated the door, and she jumped back. When she opened it, Marley threw her arms around her.

"It's so great to see you!" she squeaked.

Aubrey hugged her tiny frame. "I've missed your sweet face."

They both climbed onto the bed and sat facing each other. It reminded Aubrey of all the nights they'd stayed up late after competitions, sharing their happy moments or commiserating over their mistakes.

"I want to get something out of the way before we start catching up on gossip," Marley said. "No matter what the results are this week, I want us to have an amazing time together at the Olympics. One of us is going to be super disappointed, but our friendship is more important than any competition."

She loved Marley for being honest and direct. So many other skaters would stab their friends in the back in order to get ahead, and then they'd turn against them if they didn't succeed. She and Marley were in such a tough spot, competing for the national title and the position as the favored American team. The international judges would never put more than one American team on the traditionally-European Olympic ice dance podium, so winning the title and being the favorite was beyond crucial. She and Nick might have the slight edge since they'd won a medal at Grand Prix Final, but anything could happen in St. Louis. As she'd heard all her life, ice was slippery.

"I feel the same way," Aubrey said. "We've made it this far without a competition coming between us, so we can't let that happen now."

Marley smiled. "Good. I'm glad that's out in the open so we can talk about more fun things. I sorta have some news."

With the way Marley was grinning and her big brown eyes were shining, it had to be good news.

"Zach and I have gone out on a couple of dates," she continued. "We've been spending a lot of time together since we moved, and even though we've been partners so long, I feel like I'm only now getting to really know him. And he's pretty amazing."

Marley's situation sounded freakishly similar to hers and Chris's. There were two great things happening there — Marley had definitely moved on from Chris, and she'd fallen for a friend just as Aubrey had. Surely she would understand her feelings for Chris, right?

"That's awesome, Mar. You look really happy."

"Partner dating is something I've always thought could be disastrous, but I really think it can work with us. Maybe I'm being completely naïve... I don't know."

"If it feels right, you should go for it. Life's too short to second guess yourself."

Marley gave her a curious look. "I expected you to try to talk me out of getting involved with Zach. Knowing your views on relationships and all."

Aubrey picked at the comforter. This was her chance, the perfect opportunity to bring up Chris. Marley seemed to be totally into Zach, and it would be a huge load off her shoulders to have Marley's blessing. *Just do it.*

"I've umm… I've been seeing things a little differently lately. I've actually wanted to talk to you about it, so…" She kept her head down. "Since Chris and I moved in together, we've been hanging out, and I think it's a lot like what's been happening with you and Zach."

She peeked up from the bed, and Marley's smile had disappeared. *Oh, no.* Could she suck back in the words and pretend she'd never said them?

"If it's like me and Zach, then by hanging out you mean as more than buddies." Marley's sweet tone had turned cold.

She couldn't undo the damage now, so the best option was to forge ahead very carefully. "At first, that's all it was. But then we started getting closer and—"

"How close?"

Aubrey's response stuck in her throat, and Marley's pained stare wasn't helping her find the right thing to say.

"Have you kissed him?" Marley's voice rose.

Her heart thumped in her ears. "Yes, but—"

"I can't believe this!" Marley scrambled from the bed. "You and Chris? That doesn't make any sense."

Aubrey stood, too, needing firm ground underneath her. "It's not serious."

Never mind that she wanted it to be. She'd say anything to make Marley stop looking at her with so much contempt.

"Of course it's not serious! You're not his type at all."

Aubrey's face flamed, and she spoke quietly, "What type is that?"

"He loves doing all the things you can't stand like giving

girls flowers and teddy bears and candy hearts... showering them with attention, holding hands, singing cheesy love songs... Chris lives for romance, and you run at the first sign of it."

Every word Marley said pounded into her like nails. Spending time with Chris, she'd felt herself changing, becoming less cynical, but who knew if it would last? She was starting to think she'd been deluding herself about a lot of things.

Marley stormed past her and then spun around. "We dated for *four years*. Just because things didn't end well doesn't mean I didn't love him for a very long time. The fact that you would go behind my back and do this... I can't even..."

She marched to the door and swung it open, turning so Aubrey could see the hurt on her face. "You're not the friend I thought you were."

The heavy door slammed shut, and Aubrey stared at it, unable to move. How could she have thought getting involved with Chris was a good idea? She should've been stronger. She should've put a stop to it all on New Year's Eve after that first kiss. But no, she'd been an idiot and let herself get pulled in deeper and deeper, convincing herself it was all harmless and somehow believing Marley would be okay with it.

She sat numbly on the bed and winced at the memory of Marley's tear-filled eyes. The past couldn't be undone, but she could make better decisions starting now. Her chest tightened as she forced herself to see the truth. She and Chris had no business being together.

# CHAPTER SEVENTEEN

AUBREY BEAMED A BRIGHT SMILE TO the crowd and slowed her blades to a stop beside Nick. In her sparkling black and gold dress with a plunging back, she looked like she was ready for a Latin ballroom competition, and Nick was the perfect suave partner in his tight black shirt and pants. They had a slim one-point lead over Marley and Zach after the compulsory dance earlier in the day, and they needed to stretch that lead in this original dance. It was time to rhumba and samba their butts off.

As they waited for the music to start, Aubrey closed her eyes to bring herself into the moment. She'd been thinking about Chris non-stop since her conversation with Marley the previous night, but she had to block all that out and give the performance her full attention.

Ricky Martin's ballad "Casi Un Bolero" started their program, and she and Nick played the part of a couple in love as they performed the sensual rhumba choreography. She focused on Nick's hazel eyes and the liquid way they moved together to the music, shutting out everything else around them. As they twirled through their dance spin, the music slowed even more and then faded away, transitioning into "Por Arriba, Por Abajo" and the samba section.

They regained speed with deep strokes and moved into dance hold for the diagonal step sequence. Nick gripped her hand, and the memory of skating the samba with Chris on Frog Pond flashed through her mind, stealing her focus for just a few moments. But those few moments of lost concentration were long enough for her right blade to hit Nick's, causing her to lurch forward into him. She tensed with alarm, but she couldn't stop herself from falling and taking Nick down with her. They tumbled onto the ice, a tangle of arms and legs, as a collective gasp hushed the crowd.

Nick hurried to his feet, grabbing Aubrey's hands and pulling her up with him. She was in a daze, and she stumbled again as she tried to follow his lead. They'd missed a whole string of steps, making it seem impossible to catch up with the fast tempo of the music.

The audience clapped to spur them on, and they finally settled back into the choreography, but Aubrey had to force a smile through the dancing. Disappointment strangled her as she knew they'd just lost the title. Even with the free dance still to come, a mistake that huge would be beyond difficult to overcome.

They shook their hips one final time on the last beat of the music, and the crowd responded with a sympathetic ovation. Nick looked shell-shocked as he gathered Aubrey against him in an embrace, and she couldn't speak either. She could hardly breathe from the smothering regret. Falls in ice dance were a rare event, something she'd never done in all her years competing at nationals. Until now. The most important year of all.

Peter and Natalia wore grave faces when they greeted them at the ice door. Aubrey continued to exist in a fog as they sat in the kiss and cry and listened to their dreadful score. The only thing that registered was the number two next to their names. Not surprising but still hard to swallow since she and Nick had dominated nationals the past three years.

They trudged backstage, and Nick put his arm across her shoulders. "We can still do this. It's not over."

She appreciated his effort to stay positive, but she felt nothing but disgust with herself for making such a stupid mistake.

"I'm so sorry," she said.

"It was a fluke. It could've happened to either of us."

*No, it couldn't have because you weren't thinking about Chris while skating one of the most crucial programs of your life.*

The media coordinator summoned them to the mixed zone, and she took a few deep breaths. She had to buck up and act confident in front of the media. No matter how much she wanted to scream or break something, she wouldn't let the world see her frustration.

Following question after question whether she and Nick could rebound in the free dance three nights later, they had to face another round of inquiry at the press conference for the top three teams. Zach sat between Aubrey and Marley, and he may as well have been a brick wall because Marley acted like she didn't exist. Every time their paths had crossed that day — at the hotel, at the twenty-minute warm-up, at the draw for the original dance — Marley had refused to look at her. Being frozen out by her friend wasn't making Aubrey feel any less disgusted with herself. She fidgeted throughout the reporters' questions, counting the minutes until she could escape to her room.

As she and Nick left the media room, she checked her phone and saw she had three texts — one from Em, one from her mom, and one from Chris. Her thumb brushed over Chris's name, but she clicked on Em's first.

*Call me if you need to talk. I love you!*

Bypassing Chris's text again, she scrolled to her mom's.

*Dad and I will wait for you in the restaurant. Keep your chin up.*

She pinched the bridge of her nose. Dinner with her parents was the last thing she wanted to do. She'd make an appearance, but she wasn't going to sit through their phony "we're the perfect family" routine they put on at her events.

Chris's text glared at her, and she debated deleting it, but her fingers betrayed her before she could trash the message.

*I'm here if you need a friend.*

Her throat tightened, and she quickly erased the text and threw her phone into her purse. She had to end things with Chris. Not only had she hurt Marley, but she'd let her feelings for Chris affect her performance. It was exactly what she'd worked to avoid her entire career — having her heart get in the way of her head. And what a fantastic time she'd picked to cave to emotion.

After a quiet ride to the hotel, hiding out in the back of the bus, she rolled her skate bag through the lobby and into the restaurant. Not many diners remained at the late hour — mostly ice dancers, their families, and a few fans.

She spied her parents at a table in the far corner and wasn't surprised to see them staring at their drinks, not speaking to each other. Her mom wore her usual sweater set and pearls, while her dad had on his customary blazer and oxford shirt. They always looked like they just walked out of a country club ad. She hurried to the table and accepted quick kisses from them.

Her dad pulled out the empty chair, but she stayed standing. "I'm just gonna get room service."

"This is one of the few times we get to see you," her mom said.

"Hiding in your room isn't going to help." Her dad returned to his seat. "You need to show people you have some pride. That you're owning up to your mistake."

She let out a laugh of disbelief. "*You're* lecturing *me* about owning up to my mistakes?"

"Honey, please sit down and let's try to have a nice dinner," her mom pleaded.

"Your mother's not asking for much. Be considerate."

"Like you've been considerate of her all these years while you were—" She saw her mom's face pale, and she stopped herself from making even more of a scene. "I'm sorry, I can't be around your toxic relationship right now."

She raced to the elevator and banged her floor number with her fist. Her throat ached with screams that needed to be let out. When the elevator stopped, she barged into the hallway with her key in hand but stopped short at the sight of Chris knocking on her door.

"What are you doing here?" she blurted out.

His eyebrows rose at her harsh tone. "I just… I thought you might need to vent."

She needed to vent alright. But not to him.

She shoved the keycard into the lock and pushed open the door. "You shouldn't be here."

He followed her inside. "Did I do something wrong?"

Her back was turned to him, but she heard the heavy concern in his voice. Why did he always have to be so nice? He just couldn't make this easy for her. She dropped her bag with a thud onto the carpet as frustration and regret boiled to the surface.

"Marley hates me." She wheeled around to face him. "I told her about us and she's not speaking to me anymore."

"That's ridiculous. She shouldn't be mad at you—"

"Yes, she should. If I was any kind of a decent friend, I wouldn't have done this. It was a huge mistake."

Chris stared at her, so long she had to turn away because she was afraid he could see every emotion battling inside her.

"I can talk to her," he said.

"That's not going to make it better. The damage is done. We can't… *this* can't happen anymore." She motioned from Chris to herself. "This has to be the end of it."

His face tightened as he studied her for another long minute. "So it's over. Just like that."

"Well, we were just having fun anyway, right?" She evened her voice as much as she could to hide the pain that was throttling her.

He didn't immediately respond, and she held her breath, waiting for him to say she was wrong and he felt so much more. What would she do if he did say that? It wouldn't change how wrong they were for each other, but at least she'd know she hadn't imagined the deep connection between them.

"Right," he said, matching her emotionless tone. "It didn't mean anything."

A new wave of pain wrenched her heart, leaving her cold all over. Chris's eyes lingered on her a moment, devoid of the warmth she always saw in them, making her feel even colder. He walked quietly to the door and left without so much as a glance behind.

She wasn't a crier. She didn't cry during sappy movies or after bad skates or even when she'd seen her rink destroyed. But as she stood in that hotel room with Chris's words echoing in her ears... *It didn't mean anything... It didn't mean anything...* a burst of sobs rocked her body, choking her and shaking her so violently her legs crumpled beneath her. Tears poured down her face, and her eyes burned from the strain.

Never again would she let herself believe in love.

I STEPPED DOWN FROM the podium in the media room, and Courtney hugged me for the sixth time that evening. Her excitement couldn't be contained. She and Mark had placed third in the short program, earning them an invitation to the press conference, a first for them. Meanwhile, Chris and I had occupied the familiar center spot on the podium as the leaders.

Courtney bounced on the heels of her sneakers. "In two

days we could be celebrating making the Olympic team together."

I couldn't think about any celebration. I just wanted to get through the long program. Chris and I hadn't skated with our usual speed and confidence in the short, but we'd landed everything cleanly. We had a decent lead over Candice and Shawn, the second-place team, so we just needed to be steady in the long to win. I'd always hoped our final performance ever at nationals would be spectacular, but priorities had changed.

"Do I need to give you Sergei's famous lecture about not focusing on the results?" I asked with a smile. I was great at imparting his advice to others but not so skilled at following it myself.

"I'm trying, I swear, but we're *so-o-o* close. All we have to do is hang on to third place."

I pressed my hands to her shoulders. "No, what you have to do is fight for third place. Be aggressive, not passive."

She nodded sharply. "Aggressive. I can do that."

"That's the only thing I want you to think about between now and Friday. I have to get back to the hotel to meet Sergei, but call me anytime if you need help refocusing."

"Thanks, Em." She hugged me again. "It'll be great having you at the boards with us again next year."

"I'm looking forward to it." The only question was where those boards would be — Cape Cod or Boston. Sergei and I hadn't had a chance to talk much about SCOB's offer yet, but we were going to have to make a decision soon.

I searched the room for Chris and realized he'd split without telling me. I headed to the bus and found him sitting in the last row, a boatload of empty seats in front of him.

"You've been really quiet all day." I sat next to him. "Are you upset with me over my... situation?" I lowered my voice even though there were only two skaters near the front of the bus.

He continued to stare out the window. "It's not you."

"Is it Aubrey?"

His eyes swung in my direction. "Did you talk to her today?"

"No, she replied to my text and said she was okay, but I haven't seen her. What's going on?"

Courtney and Mark boarded the bus with loud laughter, and I avoided eye contact, hoping they'd stay in the front. Chris didn't seem to be in the mood for socializing. They took seats in the third row, and I sat up straighter.

"I won't tell her anything you say. I promise," I said.

He leaned back against the headrest and turned slightly to look at me. "You know she and I had been hanging out."

I nodded.

"Well, she told Marley and Marley got really angry. So, Aubrey said we're done." Chris's voice hardened on the last part.

A sigh sagged my shoulders. "I was worried something like this might happen."

"The thing is, I don't think Marley's the only reason she's doing this. I think she's hiding behind that because she's afraid we were getting too close."

"And you want to be even closer to her."

Chris shifted his gaze to the roof. "She has to want it, too."

It sounded like Aubrey could use a friend as well, although her general reluctance to talk about her feelings might keep her clammed up. I didn't want to get in the middle of her and Chris's issues, but I could be there to lend an ear.

"I think you just need to give her some time," I said. "With Marley being mad at her plus what happened at the OD last night, her head is probably all over the place right now."

"I don't know." Chris raked his hand through his hair. "I'm not sure if she'll ever take me seriously. It's why I didn't make a move seven years ago."

"What was seven years ago?"

The bus rolled away from the arena, and the driver shut off the interior lights, dipping us into darkness. Chris's pensive look became a dim profile against the window.

"When I moved to the Cape and first met Aubrey, I thought she was the most beautiful girl I'd ever seen. And she was so funny and sure of herself..." A hint of a smile showed through the darkness. "I wanted to ask her out so bad, but I saw the types of guys she went out with... older, edgier, way cooler than me. I didn't think I had a chance. So, I chickened out."

"I had no idea you were interested in her back then."

"She never gave me a second look, so I didn't really wanna broadcast my feelings."

I thought back to the conversation I'd had with Aubrey when she'd told me about the New Year's kiss. I'd never seen her smile that big when talking about a guy. Chris definitely had her attention now. Whether she was ready to admit it was another matter.

"Things have changed a lot between you guys since then. It might be a mess right now, but don't give up on her." I patted his leg, and he slowly bobbed his head. "And for the record, there's no one cooler than you."

He slid his arm behind me and hugged me to his side. "Thanks, Lil Mama."

"Lil Mama?"

"That's my new nickname for you." His smile reappeared. "Since you're little and you're gonna be a mama soon."

I shook my head. "No. Just no."

"Come on. It's cute."

"If anyone hears you saying that..."

"No one will know what I'm talking about."

I wasn't so certain. Ever since my episode at practice, I'd been paranoid the reporters were watching me closely and taking note of my tentative skating. It would be a stretch for them to connect all the dots, but I still worried. Someone was always looking to break a hot story, and it didn't get much hotter than the two-time defending world champion being pregnant on the eve of the Olympics.

# CHAPTER EIGHTEEN

The crowd was too quiet.

I paced backstage, trying to stay in my zone, but I needed to know what was happening on the ice. Courtney and Mark were in the middle of their long program, and I hadn't heard much applause. The knot in my stomach grew tighter with each quiet moment that passed.

"Emily, Chris." Our team leader Lynn beckoned us forward. We had to skate next, and since Sergei was at the boards with Courtney and Mark, Lynn was watching over us.

We edged into the tunnel to the ice, and the soaring score from *Pearl Harbor* streamed louder toward us. When we reached the entrance, I stole a glance at Sergei standing nearby. His eyes were trained on the ice, and I knew from the tight set of his mouth things weren't going well.

I turned my back to the action, and Chris took both of my hands. His were always so warm. I remembered our first nationals when I was so nervous my hands wouldn't stop shaking, and Chris had held them in his warm grasp our entire time backstage, not letting go for one second. Before I'd met him, competing made me physically ill. But since we'd paired up, I'd learned from him how to find the fun side of competition. I could never thank him enough for that.

The music ended, and the audience applauded respectfully but not wildly — unfortunate clue number three that the performance hadn't been a success. I kept my head down as I turned to take the ice. I had to avoid seeing Courtney's face because if she was in tears, I'd fall apart, too. I was already battling too many other emotions — sadness over this being our last nationals, my usual competition jitters, plus the extra anxiousness about being cautious and staying on my feet.

We circled the rink while the scores were read, and I set my tunnel vision on the ice. Markings from the previous teams in the final group scarred the white surface. I stared intently at the swirling lines, waiting for the announcement of Courtney and Mark's fate.

"… and they are currently in third place," the announcer declared.

My heart dropped into my stomach. They weren't going to be on the Olympic team. Well, not unless Chris and I had an implosion of epic proportions and dropped behind them in the standings. Goodness, I shouldn't even think about something like that.

*You can be there for Courtney later. Right now you have to give all your attention to this program you know and love dearly.*

The building erupted as their focus shifted from Courtney and Mark to Chris and me, and we skated to the boards for a moment with Sergei. He hurried forward from the kiss and cry, but he didn't speak right away. It had to be difficult for him to go from that heartbreaking scene to standing at the boards, where he needed to be strong for us.

He looked around at the raucous crowd, and his expression lightened. Focusing back on us, he leaned closer so we could hear him over the booming cheers.

"You have the love and support of everyone here. Just

have fun and enjoy skating with each other. Enjoy this moment."

Chris and I smiled at each other, and we left Sergei to glide into our starting position. I was already sweating under my black velvet dress. I needed to get moving so the rush of air would cool me down. As the first deep piano notes sounded, I reminded myself again and again, *Enjoy this moment.*

We stroked together in perfect unison, preparing for the first major element, the triple twist. Normally, we'd fly around the rink to set up, but we decreased our speed by a few cautious degrees. Chris tossed me upward, and I pulled in tight to spin three times. Dropping neatly into his catch, I ticked off the element on the checklist in my head.

*Keep it up exactly like that — clean and safe.*

The side-by-side triple Lutzes brought no problems, and I checked off another item. With strong crossovers, we rounded the corner of the rink, approaching the spot in the program where the quad had been. We'd replaced it with the easier triple loop throw. Chris set his hands on my hips, and I used my right outside edge to help propel myself into the air.

The cold air swished around me as I spun, and my right foot came down in a clean landing. I started to smile and spread my arms out, but then the heel of my blade stuck and I went flying backward. My butt crashed to the ice, sending a blow of pain to my tailbone.

*Oh, no, no, no.*

I hadn't fallen since I'd found out I was pregnant. This wasn't a fall on my stomach, but it was a hard one regardless. Chris held out his hand to help me up, and the stricken look in his eyes didn't reassure me. We caught up to the music, rushing to get into place for the transition to the slow section.

Chris pulled me close as the romantic adagio movement of the concerto began. "You okay?" he whispered.

I gave him a slight nod, but my heart was still pounding,

shaking me to my core. The soft, beautiful music didn't relax me as it usually did. My body was tight, and I had to complete a jump combination in a few seconds.

Chris released my hand so we could set up side by side for the jumps, and the only thing running through my mind was, *You can't fall again!*

I jabbed my toepick into the ice, but instead of rotating three times, I made two easy turns, lowering the difficulty of the jump from a triple to a double. I completed the second double toe loop to finish the combination, but I'd just thrown away valuable points by not doing the triple on the front end.

We joined hands, and Chris asked me again, "Feel okay?"

I nodded. I didn't feel sick to my stomach like I had at practice. I felt paralyzing panic because I didn't want to fall again.

One jump remained — the throw triple Lutz, which we'd choreographed on one of the strongest notes of the concerto. It was our big wow moment near the end of the program that always garnered a huge response from the crowd and gave me goose bumps. But now I feared it. The height, the distance, the impact if I fell... all of my muscles stiffened once more.

"Double. Double," I hissed to Chris.

He understood and threw me into the air with less power, just enough for me to complete two revolutions. More points lost.

We skated past Sergei, and his hands gripped the boards as if he was riding a roller coaster. With no more jumps ahead, I breathed easier through the last thirty seconds of the program. Chris held me in his arms for our final pose, and I started doing the math in my head, calculating just how many points I'd given away.

Chris hugged me as applause rang out. "You sure you're okay?"

"I think so. I don't know what..." I gasped, searching for air. "I panicked."

We separated to take our bows, and I looked at all corners of the arena, taking in the appreciation from the crowd. I'd wanted to give them so much more, to leave them with the lasting memory of a performance they'd talk about for years to come. Instead, it had been my worst skate ever at nationals.

Chris locked his arm around my waist as we glided to the ice door. Sergei stood next to it, still hanging on to the barrier with a white-knuckle grip. As soon as I stepped off the ice, he let go and took me into his arms.

"Are you hurt?"

"I'm okay." I put my mouth next to his ear. "I just got spooked."

He hugged me tighter and kissed my forehead. "It's alright." He repeated it a couple more times as he refused to let me go.

We finally retreated to the bench in the kiss and cry, and I stared at the replay of my fall on the throw. My heel had clearly caught a bad spot in the ice. A total fluke. Then the video showed me bailing on the triple toe. I bent forward and held my head in my hands. I couldn't be afraid of the ice if I was going to continue skating. I had to be stronger or all the risks I was taking would be for nothing.

The announcer read the low technical score, and I cringed. Maddy and Damien were probably watching the live results on a computer in Canada and high-fiving each other. As usual, our program component score reflected the high quality of our skating skills and intricate choreography. I peeked over my steepled hands at the monitor to see if it would be enough to give us the title.

*First place.*

I exhaled and hugged Chris, pressing my face against his silky shirt. We'd really done it. Six national titles in a row. More than anyone in the past eighty years. My eyes watered as I realized what we'd accomplished.

Sergei gave us both long hugs before we moved

backstage. A parade of congratulations followed from our competitors and various federation personnel. I spied Courtney waiting behind the crowd, and tears came to me again as I saw her red, puffy eyes.

I went over to her and wrapped my arms around her. She started crying, and I lost it, too. When I was able to speak, I held her hands and looked her firmly in the eye.

"I want you to listen to me. Twenty-ten in Vancouver will be your time. For the next four years, Sergei and I will do everything we can to help you and Mark get to the Olympics. It's going to be one of my most important goals as a coach. I promise you."

She gave me a shaky nod as fresh tears trickled down her cheeks. I dabbed at my own eyes and took a deep breath. This was only the beginning of what promised to be a very emotional day. Aubrey and Nick were skating their free dance in a couple of hours. If they couldn't pull out the win, Aubrey was going to be devastated, and from what I could tell, she was already an emotional wreck. I'd asked if she wanted to talk about what went down with Chris, and as expected she'd quickly dismissed the topic.

"Hey." Chris touched my back and steered me away from the traffic in the corridor. "When we get asked about our skate, I'll say we knew this would be a tough competition, we're working to peak at the Olympics, yada, yada."

"I just want you to know that I'm not going to let this happen again. I think I was so shocked by the fall and the way it came out of nowhere that I freaked out, but I'm still one hundred percent committed to seeing this through."

"I was kinda freaked out, too. And seeing how Sergei looked, so was he."

I glanced back at Sergei, who watched me closely. My mistakes may not have cost us gold, but they hadn't helped me make my case for continuing on to the Olympics. I'd asked Sergei not to be so anxious, and I'd just given him more reason to worry.

AUBREY SHOVED HER ROOM key in her jeans pocket and brushed her hand through her hair as she made her way to the elevator. She usually spent a ton of time getting ready for the post-competition parties, but she didn't feel like making the effort this year. After losing the title to Marley and Zach the previous night, she wasn't in the mood for partying at all, but Em had insisted she go since it was their last nationals.

The official competitors' party was in the hotel's big ballroom, but the unofficial one was in Nick's room. After their friend Trevor had quit skating, Nick had become the new party host. Aubrey paused at his door and debated turning around and leaving. Chris was likely inside, which would make the night even more difficult. But she had to live with him for the next three weeks until the Olympics, so she might as well get used to seeing him.

Nick answered her knock and reached for her hand. "I've got a drink with your name on it."

"Perfect."

She followed him through the bodies packed into the small space, and he stopped at the desk covered in liquor, juice, and soda bottles. Also jammed onto the desk was a laptop playing music. While Nick mixed bourbon and coke in a red plastic cup, Aubrey scanned the room and found Chris near the window. His back was to her as he talked to Shawn and Mark.

Em squeezed around the crowd and gave her a hug, warming her with her fuzzy sweater. She was holding her own plastic cup.

"What are you drinking?" Aubrey whispered in her ear.

"OJ," Em mouthed and showed her the orange liquid.

"Here you go, my lady." Nick handed over her cocktail

and turned to fiddle with the computer.

She took a long gulp and leaned against the desk as the liquor went down with a deep burn. A couple more drinks like that one and she wouldn't remember any of her troubles.

"Sergei didn't wanna come to the last hurrah?" she asked Em.

"You know he doesn't think he should mingle with the group since he's a coach. I was surprised he didn't change his tune this year, though, so he could keep an eye on me. He's been hovering over me so much lately."

"Well, better to have someone paying too much attention to you than not giving a crap," Aubrey said and gulped down more of her drink.

"Yeah... that's true."

"You'll have a little breathing space at the Olympics since you'll be rooming with me. Aren't you glad I insisted we do that?"

Em smiled. "That's gonna be fun. It'll be just like old times. And maybe Chris can calm Sergei's nerves since they'll be rooming together."

"Emily!" Candice laughed as she and one of the ladies' medalists surged forward. "You have to tell Jenna the story about the fire alarm at nationals in Atlanta... when Trevor almost got in a fight with that old guy? You tell it better than anyone."

Em launched into the story, and Aubrey snuck a glance at Chris, who was still facing the window. His broad shoulders filled out his red polo. It looked like the same shirt he'd worn on their date. That night seemed so long ago, more like two years than two weeks. She downed the rest of her drink and made herself another.

The bottle of bourbon became her closest companion at the party. She stayed parked next to the bar, letting the buzz take hold of her as conversations floated around her. Em suggested she slow down, but she waved her off and went back to pretending to listen to Jenna. By the time Chris approached her, she needed the wall behind her to keep her steady on her wedge heels.

"How are you doing?" he asked.

With her brain being a little woozy, she wasn't sure at first if it was a general question or if he was asking for a specific reason. As she squinted at him, she realized he was probably referring to the competition results.

"I'm fantabulous." She rested her head against the wall.

He looked down at the bottle beside her then back up at her again. "I know it's not easy to be positive right now, but you still have a chance to get a medal in Torino. It might seem harder with the way things shook out here, but don't stop believing that you can do it."

Harder? Try near impossible. She'd ruined her and Nick's status as the top U.S. dance team with one click of her blade.

"I'm not really in the mood for Mr. Brightside." She pushed off from the wall, and a wave of dizziness knocked her against the desk.

"Whoa." Chris grabbed her arm.

She looked up into his eyes. Those gorgeous, caring eyes. If he wasn't so nice, she never would've fallen for him. And if she hadn't fallen for him, she wouldn't feel such a painful ache every time he was near. Like right now.

"I'm fine." She stumbled out of his grasp.

Swaying toward the bed, she plunked down next to Nick. He tapped her cup with his and then halted with his drink in mid-air.

"We need to make a toast. With Team Cape Cod." He curved his neck to search the room. "Emily, Chris, Mark, Courtney! Get over here!"

It took a few minutes for them all to gather. A slight flush colored Courtney's cheeks as she sipped from her cup. She'd probably never drank alcohol before. Em was holding a bottle of water, and Nick took it from her hands.

"You can't toast with water. It's bad luck."

Aubrey snatched the bottle and handed it back to Em. "Enough with the superstitions. They're ridiculous."

"We can't have any more bad ju-ju," he said.

"I did your stupid New Year's kiss and we still had bad ju-ju, so what's the point?" she said, her voice rising.

"Why are you making such a big deal? Will someone just get Em a drink?"

"She can't have a drink! She's pregnant!"

Not only did everyone in the circle gape at her, but she'd yelled loud enough for everyone in the room to stop and stare. Em's face turned ashen, and the silence seemed to stretch for days.

*Oh crap. Oh crap. Oh crap.*

"Pregnant. That's funny. You have a good imagination when you're drunk." Chris pried Aubrey's cup from her shaky hand. "No more for you. Who knows what you might make up about the rest of us."

What was he doing? He thought he could cover it up? Her head spun as she watched all the wide eyes swing back and forth between her and Em.

"Why don't we go get some air?" Chris set down their drinks and led her by the elbow. She glanced back at Em, who was still pale and speechless.

As soon as they hit the hallway, Chris pulled at his hair. "How could you just blurt that out?"

She squeezed her head between her hands to try to clear her blurry focus. What had she done? She'd just hurt another one of her best friends. Em was going to hate her, too.

The door flew open, and Em came out with fire in her big blue eyes. "Are you seriously that drunk that you have no control over what's coming out of your mouth?"

"I'm so sorry! I'm so, so sorry!" Aubrey threw her arms around her. "Please don't hate me."

Em let out a deep sigh. "I don't hate you. But I'm not very

happy with you right now."

"Do you think people believed me when I played it off?" Chris asked.

"I don't know." Em wiggled out of Aubrey's tight embrace. "I should probably go do some more damage control."

"I'll tell everyone I was joking." Aubrey moved toward the door, but Chris stepped in front of her.

"You're not going back in there. You've said enough."

"I have to do something to make it better!"

"I don't know if there's anything that can make it better." Em glared at her before disappearing inside.

Aubrey stared at the closed door and then slowly turned toward the elevator.

"Where are you going?" Chris asked.

"My room." She continued forward. "Where I can't hurt anyone else."

"I'll walk you there." He quickly caught up to her slow, weaving steps.

"I can make it on my own."

"I'm going with you," he said more forcefully.

Inside the elevator, Aubrey caught a glimpse of herself in the mirror on the back wall. Her eyes were glassy, her hair tangled from pushing it out of her face all night. She was such a mess. Not the kind of girl for a guy like Chris. At least not for anything more than a fun time.

She pulled out her room key as they approached her door, and she leaned against the frame for support. The elevator ride had thrown her wooziness into overdrive. She fumbled to stick the card into the lock, and Chris wrapped his strong hand around hers, gently guiding the key into the slot. His warm touch made her even more lightheaded. Turning the handle, he slowly released her hand, and she backed against the door to hold it open.

She gazed at him, blinking the fog from her eyes. "Did

you walk me here hoping to get invited inside?"

"I walked you here to make sure you got here okay."

She smiled a little. "You're such a good guy. You really, really are." She tapped his chest with the key. "You're gonna find your Miss Brightside... a nice, sweet girl who doesn't get drunk and do stupid things."

His eyes darted over her face, and her cheeks heated. She stumbled into the room, and as the door shut, she thought she heard Chris say her name. She waited a moment and then looked through the peephole. But he was gone.

Collapsing onto the bed, she closed her eyes to make the world stop spinning, but nothing could stop her heart from aching. No amount of alcohol could drown that pain.

# CHAPTER NINETEEN

AUBREY ROLLED HER SKATE bag inside her room with Nick trailing close behind. They'd struggled through early morning practice for that afternoon's Skating Spectacular, the show where all the medalists would perform their exhibition programs. Their program was to "Fix You" by Coldplay, which Aubrey found fitting since many things in her life these days needed fixing.

She stretched out on the king-sized bed, and Nick claimed the opposite side. If they could work in a nap before the show, they might not resemble zombies under the spotlights.

"So you haven't told me…" Nick lifted up and pulled a second pillow under his head. "Is Em really pregnant?"

She rolled onto her side so her cheek pressed against the cool pillowcase. "What was everyone saying after I left last night?"

"Em denied it, but I don't think anyone was buying it."

"I can't believe I did that to her." She rubbed her forehead. "She's been so worried about people finding out, and I announced it to the entire room."

"I had a feeling something weird was up with her, just from the way she's looked at the rink."

"She gets morning sickness at random times during the day."

Nick made a face. "Girl's got some guts. I guess it would be hard to quit at this stage of the game, but it has to be pretty scary flying across the ice when you're pregnant."

"Yeah, our problems don't seem so bad in comparison."

Nick closed his eyes, so Aubrey did the same until he started talking again a minute later. "I've been thinking about the Olympics. Do you realize how lucky we are that we're getting to go not just once but twice in our career? It's really pretty incredible when you stop and think about it."

Aubrey thought back four years to the Opening Ceremony in Salt Lake City and how her feet had barely touched the ground as she'd marched with all the other athletes. She'd felt so honored, so special walking behind the American flag. That feeling had stayed with her the entire two weeks of the Games. She wanted the same experience in Torino. She wanted more wonderful memories she could hold onto for the rest of her life.

"Let's make our goal to have three amazing skates at the Olympics," she said.

"I'm down with that."

"From now until we compete in Torino, my sole focus will be on working toward those three performances. Nothing is going to distract me."

Nick shifted slightly toward her. "Did something distract you the other night during the OD?"

The image of Chris saying, *It didn't mean anything* popped into her mind, and she lowered her eyes to the bed. She cleared her throat and looked back up at Nick.

"It wasn't anything that will ever trip me up again."

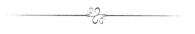

"IT'S NOT TOO LATE for you and Chris to pull out of the gala," Sergei said as he stood in the doorway of the bathroom. "We can say you're not feeling well."

I paused in the middle of brushing purple eye shadow on my lids. "There's no reason to pull out. That would only make people more suspicious."

Sergei retreated into the room while I resumed creating smoky eyes. Our show program to "Overcome" by Better Than Ezra was dark and intense, so I liked my makeup to match the mood of the music. My personal mood was a bit dark at the moment, too. After Aubrey's outburst at the party, my attempt to do damage control hadn't seemed too effective. I'd told people Aubrey and I had talked about me trying to get pregnant right after the Olympics, and she'd just gotten it all screwed up in her drunk brain. I'd received lots of curious looks, and Courtney had been especially probing, to the point where I'd caved and admitted the truth to her.

Sergei reappeared and came closer to the vanity. "I don't want you doing the twist or the throw under spotlights. It's too dangerous."

"If we take stuff out of the program, it'll raise a lot of questions."

"I don't care. I don't want you doing them. I'll tell Chris, and you can make an adjustment."

I snapped the eye shadow shut and looked at Sergei in the mirror. "We've never had a problem hitting our elements under spotlights."

"It's better to be safe in this situation."

*Safe.* That was a word with which I'd become very familiar. Safe was how things needed to be, but what would happen once we got to Torino? We couldn't be cautious there. We had to go all-out, no holding back. Without the quad in our arsenal, it was even more important that we do every element not just cleanly but spectacularly.

As I coated on multiple layers of mascara, a hard knock

sounded on the door. Sergei answered it, and Mom's voice filled the room.

"Is Emily here? She needs to see this."

I stepped out of the bathroom and saw Mom carrying her laptop. "What is it?"

She set the computer on the desk. "Read this post on the Skate World message board."

I sat in the chair and looked at the screen. A poster had written:

*I heard from a reliable source that the reason Emily wasn't feeling well at practice and hasn't been skating great isn't a migraine or an injured hip. She's pregnant.*

"Who is this source?" Mom cried. "Which one of your friends went behind your back and blabbed?"

I rested my elbows on the desk and pressed my fingertips to my temples. "The federation and the media read this board religiously. I'm surprised I haven't gotten a call yet."

"I'm going to let Aubrey have it when I see her," Sergei fumed.

"Aubrey did this?" Mom gasped.

"She didn't mean to leak it. She was drunk," I said.

"Oh, well that makes it so much better."

Sergei paced behind me. "If you get questioned about it, you can deny it, say it was a false claim."

"But what if someone starts digging and finds out I'm lying? I think that would make the situation even worse."

I looked up at the mirror above the desk. My hair was still in a sloppy bun, and I had mascara on only one eye. I needed to be glammed up and at the Savvis Center in less than an hour. What kind of mess I might walk into remained to be seen.

My cell phone trilled, and I took two slow steps toward the nightstand to retrieve it. I let out a breath when I saw Chris's name.

"Have you seen the message board?" he asked.

"My mom showed me."

"I was hoping everyone was too buzzed last night to remember what happened."

"I knew it would get leaked. Too many people there and too juicy of a story."

"Liza!" Sergei burst out, his hand to his forehead.

I moved the phone away from my mouth. "What about her?"

"I don't want her hearing about this from someone at her rink. We need to tell her first."

I glanced at the clock. I had to finish getting ready, call Liza and give her the news, and hopefully escape any media inquiries all in a very limited amount of time. After saying a quick goodbye to Chris and then Mom, I started brushing my hair while Sergei dialed Elena on his cell.

He breezed through the pleasantries with Elena and switched to the speaker function on his phone once Liza was on the line.

"Hey, sweetheart, we have some exciting news," Sergei said. "We were going to wait until we see you at the Olympics, but we thought we'd call and tell you now."

"Ooh, what is it?" Liza's voice crackled over the speaker.

Sergei looked at me as I fastened my hair with a barrette. I nodded for him to continue doing the talking.

"You're going to be a big sister." He grinned.

"What! You're having a baby?" she screeched.

I could only imagine Elena's face in the background upon hearing that information. She was surely thinking back to finding out she was pregnant with Liza and realizing it was the end of her skating career.

"The baby is due in September," Sergei said.

"That's so awesome!"

"We knew you'd be excited," he said.

"So, it's okay for Emily to still skate?"

Sergei made a rapid transition from smiling to looking

worried. I spritzed my hair with hairspray and leaned closer to the phone. "I'm being very careful."

"And I'm keeping a close eye on her," Sergei said.

"I hope it's a girl. I really want a little sister," Liza said.

I hadn't thought much about the sex of the baby. With skating at the forefront of my mind, I'd been viewing my pregnancy more as a medical condition than anything else. Maybe when I'd eventually start showing I'd feel more like an expectant mom?

"Another amazing daughter like you would be wonderful." Sergei regained his smile.

"Aww, thanks, Dad."

He and Liza chatted for a few more minutes while I finished my makeup. After double-checking my bag for my exhibition costume, we headed down to the shuttle, and I began revising the choreography of the program in my head. Taking out the twist and the throw would look suspicious, but that was probably a moot point now.

My phone rang as Sergei and I claimed two seats on the bus. Seeing the name of the federation's PR coordinator on the screen made me hesitate before answering.

"Hi, Jessie," I said, trying to sound casual.

"Hi, Emily." She didn't sound nearly as casual. "Will you be here soon? I've been getting some questions about an internet report that you're pregnant? I'm hearing there are multiple sources."

Goodness gracious, how many people from the party had loose lips? News always traveled fast in the skating world, but this was ridiculous.

"I don't want this discussed in the media. I didn't want this discussed *anywhere*," I said as Sergei watched me intently.

"I think it's unfortunately too late for that. The best thing we can do now is address it and control how we want the story presented."

I leaned my head against the seat and closed my eyes.

*And so it begins.* My Olympic quest was about to become all about my pregnancy. Not about the lifetime of work I'd put in or my incredible partner or how we'd raised the bar technically in the sport. No, all the focus would be on my body and a baby I hadn't even emotionally come to terms with yet.

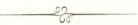

"MARLEY!" AUBREY CALLED.

Marley looked over her shoulder but kept walking through the hotel lobby toward the elevators. Aubrey quickened her pace and wheeled her bag around the fancy furniture. She hadn't been able to corner Marley on the bus ride back from the gala, but she could hopefully catch her now.

"Can we please talk for a few minutes?" Aubrey asked as she joined her in stride.

Marley stopped before the elevator bank and let the crowd of other returning skaters pass them. "If this is about Chris…"

"There's nothing going on between us anymore. I never should've let it happen in the first place, but I wanted you to know that it's done and it's over." She patted the handle of her bag for emphasis. "I can't stand the thought of losing our friendship over this."

Marley stared at her, her eyes sad under the heavy stage makeup. She backed toward a quieter spot away from the people traffic, and Aubrey followed.

"It's just hard for me to think of you guys together. He was my first love. He's always going to have a special place in my heart."

Aubrey could hear how upset she still was. "I'm so sorry, Mar. I don't know what I was thinking."

"You could have any guy, so why him?"

There were so many reasons why, but listing all Chris's

wonderful qualities wouldn't help her get back in Marley's good graces.

"We... we were just spending so much time together at the apartment, and... I don't know. He was just... different from other guys." She avoided Marley's questioning gaze.

"Which is why I never thought you would go for him. When you said you were moving in together, I didn't think for a minute that anything would happen between you."

"I didn't think anything would happen either. It was like... it was like how you described you and Zach. You were just hanging out and then something changed before you could even realize it."

"But there was no reason for me to stay away from Zach. There was a very good reason for you to stay away from Chris. One you should've thought of from the beginning."

"I did think of it, but I couldn't stop these feelings—" Aubrey shushed herself, realizing she'd said too much.

"So, you do have feelings for him," Marley said quietly.

She fought for words and stuttered, "That's... that's not important. What's important is our friendship and—"

"Hi, girls." Her mom walked up. "Marley, I can't believe this is the first time I've seen you all week."

She hugged Marley, and Aubrey silently cursed her timing. She wanted to patch things up with Marley while they were face-to-face. It would be easier than trying to repair their friendship long distance.

"It's good to see you, Mrs. London," Marley said.

"Why don't you come to dinner with Aubrey and me? I want to hear all about Seattle."

Marley grabbed her bag. "I'm meeting my parents, but thank you for the offer. They're probably waiting for me, so I'd better get going."

"Mar, wait," Aubrey said. "Can we talk more later?"

She gave her a long pensive look. "I don't think there's a whole lot more to say."

Her mom watched Marley curiously as she walked away. "Are things tense between you because of the results? I know you and Nick aren't used to losing to them, but I hope you've been gracious."

"Of course I've been gracious. They deserved to win."

"Then what's going on? She's obviously not happy with you about something."

Aubrey decided to evade the question and ask one of her own. "Where's Dad?"

Her mom straightened her pearl necklace. "He left last night. He had some work he needed to do today."

"On a Sunday? He couldn't stay one more day for the gala? Or even tell me he was leaving?"

"You've been so busy here that we've hardly seen you. He didn't think you'd mind."

"I'm sorry that I have obligations to the federation and to the media that I can't skip out on. Unlike his *work*." She made air quotes on the last word.

"Your father does work hard."

"And he plays hard too, doesn't he?" She bit down on her lip, but she'd already said more than she'd planned to.

Her mom's face froze, and she hugged her arms over her chest. "I think we should go to dinner now."

But the door had been opened, and after all the years of keeping quiet, Aubrey didn't want to shut it again. "Mom, you don't have to pretend with me."

She avoided her gaze and returned to fiddling with her pearls. "I'm not going to talk about this here."

"Can we go to my room?"

After a short pause, she received a slight nod in response. Neither of them spoke during the elevator ride or when they reached the room. Aubrey waited tensely for her mom to start the conversation.

"You know about the other women," her mom said, reluctantly making eye contact.

Aubrey sank onto the edge of the bed. "How many have there been?"

Her mom joined her, and Aubrey noticed she was twisting her platinum wedding band around and around.

"Three that I'm sure of," she said. "But there were probably more."

"Why are you still with him? How can you stand it?"

"Because it's the only life I've known for thirty years. I don't know who I am if I'm not Mrs. Scott London. Trust me, I've thought many times about what it would be like if I left him, and it's just easier this way. I have everything I need…"

"You don't have love or respect. Aren't those two of the most important things between a husband and wife?"

"I believe your father does love me." She stopped turning her ring. "He's just always needed more."

Aubrey bent forward and covered her face. "Please don't make excuses for him. You deserve so much better. *I* deserve better. Did you ever think about how it might affect me? To have to watch my parents in this sham of a marriage?"

"Don't let my choices affect yours. I want so much more for you. I want you to find someone who will truly be your partner, who'll make you feel like you're the most special person in the world."

She'd thought for a brief shining moment she might have found that someone, but that dream had come crashing down. She wasn't interested in feeling that kind of heartbreak again anytime soon.

"I'm good being on my own." She lifted her head. "That's the easier way for *me*."

"Honey, you can't be afraid of getting hurt. You have to open up your heart and take chances."

"How can you tell me to take chances when you won't do it yourself?"

"I'm content with the choices I've made. I know that's hard for you to understand, but…"

She didn't think she'd ever understand. She never wanted to feel trapped in a life that was passing her by. She'd rather be alone forever than to fall for the wrong guy and have her heart lead her down a road of bad decisions. She'd already made enough of those.

# CHAPTER TWENTY

I SQUINTED UNDER THE BRIGHT TV camera lights and fidgeted in my chair. We'd only been back at the rink in Boston for a few days, and Chris and I had already sat for ten interviews. Everyone from *People* magazine to the local university newspapers had jumped on our story. I'd been asked everything from whether my pregnancy was planned to which baby names I was considering. The reporters knew no boundaries as far as getting personal with their questions.

Sergei stood near the boards, a few feet from where the TV reporter had set up his camera. He'd been asked to participate in the interview, but he'd declined, just as he'd done with every other request he'd received. I had a good idea why he didn't want to be questioned.

Currently interviewing us was the young sports anchor from one of Providence's local channels. He didn't seem to know much about figure skating as he kept referring to his notebook for the most basic information like which city had just hosted nationals.

"Chris, how has your approach on the ice changed with Emily's condition?" he asked.

*Poor Chris.* He could probably recite the answer in his sleep.

"Emily's safety has always been my top priority, so my approach hasn't changed."

His responses had grown terser with each interview, and I could see him fighting not to roll his eyes at some of the questions. I didn't know how I would ever repay him for putting up with this circus.

"So, Emily, do you think skating pregnant at the Olympics means your child will be a champion skater when he or she grows up?" He flashed one of those phony TV smiles.

*Are you serious?* I had to stop my own eyes from rolling into the back of my head.

"If my child has a passion to skate, I'll be very excited, but if he or she doesn't, then that'll be okay, too. I'll support whatever passion the child has."

The reporter flipped his notebook shut, and Chris and I both shot up from our chairs. Finally we were free. Well, until the next day at least, when more media would come calling. Our agent Kristin had been working overtime, too. Some of our sponsors were nervous that we weren't prime gold medal contenders anymore, while on the flip side, a whole new group of companies wanted a piece of us. Me, specifically. Most of the products were related to women's health or motherhood. Kristin had even received a call from one of the pregnancy test manufacturers, to which I'd emphatically said no.

I escaped to the upstairs lounge and took my bag of carrot sticks out of the fridge before joining Aubrey at one of the small tables.

"I haven't apologized yet today for my big mouth," she said, her voice raspy. "I'm so sorry you're getting bombarded by the press."

"You don't have to keep apologizing. It probably would've come out some other way if you hadn't said anything." I watched her sip a cup of hot tea. "You sound worse today. Do you feel worse?"

She nodded and touched her palm to her forehead. "It's like clockwork. Every year I get sick right after nationals."

"You should ask Chris to make you his special cold remedy concoction." I pointed a carrot stick at her. "It's nasty to drink, but it's got some killer vitamins in it."

She huddled over her cup, breathing in the short wafts of steam. "I'm not asking Chris to do anything for me."

"Are things that bad between you guys?"

"They're not bad. They're just... nonexistent. We've said about ten words to each other since we've been back."

"That can't be easy, living in the same house and barely speaking."

"I've had a lot of experience watching my parents do it. It's not as hard as it sounds."

I frowned. "You'd become such good friends. There has to be some way you can get back to that."

"Things are too weird now. We should've never crossed that line." She sighed and rested her head on her fist. "It screwed everything up."

I chewed slowly as I recalled my conversation with Chris on the bus. He didn't think Aubrey took him seriously, but I could see the droop in her eyes as she talked about him. And it wasn't just from not feeling well.

"Have you heard from Marley at all?" I asked.

"I've texted her a few times, but she hasn't responded."

"I wish there was something I could do. I hate seeing all my friends hurting."

"You have enough to deal with right now without worrying about us."

"That's right," Sergei said as he walked up to the table. "No thanks to your drunken outburst."

"I apologized again to Em. I'm sorry I caused such a mess." Aubrey pushed back her chair and stood with her tea.

"I have to go find Nick. Em, I'll talk to you later."

"Feel better," I called after her and then turned to Sergei as he sat in her chair. "She really is sorry for what she did."

"She should be. Our baby shouldn't be national news, but now it is."

I plucked a carrot stick out of the bag and broke it in half. "That guy from Providence was really insistent about interviewing you. I didn't think he'd let it go."

"There's no way I'm talking to any of them."

"You're afraid they'll bring up what happened with you and Elena."

Sergei rubbed the back of his neck. "I don't want Liza getting pulled into this. With the issues she's had at her rink recently, she doesn't need this kind of attention on her."

"I hope they wouldn't dig that far and drag Liza into the story."

"I don't trust these people not to bring it up. They'll look for any angle they can get."

I pulled my phone from the pocket of my warm-up jacket and clicked to the calendar application. Scrolling through the rest of the week, I counted eight more appointments with three more tentative ones. I shook my head and slid the phone onto the table.

"I understand Jessie and Kristin's strategy that we do all these interviews so it seems like my pregnancy is no big deal and I'm still just as prepared for the Olympics, but we can't keep this up for the next three weeks. It's just too much. Every interview stresses me out because I'm scared my words might get twisted around. Some of the stuff they're asking is so personal…"

Sergei clasped my hand. "It won't go on like this. I won't allow it. You and Chris need time to prepare for Torino, and you need extra time to rest."

"I never knew being pregnant would make me so tired. I'm kinda worried what the jet lag will do to me in Italy."

"The good thing is you'll have almost a week to get settled there before you have to compete. I'm telling Jessie and Kristin that you are not to be hounded by the media that week. Standard press conferences only."

"I can talk to them about it."

"No, I'll handle it." He sheltered my hand between both of his. "You should just concentrate on relaxing and keeping up your strength."

I wasn't surprised he insisted on taking care of it. He'd been doing that every chance he had lately. I loved Sergei from the depths of my soul, but if he was going to treat me like an incapable person for the duration of my pregnancy, I might strangle him.

AUBREY SLOWLY OPENED HER eyes and lifted her head from the smooth leather couch. She'd come home from the rink and hadn't had the energy to climb the stairs to her bed, so she'd decided to lie on the couch and close her eyes for a few minutes. But darkness had replaced the daylight previously streaming through the windows, and she was now covered with a blanket. From the kitchen came the whirr of the blender.

She took her time standing and then wobbled her way through the living room. Every inch of her body ached, and chills waved through her. In the kitchen, Chris stood next to the counter, watching the blender. A thick green liquid spun inside. He spotted her in the doorway and shut off the machine.

"Did I wake you?"

"How long was I asleep?" she croaked.

"A few hours. I was making something for you to drink when you got up."

She stared at him. Were they friends again? Everything

had been so awkward the past few days that she didn't think they could return to normal. It was still deeply painful to be around him, but it hurt even more not having his friendship.

She stepped toward the counter and peered at the blender. "Is this your cold remedy concoction?"

"It's all natural and proven to be highly effective." He gave the mixture one more whirl. "You'll feel much better if you drink this."

"It looks like the Incredible Hulk's blood."

He laughed, and she smiled a little. She'd missed that infectious laugh.

He poured half of the contents into a tall glass and held it out to her. "Close your eyes if you have to."

She shook her head, and it throbbed in response. "No way."

She went back into the living room and curled up in the corner of the sofa. Chris followed with the concoction and sat on the other end. He brought one leg up onto the cushion and spread his arm across the back of the couch.

"Come on, it's not that bad," he said.

She eyed the drink warily. "You shouldn't have gone to all the trouble of making it. I can get better the old-fashioned way — OJ and chicken soup."

"It wasn't any trouble. You looked like you could barely make it around the rink today, so I figured you could use some help."

There he was, being the nice guy again. At least now she knew not to confuse his gestures as being anything more than friendly.

"You 're not gonna leave me alone until I drink it, are you?"

One side of his mouth twitched upward as he extended the glass to her. She scrunched up her nose and reached for the drink. Her fingers brushed Chris's, and the brief tingle made her grab the glass too quickly, almost sloshing green goo over the rim.

"Whoa, got it?" Chris smiled.

She clutched the glass with both hands and brought it under her nose, holding her breath as she cautiously sipped. The thick mixture sat in her mouth, tasting viler than any medicine she'd ever taken. She forced herself to swallow without gagging.

"It tastes like... grass and feet!"

Chris laughed. "I'm not sure how you know what those two things taste like, but I'll take your word for it."

"I can't drink this." She stuck out her tongue.

"You have to chug it, not sip it. Take it down fast."

She raised the glass to her lips and took a bigger gulp, squeezing her eyes shut as the liquid slimed down her throat.

"That's better," Chris said. "A few more like that."

Her phone rang with "Mamma Mia" on the coffee table, and she leaned forward and pressed the button to send the call to voicemail. She felt sick enough without listening to her mom rationalize staying married to her dad.

"Did something happen with your mom at nationals?" Chris asked.

Even with all the weirdness they'd been through, she still sensed deep down that she could trust him as a friend, and he was the only person who knew all her family drama. She found herself slipping back into the familiar comfort she'd once had with him.

"She admitted my dad's been cheating on her, and then she tried to make excuses for him."

"Oh, man. I'm sorry."

"Yeah, last week sucked six ways from Sunday." She drank more of the nasty goop and made a face.

"I'd say something encouraging, but Mr. Brightside doesn't wanna get yelled at again." He gave her a knowing smile.

She lowered her head and shielded her eyes. "I don't

know half of what I was saying that night."

"There was some fascinating stuff."

She unfortunately remembered the rambling she'd done when he'd walked her to her door. Afraid he might bring up that moment, she drained the glass and set it on the table. "I expect to be fully cured when I wake up in the morning."

Picking up her phone, she unfolded her achy joints and headed for the stairs. "Have a good night."

"You, too. I promise you'll feel better tomorrow."

She paused and started to turn around but thought better of it. Seeing the softness in his eyes that she heard in his voice would just tear away another piece of her heart. If only there was a disgusting green potion she could drink to make her feelings for Chris disappear. She'd chug it down in one gulp.

After a hot shower with lots of steam to clear her chest, she crawled into bed and burrowed under the two layers of blankets. The chills had become worse after departing the warmth of the bathroom. She thought about putting a long-sleeved T-shirt over her tank top, but she was too cold to leave the blankets.

Beside her bed sat Frosty the stuffed snowman, his fluffy white fur looking very warm and cozy. She reached over and pulled him under the covers with her, wrapping her arms around him. Her eyelids sagged, and darkness slowly took over.

When she next opened her eyes, she jumped at the sight of a figure sitting on the bed. Once her vision adjusted, she saw the figure was Chris… wearing nothing but his boxers… the plaid ones she'd seen in his laundry once.

He peeled back the blankets and removed Frosty from her grasp. Taking the snowman's spot himself, he hugged her close to him. "I thought I could keep you warm instead."

*What?* Had there been something in the drink that was making her hallucinate? She had no idea what was happening, but she'd never experienced a more electrifying feeling in her life. The chills and aches had completely vanished. All she felt was Chris's strong arms around her, the smooth skin of his chest under her palms, the long, hard length of his body pressed against hers.

He tilted her chin up, and his breath heated her lips. "I need to tell you something."

His mouth drew nearer, the tip of his nose brushing hers. The hammering of her heart vibrated down to her toes.

"I need you to know how I feel," he said, rubbing his hand over her bare shoulder and down her back.

Her entire body trembled with anticipation. She was too overwhelmed with shock and the sensory overload of being in Chris's arms to find any words. Her eyes strained in the dark to see his, to find the tender look she knew was there.

"Aubrey, I..." He paused, and she pressed her fingertips into his chest.

"Yes?" she whispered.

He licked his lips and pulled her closer. "I want—"

Her body jerked, and her eyes flew open. Blackness surrounded her. Sweat caked her face and neck. And nestled against her was the stuffed snowman. Not Chris.

She threw the blankets aside and inhaled deep breaths. Her heart apparently didn't know the difference between dreams and reality because it was beating in double time. She couldn't blame it, though. All the sensations — the warmth of Chris's touch, the clean scent of his skin, his husky voice — they'd seemed so real. Torturously real. Tears pooled in her eyes, and she flung the snowman onto the floor.

Talking to Chris earlier had messed with her head. They couldn't be buddies. Not as long as this agonizing desire to be with him haunted her.

# CHAPTER TWENTY-ONE

OUTSIDE THE WINDOW OF SERGEI'S SUV, row after row of charming Victorian homes rolled past. It was one of those beautiful clear winter days on Martha's Vineyard when the sky gleamed crystal blue. Everything in Edgartown sparkled under the brilliant sunshine.

"Escaping for the weekend was the best idea ever," I said to Sergei in the driver's seat.

He smiled. "I know how much you love it here."

"It always feels like the rest of the world is so far away when I'm here."

"That's exactly why I thought it was the perfect time to come."

I couldn't agree more. After the week full of interviews, photo shoots, and conference calls, there was no better way to unwind. I had so many great memories of the island from spending childhood summers at Aunt Debbie and Uncle Joe's vacation home in Chilmark. I also had some pretty awesome recent memories like Sergei's and my first kiss at the clay cliffs in Aquinnah.

"If we move to Boston permanently, it'll be a longer trip

whenever we want to come out here," I said.

"That's one for the cons column on our pros and cons list," Sergei said.

"We don't have to give the club a decision until after the Olympics, right?"

"Yeah, I told them we needed time."

I shifted in the smooth leather seat so I was angled toward Sergei. "It would be great to be closer to my family, but then there's the danger of them dropping in at any time."

"Your mom coming by unannounced? Never!" He laughed.

Sergei's cell phone rang in the cup holder between our seats, but he kept his focus on the winding road. "Can you grab it?"

I answered and Elena asked, "Where is Sergei?"

"He's right here, but he's driving."

She let out an audible breath. "Well, I should speak with you both anyway."

"I can put you on speaker." I pressed the button and laid the phone face-up on my palm.

"Is Liza okay?" Sergei's brow creased.

"She was in fight at the rink. Her face and arm have cuts."

"What?" Sergei exclaimed.

I gave my own concerned look to the phone as if Elena could see us. "Are the kids still giving her a hard time about junior nationals?"

"Not only nationals. Now they have new thing to taunt her. They talk about you and Sergei."

A sense of dread filled me, and the arm I was using to hold up the phone weakened. I rested my elbow on the console.

Sergei's jaw clenched as did his grip on the steering wheel. "What did they say?"

"She does not tell me except it is about Emily's pregnancy."

"Did Liza start the fight?" he asked.

"Yes. Other girl, Olivia, have cuts, also. I speak with her mother and tell her how she has been so cruel. I think it get better before but now this."

"I'd like to talk to Liza," Sergei said.

"She is in her room. I call her."

Silence came over the line, and I looked at Sergei. "Whatever they said must've been pretty bad for Liza to get in a fight. I've never even heard her raise her voice to another kid."

He shook his head and stayed quiet, eyes firmly on the tree-lined road. We'd entered a more rural section of the island on the way to Chilmark. The sunlight didn't seem as bright as it had before.

A brief shuffling sounded on the phone, followed by Liza's tiny voice. "Hi."

"Your mom told us everything," Sergei said. "Are you okay?"

"I just have a few scratches."

"What did Olivia say to you?" he asked.

Nothing but dead air came in reply. The feeling of dread became more overwhelming.

"Sweetheart, tell us what she said," Sergei prodded.

Liza sniffled. "She said... she said Emily is going to kill the baby if she keeps skating."

My stomach dropped, and my hand flew to my mouth. Sergei had the same reaction, rubbing his mouth and then his face. The car suddenly seemed to be moving at a much higher speed as the barren trees whizzed by. It didn't take a lot to make me woozy these days.

"Can you slow down?" I murmured between my fingers.

He glanced at me and eased way up on the gas pedal. I pressed the window button, cracking open the glass a few inches to bring in some fresh air. I didn't care that it was forty degrees outside.

"Liza," Sergei started but then paused and rubbed his face again. He took a deep breath and began once more, "Liza, the baby will be fine. This girl... Olivia... she's just trying to upset you. I want you to stand up to her, but getting into a fight isn't the right way."

"She's so mean, Dad," Liza cried. "The stuff she was saying was so horrible. I just wanted her to stop."

"I know, but the best way to make her stop is to stand up to her and tell her you know what she's saying isn't true. If this ever happens again, promise me you'll do that."

Louder sniffling mixed with the static on the line. "I will."

Elena returned to the phone, and while she and Sergei discussed Liza's punishment, I remained silent. The sickening sensation in my stomach had tied itself into a tight knot. I couldn't help but wonder how many people thought I was an unfit mother-to-be. I'd avoided reading the internet message boards the past week for my own sanity, but I didn't know if I had the willpower to stay away from them any longer.

After I hung up the call, I dropped the phone into the cup holder and turned toward the window. A cold whistle of air streamed across my face, drying the moisture that had gathered in my eyes.

"Em." Sergei squeezed my knee. "Don't give a second more of thought to what some stupid kid said."

I nodded but didn't look at him. The side road to Aunt Debbie and Uncle Joe's summer home came into view, and Sergei turned us down the narrow lane. He parked in the long driveway in front of the two-story house, and we met at the rear of the SUV to retrieve our bags.

Sergei popped open the back and then put his hands on my waist. "From this moment on, the rest of the world doesn't exist. It's only you and me and this quiet, peaceful island."

I nodded again, still not speaking. How I wished I could snap my fingers and forget what I'd heard, but it was stuck in my brain on repeat.

Sergei grabbed both of our overnight bags, and I carried my laptop case. I'd brought my computer so I could finally organize all the photos I'd taken at our events that season. Now I was thinking I could also use it for another purpose. The house had wi-fi...

We brought our stuff up to the guest room, and I sat on the bed and unzipped my tall boots. "I think I'll lie down for a little while. The ferry plus the car ride made me kinda queasy."

"Do you want some crackers?" Sergei opened his duffel bag and pulled out a box of saltines. "Or I can go to the store and pick up something else."

The fact that he'd thought to pack crackers for me melted my heart. I stood and wrapped my arms around him.

"I'm okay. I'm not really hungry. I just need to be still and it'll pass."

He kissed my forehead. "Okay. I'll be outside getting wood for the fireplace. Yell if you need me."

I took off my boots and lay on top of the burgundy comforter, closing my eyes, but I couldn't stop thinking about the computer a few feet away. I got up and brought it onto the bed with me. Lying back against the pillows, I watched the screen come to life with the background photo of Sergei and me in Red Square in Moscow. We'd taken it during the world championships the prior year, and I wore a huge smile as I showed off my gold medal. When would I finally look that happy about being pregnant?

I clicked on the internet and went to the Skate World message board on my favorites list. Not surprisingly, there was a whole thread dedicated to my situation, and it was already ten pages long. My finger hovered over the touchpad as I hesitated to tap on page one. How many times over the years had Sergei told me not to read the board? The posters never held back in their comments, which were sometimes downright cruel. But morbid curiosity caused my finger to click.

The first few comments were all by supportive fans who thought Chris and I could maintain our performance level even with the reduced training. I scrolled down the page and read the next comment:

*What in the world is Emily thinking, trying to skate at the Olympics? How can an Olympic gold medal be more important than the health of her baby?*

My throat ached with tears, but I couldn't rip my eyes away from the screen. I clicked the next page, and the first poster said:

*Talk about misplaced priorities. There's no way I'd put my body at risk like that even with the Olympics at stake. If something happens to the baby, a gold medal isn't going to make it all better.*

And then another:

*I don't know if she's ready to be a mother if she's this reckless.*

I slapped the computer shut and muffled my cry into the pillow. Why hadn't I been more worried, more insistent on putting the baby first and my competitive dream second? I'd been so obsessed with my Olympic dream for so long, and it consumed so much of my emotional energy. Shouldn't I feel just as strongly about the baby? What was wrong with me? My queasiness grew heavier as my tears flowed faster, and the rising bile added to the burn in my throat.

Since I'd found out I was pregnant, my focus had been all on skating, skating, skating. I'd convinced myself that I couldn't think about anything else until after the Olympics, but was that how someone carrying a child should feel?

I curled into a ball, clutching my stomach. When I looked up, I saw Sergei peering around the door frame.

"Em?" He rushed onto the bed and brushed my hair away from my face. "Are you feeling worse? Are you hurting?"

I shook my head slightly and mumbled through the tears, "It's not that."

"Then what—" He noticed the laptop next to me. "Oh, no. Were you on the Internet?"

I swallowed hard. "Do you think I'm horrible for putting the baby at risk?"

"No, of course not." He pushed the computer away so he could scoot closer to me. "You're listening to the doctor, taking good care of yourself…"

"But something could still go wrong. There could still be an accident."

"You're doing everything you can to keep yourself safe and healthy. You're amazing me every day with how you're fighting through this."

I blinked away the blurriness from my tears and gazed up at him. "You've been so worried, though. Deep down, don't you wish I would quit?"

"No." He didn't hesitate to answer. "Because you would be devastated if you had to stop now, and I couldn't stand to see you hurting like that. I do worry, but I'd feel the same even if you weren't skating. That's just me being a protective father-to-be." He smiled and wiped a tear from my cheek. "I believe in you and that you can still make your dream happen. Just think about the story we'll be able to tell our little boy or little girl… how he or she was a part of this incredible experience."

I tried to smile, but my quivering chin wouldn't cooperate. Sergei's connection to our child and his protective instincts had already kicked in full force, but mine hadn't blossomed yet. That seemed so backwards.

I sat up, and he cradled me in his arms. "What people on the Internet say… what people anywhere say doesn't matter. All that matters is what I've known about you since the day I met you. You are strong and determined, and you put your beautiful heart into every single thing you do. That's how I know you can have it all. The baby, the Olympics, everything."

His shining blue eyes held so much love. For me *and* the

baby. I couldn't tell him I was still grappling with my own emotions. I didn't want him to know I wasn't the excited expectant mother I should be.

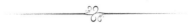

AUBREY SIPPED HER GREEN tea and let her gaze wander from her laptop screen to the busy rush hour scene outside Starbucks. A constant stream of cars hummed down Beacon Street as did people on foot. Since she'd spent almost every evening in the coffeehouse the past couple of weeks, she'd begun to recognize some of the faces of the professionals on their way home from work.

She looked further down the street toward her apartment. Chris had to have noticed she'd been avoiding the place as much as possible, but he hadn't said a word. When she wasn't at Starbucks, she was either hanging out with Nick or holed up in her bedroom. Only a few days remained before they'd leave for Torino, so she just had to keep it up a little longer. As soon as the Olympics were over, she could move back to the Cape and start making plans for the rest of her life.

Her eyes lowered to the computer screen and one of the possibilities for that future life. Boston Architectural College. It had a highly-ranked design program and was located just a few blocks away on trendy Newbury Street. She'd walked by the school a few times since she'd been in the city, but she never knew it had a School of Interior Design until she'd done some online research.

She clicked on the admission requirements and was halfway down the list when her phone chirped. She picked it up, and her eyes widened when she saw Marley's name above the text. It read:

*Do you have some time to talk?*

She couldn't type fast enough in reply:

*Definitely! I'll call you in a few minutes.*

After packing her laptop into her messenger bag, she threw on her jacket and grabbed the phone and her cup of tea. She joined the other hustling people on the sidewalk and raced to the apartment. Stopping on the stoop of the brownstone, she sat on the stairs and set her cup next to her. Chris was home, so she'd have more privacy outside.

Marley answered on the first ring. "Hey."

"Hey." Beyond that, she didn't know what to say. It felt strange to be tongue-tied while talking to one of her best friends.

Marley broke the silence. "I've been thinking a lot about what happened between you and Chris and what you said about not being able to stop your feelings."

"I was just babbling and not making any sense."

"No, I think you were. It made a lot of sense once I had time to really think about it. We've been friends a long time, and I've never heard you mention the word feelings when you've talked about a guy. That meant this had to be a pretty big deal for you."

"I don't know what I was saying—"

"It's okay," Marley interrupted her. "I realized you wouldn't have gotten involved with Chris unless you really fell hard for him, and I can't blame you because I know what that feels like."

She let what Marley had said sink in, hoping she'd correctly heard the understanding in her voice.

"Are you saying you're okay with what I did?"

She didn't immediately reply, and Aubrey huddled her knees to her chest. The evening was growing darker and colder by the moment.

"I'm saying I know the kind of friend you are, and I know you didn't want to hurt me," Marley said.

Aubrey tilted her head back and exhaled. "I'm so glad to hear you say that."

"It's still really weird for me to think of you and Chris

together, but if you make each other happy, you deserve to have that."

The heaviness in her heart that she couldn't seem to shake flared stronger and deeper. She hugged her knees tighter.

"There's no chance of us getting together. Chris wasn't ever serious about me." She felt a waver in her voice, so she took a breath. "I think I was more of a rebound thing for him."

"That doesn't sound like Chris." Marley hesitated. "Maybe you should tell him how you feel."

"No. That would be another huge mistake. He made it clear we weren't..." She bit her lip. "That it didn't mean anything."

"I'm sorry."

"It's fine. You were right. We don't make a whole lot of sense together anyway, so... and I have bigger things to focus on right now. Are you ready for Torino?" She had to change the subject before she became any more strangled by emotion.

"I already started packing. I'm *so* ready to go."

"If it's anything like Salt Lake, it'll be an amazing couple of weeks."

"I wish we could be on the podium together. That would make it even more amazing."

Aubrey picked up her tea and then set it back down. It probably wasn't very warm anymore. "Well, we know the Russians will win, and then it's me and Nick, you and Zach, and the Italians all going for two spots. I don't think there's much hope of both of us making it up there. The European judges won't let it happen."

"I know it's not likely, but I still wish there was a way..."

"I just want to skate fabulously. That's all I'm thinking about. Ending my career with the best performances we've ever had."

A glance down the sidewalk made her look twice. Chris was coming toward the apartment, his head down and his hands stuffed in his jacket pockets. A black beanie covered his dark hair.

As he came up the steps, Aubrey gave him a curious look. "I thought you were inside."

"It was too quiet, so I went for a walk."

Was that a subtle comment on her frequent absence?

"It's kinda cold," she said, noticing his red nose and cheeks.

"Says the girl who's sitting outside talking on the phone."

She turned away from his adorable crooked smile and put the phone back to her mouth. "Hey, Mar. Sorry about that."

Chris waited a second on the top step and then went into the building. Marley said, "I'll let you get inside. I need to finish cleaning my apartment. I don't want it to be a mess when I come home from the trip."

Aubrey stood and slung her bag over her shoulder. "I'm so, so happy we talked."

"Me, too. I can't wait until we get to hang out in Italy. At the Olympics!"

They said their goodbyes, and Aubrey was still smiling as she walked into the apartment. Chris looked up from the take-out menu he was reading, eyebrows raised.

"That was Marley on the phone?"

Aubrey stopped at the foot of the stairs. "She asked me to call her, and we had a great talk. Everything's good between us now."

"That's awesome."

"I know. I'm so glad we have this all behind us before the Olympics."

The few moments of silence that followed felt more awkward than they should. Weeks of barely conversing had made all their brief encounters slightly uncomfortable.

"I had a feeling you'd hear from her," Chris said. "Your friendship is super important to her."

She didn't have a response and didn't want to endure

another awkward pause, so she nodded and quickly started upstairs.

Chris called after her, "Do you wanna order Chinese with me?"

She halted and yelled down, "No, thanks. I'll make something later."

*Just a few more days*, she thought as she continued on to her room. Once she was in Torino, she'd be swallowed up by Olympic excitement and Chris would be just another athlete in the Village.

# CHAPTER TWENTY-TWO

I STOOD UP FROM MY SUITCASE and bumped into Aubrey, sending us both into laughter.

"We've shared a lot of rooms over the years, and this is definitely the smallest," I said.

Our dorm room in the Olympic Village was half the size of a hotel room, and the twin beds were so close together we could reach out and touch each other when we lie in them. It was worlds different from the apartment we'd had in the Village in Salt Lake City.

"I feel bad for the people who aren't familiar with their roommates," Aubrey said. "I wouldn't want to be this cozy with a stranger."

"Sergei said Chris got up during the night to go to the bathroom, ran into his bed, and almost fell on top of him." I laughed.

Aubrey put her head down at the mention of Chris and then knelt in front of her own large suitcase shoved against the wall. "If you and Sergei ever want some private time, just let me know and I'll go hang elsewhere."

"We might, especially after my competition's over." I

paused and shifted my weight. "You can hang out with Chris while our room's occupied."

"You know he and I aren't buddies anymore."

"But there's no reason you shouldn't be. You and Marley are cool, and maybe if you and Chris start spending time together again, it could turn into something more."

"He doesn't want anything more, and I'm not putting myself out there again."

Her hair fell around her face so I couldn't see her expression, but I could hear the hurt in her voice. I didn't want to blab what Chris had told me — how he'd been interested in her years ago — but I wanted her to know there was a chance something good could happen between them.

"I think he might be more into you than you realize," I said as I stepped into my pencil skirt.

"He was into me because I was a good distraction, and he liked making out with me every night." She stood and tossed a pile of T-shirts onto her bed. "I don't wanna think about this. I'm here to skate and to enjoy my final event with my friends."

"I'm sorry. I didn't mean to push."

"It's okay." She sighed. "I didn't mean to get all cranky on you."

"Don't worry. I've been having some crazy hormonal swings lately, so I might be having my own cranky moments while we're here."

I zipped up my skirt and pulled the button toward its hole, but it wouldn't reach. I sucked in my abdomen and tugged harder until the button connected. The waistband of the skirt hugged me so snugly I could hardly breathe.

"Why is this so tight?" I winced. "I've only gained a couple of pounds."

Aubrey gave me a once-over. "You don't look any bigger."

I unhooked the button and let out a long breath. "What if my costumes don't fit? I haven't worn them since nationals."

"They'll fit. The material will stretch."

I ripped off the skirt and glanced down at my stomach. It seemed as flat as always, but apparently it wasn't.

"No one would ever know you're pregnant looking at you," Aubrey said. "You still have a rockin' body."

"This rockin' body can't put on any more weight in the next couple of days." I pulled a red sweater dress from the closet and slipped it over my head. "I'll have to lay off the pasta in the dining hall."

I finished getting ready so I could meet Sergei. We'd made plans to join my parents, Liza, Aunt Debbie, and Uncle Joe at a restaurant just outside the Village. I hadn't seen any of them yet since they'd arrived only that afternoon. Sergei's mother Anna was due from Moscow the next day, shortly before the Opening Ceremony.

Sergei smiled as we met in the hallway. He helped me put on my coat and then circled his arms around my waist as he stood behind me.

"I miss you," he said.

I turned to face him. "You're only a few doors down."

"That's not close enough. I miss you next to me at night... how soft you feel in my arms, how sweet your skin tastes," he said low in my ear.

Goose bumps tickled the back of my neck, and I clutched the front of Sergei's leather jacket. "As soon as the competition's over, you and I have a date. In my room."

"I can't wait," he said, resting his forehead against mine.

We made the quick walk through the Village and found the restaurant suggested by one of the event volunteers. Mom waved to us from a table in the middle of the room, and Liza jumped up to greet us with hugs.

Sergei looked up at Mom and Dad as he brought Liza in for a longer hug. "Thank you again for letting her travel with you and stay with you."

"It's our pleasure," Mom said.

I sat across from Mom and pushed up the sleeves of my wool dress. After the brisk walk through the cold night, the warm room should've felt good, but it was *too* warm. I wished I'd been able to fit into my much cooler skirt and silk blouse.

I fanned myself with the menu, and Dad asked, "You okay, sweetie?"

"Yeah, it's just my usual pre-dinner spell."

"They should be bringing out bread after they take our orders," Mom said.

Aunt Debbie gave me a sympathetic smile. "I was sick all the time when I was pregnant with Bella. Not for Trey or Bri, though. I think the first child is always the worst."

"Why does a baby make you sick?" Liza asked.

Sergei unfolded his napkin. "Well…a lot changes in the body when there's a baby inside, and all those changes sometimes cause a woman to feel sick."

"I hope by the time I have a baby there'll be a cure for that," Liza said.

Everyone laughed and then settled down to give their order to the waiter. He was the typical Italian waiter I'd expected — young and handsome with dark hair, dark eyes, and a swoon-worthy accent. Liza's ivory cheeks turned pink when he smiled at her.

When he returned with our drinks, Dad asked about the bread and he apologized and said he'd be back shortly. My stomach rolled and sent another wave of nausea through me. I was about to ask the next table if I could have a slice of their ciabatta loaf.

"Your mom said you might be moving to Boston," Uncle Joe boomed from the other end of the table.

"You are?" Liza's eyes widened.

*Here we go.* Mom had probably told Aunt Debbie and Uncle Joe so they could gang up on us with the hard sell.

"Nothing's been decided yet," Sergei said. "We still have a lot to talk about."

"You would have a free babysitter if you're in Boston." Mom pointed to herself.

"You'd have me, too," Aunt Debbie added.

I took a small sip of water, afraid it might come back up. "We'll put that on our list of pros."

Mom and Aunt Debbie proceeded to start a discussion about the benefits of raising children in Boston. Dad and Uncle Joe only got a few words in as they went on and on, back and forth, sounding like official ambassadors for the city.

"There are more choices for schools."

"And after-school activities — so many different sports and arts programs."

"Great museums for kids. The whole city is a living history lesson."

"Right. And so much culture everywhere. There's always something going on."

Sergei drank his wine quietly, and I kept scanning the room for our waiter. Between the head-pounding chatter of Mom and Aunt Debbie, the sweltering temperature, and my empty stomach, I thought I might faint onto the decorative tile floor at any moment.

"I'm going to look for the waiter." I pushed my chair back from the table.

Sergei did the same. "I'll go."

"I can do it," I said louder and stood.

"You're not feeling great." He stood, too, and touched the small of my back. "You sit and I'll find him."

My face grew hotter and not from the warmth in the room. "I'm not an invalid. I can do it myself!"

Sergei gaped at me, and likely so did everyone else at the table, but I didn't stick around to see the reactions. I rushed toward the back of the restaurant where the waiters exited the kitchen. Nearby was a side door that led outside, and I decided fresh air might be more of a relief than food at the moment.

I charged into the night and inhaled the cold. Below-freezing had never felt so good. I stood there taking deep, slow breaths until Mom opened the door.

"Sweetie, what are you doing out here?"

"I couldn't breathe in there."

"The waiter just brought the bread. I gave him a nice little lecture in Italian to make sure he understood."

I smiled to myself. Leave it to Mom to pull out her Italian-speaking skills for a lecture. That poor waiter didn't know who he was dealing with.

"I just need a few more minutes of quiet," I said.

"I've never seen you snap at Sergei like that. Is everything okay with you two?"

"He's just been a little too alpha male lately. I appreciate him wanting to take care of me, but just because I'm pregnant, it doesn't mean I'm incapable of doing simple tasks."

Mom let the door close, and she hugged her arms to her body. "He's pretty excited about the baby, isn't he?"

I toed a crack in the sidewalk with the pointy end of my boot. "Yeah, and I'm not exactly the glowing mother-to-be."

"Well, you weren't expecting to get pregnant now. I'm sure you're still getting used to the idea."

"I'm just worried I'm missing the maternal gene or something," I said, continuing to stare at the concrete.

"You're not missing anything. I watched you with Liza over the holidays, and you're so good with her. You're caring and selfless, and you treat her as if she was your own daughter. Sounds like some strong maternal instincts to me." She put her arm around my shoulders.

"When am I going to start feeling those for the baby?"

"I think you already have. When you pulled out of those jumps at nationals because you were afraid to fall, that was you being a protective mom. You're feeling it whether you realize it or not." She cuddled me to her side. "Give yourself some time. You have a lot going on right now, so don't feel bad that you're not thinking about baby names or picking out nursery colors yet."

I smiled and rested my head against hers. She might drive me bananas sometimes, but she usually had valuable advice when I needed it.

"Thanks, Mom."

"Anytime, sweetie. Now can we go back inside? I'm freezing."

She opened the door, and I held up my finger. "One thing. Can you nix all the Boston talk? Sergei and I have tabled the discussion until after I compete."

"Sure. You just tell me when you're ready to talk more about it."

She didn't seem to understand that the discussion wouldn't involve her, but I wasn't going to get into that at the moment. I had an important date with a loaf of bread.

Sergei stood when we returned to the table, and he watched me with a hesitant look. I leaned in close to his ear.

"I'm sorry," I whispered and took his face between my hands, following with a soft kiss on his lips. "I love you."

He smiled. "I love you, too."

We sat, and I reached for the bread basket. "I hope everyone took a piece already because this is all mine!"

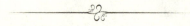

AUBREY PICKED UP HER salad and bottled water and turned toward the crowded tables in the Village dining hall, searching for an empty seat. The dining hall in Salt Lake City had been her favorite place in the Village because it was the best spot to meet the other athletes. It didn't matter which country an athlete represented; everyone mingled and struck up conversations with each other.

She spotted Marley and Chris sitting across from one another, deep in conversation, so she headed in the opposite direction. She hoped Marley wouldn't tell Chris she'd been upset over how things went down between them. Their interactions were already uncomfortable enough without adding pity to the mix.

She snaked between the tables and came upon a couple of seats next to some athletes in Japanese team jackets. They were all laughing and speaking loudly in their language.

"Hello." She smiled and nodded to the two girls and two guys as she sat.

They all nodded and greeted her in return. The guy with spiky black hair examined her with one eyebrow bent. "I guess... you are figure skater."

"You guess right. Which sport are you?"

"We are speed skater."

She uncapped her water bottle. "Awesome. I love watching speed skating."

"There she is," a familiar annoying voice said behind her. "My favorite ice dancer."

She closed her eyes and wished for the power to teleport out of the dining room and clear across the Village. Or maybe the ability to turn into a fly and buzz her way past Damien's head.

He came around the table and eased into the chair across from her. His dark hair curled over the high collar of his red and white Team Canada jacket, and he wore an irritatingly huge grin.

"Ms. Aubrey London," he said, resting his forearms on the table. "How have you been?"

"I was marvelous a minute ago and I'll be marvelous again if you leave."

His hand went to his heart... as if he actually had one. "Why can't we get back the vibe we had in Paris? We were so hot together."

Anger and shame burned its way onto her cheeks and up to her scalp. The Japanese skaters watched them curiously, and she hoped their English wasn't very good.

"I don't remember any part of that night," she seethed. "How many times do I have to tell you to leave me alone?"

"I think you'd gladly do it again, but you don't want your friends to know you slept with the enemy."

"You're disgusting. Don't say another word to me or this bottle of water will be all over your face."

"Hey." Chris dropped into the seat next to her and glared at Damien. "What did I tell you about harassing my friends?"

Aubrey gripped her chair. Damien wouldn't hesitate to tell Chris about their night together.

"Shouldn't you be off taking care of your pregnant partner?" Damien laughed. "Brilliant timing on her part, by the way."

"It's just going to make it even sweeter when we beat you," Chris said.

She tapped her fingers on the bottom of her seat. Why did Chris have to butt in? The more he provoked Damien, the more likely Damien was to spill her secret.

"I'm not really interested in listening to you try to one up each other, so if you could both let me eat in peace..." She stabbed a piece of lettuce with her fork.

Neither of the guys moved as they continued to stare each other down, but then they both slowly stood. Damien leaned forward, pressing his palms to the table.

"I'll see you around," he said, giving her a long look before walking away.

She put down the fork and looked up at Chris. "I didn't need you to rescue me."

"I was just trying to be a friend."

She turned back to the table and grabbed her water, keeping her eyes straight ahead. "I don't need any more friends."

# CHAPTER TWENTY-THREE

I STEPPED IN FRONT OF THE locker room mirror and smoothed my hand over my costume. The slate blue dress hugged my middle a tad tighter than I remembered, but I could still breathe — good news since I had to skate a short program in a few minutes.

The previous night we'd experienced the exhilarating pageantry of the Opening Ceremony, including a goose bump-inducing performance by Luciano Pavarotti. As he'd sung one of opera's most famous arias, I'd thought about all the amazing experiences I'd had in my life because of skating. I owned the power to create another amazing memory starting now.

I draped my team jacket over my shoulders and went to find Chris. We'd had solid practices all week and a good six-minute warm-up, so there was no reason to feel uneasy, but my insides still churned. I'd been landing my jumps, but we hadn't done many full run-throughs. I needed to trust that my body would respond under the stress of competition.

Chris sat in a flimsy chair along the wall of the bustling corridor. He was bent at the waist, staring at the ground.

Normally, I'd find him yapping with Sergei when I came out of the locker room. Nervous energy danced wilder in my stomach as I watched him remain quiet. He couldn't be anxious. I needed joking, confident Chris now more than ever.

I paced in front of him, skating the perfect program in my mind. I saw every step, every turn, every jump in vivid color. When Sergei approached us a minute later, my pulse quickened knowing our moment had come. No more visualizing the program. It was time to *do* the program.

We walked to the end of the tunnel, and Chris grasped my hands. I looked into his eyes, and he held my gaze, sharing the confidence I'd been seeking.

"We are champions," he said.

I nodded sharply and squeezed his hands. Skating like champions meant attacking every element and every moment of the choreography and taking the audience on the emotional journey with us. I wanted everyone in the building to feel like they were part of the program.

As soon as the French team exited the ice, Chris and I shed our jackets and skate guards and took their place. I made long, smooth strokes, letting my knees settle into the ice. The low buzz of the crowd whooshed through my ears as I circled the rink over and over.

*Attack, attack, attack*, I reminded myself. I couldn't allow the cautious mentality I'd had in practice to seep into the performance.

Chris caught up to me, and we joined hands again on our way over to Sergei. As our blades slowed, I took a mental snapshot of him standing at the boards in his crisp gray suit and red tie. It was one of the images I wanted to file away and remember when I looked back on our final event. My coach… my husband… always there to support me.

Sergei gave us a warm smile. "You know this program so well. You've given it all your hearts time and again, and tonight will be no different. It's ready for you to bring it to life once more, to show how beautiful and powerful your skating is."

The fact that he said "powerful" gave me added confidence. He expected us to skate full-force, not to hold back like we'd done at nationals. I felt free to be the fierce competitor I'd learned to be under Sergei's years of guidance.

Upon our introduction, the audience treated us to a hearty ovation, including a number of "USA!" chants sprinkled through the applause. Chris and I faced each other at the center of the rink, and I inhaled and exhaled a long breath as the music began. To the haunting strains of Barber's *Adagio for Strings*, we moved across the ice with invigorating speed, not letting a note go by without expressing it with our bodies.

We completed the triple twist with a smooth toss and catch, and we separated to prepare for the side-by-side triple Lutzes. Adrenaline surged through me as the moment to jump grew closer. *No fear*, I commanded. *Take control.*

I switched to the back outside edge of my left blade and picked into the ice with my right. Holding my arms tight to my chest, I spun three times and unwound for the landing. My body relaxed as my foot hit the ice with a clean edge, but then my peripheral vision caught sight of something I rarely saw — Chris stumbling on the landing. Not a fall or even a hand down but enough of a misstep for the judges to mark down the element.

Chris's eyes were wide as our hands reconnected. He had to be just as shocked over his mistake as I was. I squeezed his hand extra hard to let him know I had his back like he always had mine.

We regained speed into the overhead lift, where I stretched my limbs as if I was trying to reach the top row of the arena. Chris set me down, and the soulful music carried us through the circular footwork, leading us toward the last big element, the throw triple Lutz. We needed the jump to be huge and clean.

Chris gripped my hips, and I jabbed my right toepick into the ice once again. With a world of air under me, I soared across the ice, turning three times and then reaching for the ground with my right blade.

*Swish!*

I spread my arms out and held my posture perfectly upright. The jump had been more than huge! I'd felt like I'd flown two miles through the air. We finished the program with a crisp and fast pairs spin, and the moment the music ended, Chris slapped his hand to his forehead.

"I can't believe I did that," he said.

"Hey." I patted his chest. "It was just a little thing. We owned the rest of the program."

He pulled me into a hug, and I rubbed his back. The calculator in my head began to spin the numbers. Maddy and Damien would skate later, so we didn't have a comparison score yet. Our marks should be big even with the tiny mistake. The performance had felt immensely better than the short program we'd done at nationals.

When we met Sergei at the boards, he embraced Chris first. "It's okay. It didn't affect the program at all. You put everything you had into it."

He turned to me and touched my face before swallowing me in his arms. "You were so beautiful."

I held onto him a little longer than usual. I only had one of those moments with him left in my career — the special time of thrill and relief after finishing a program — and it was another memory to put in my mental scrapbook.

Chris continued to shake his head and mutter to himself as we sat in the kiss and cry. I put my arm around him and looked around at the stands. A few American flags waved, and I squinted to see if any of them were attached to my family.

The announcer came over the loud speaker, and I

clenched my hand around Chris's shoulder. The total score came in a bit lower than our season's best, but it was still an excellent number, far ahead of the next team in the standings. It meant nothing, though, until Maddy and Damien skated.

We stepped into the mixed zone backstage, and I answered question after question about how I felt physically, if I would have as much energy in the long program two nights later.

I gave the same answer every time. "I feel great. This is our last competition, so I'm going to give the long every ounce of energy I have."

Meanwhile, the reporters asked Chris if he'd stumbled because he was busy worrying about my physical state. He laughed off those questions.

"I might've been too amped up going into the jump," he said. "That's the only explanation I can come up with."

By the time we finished with the long line of press, Maddy and Damien had skated. We stood with Sergei in front of the monitor backstage and watched their score flash onto the screen. It was higher than ours but by less than a point. My nerves started twitching, and we still had forty-eight hours until the free skate.

"Almost even," Sergei said. "That's what we expected, so nothing's changed. If you skate the long as well as you skated tonight, you'll be in a great position."

I remembered Sergei saying something similar when we'd been in second place after the short in Salt Lake City. And we did skate well in the long. We skated the best program of our lives, and we still hadn't won. Fate wouldn't be cruel enough to deal us that hand again, would it?

THE NEXT MORNING CHRIS and I stood on the ice of the Palavela Arena once again but only in practice mode. Maddy and

Damien zoomed toward us, and we backed closer to the boards to give them space for their free skate run-through. They'd nailed everything so far and looked supremely confident.

"Did you hear what Damien said to one of the Canadian TV stations?" Chris asked. "He said, 'We're bringing home gold.'"

I let out a single laugh. "He gives us such good bulletin board material."

They finished their program with a furious spin and then vacated center ice, allowing the Chinese team to get into position for their run-through. We were next, so we skated slowly along the boards, warming up our legs. We didn't plan to do a full run-through but rather sections with the key elements.

I glided over to Sergei at the boards for a drink of water, and he smiled. "It's hard to believe this is one of the last times I'll watch you practice."

"I know. I'm trying not to think about it too much or I'll be really sad."

Chris skidded to a stop beside me. "You're not gonna start crying, are you?"

"Not now, but tomorrow night after the event I'm going to be waterworks central."

"Hey, I'll probably be crying right along with you. Hopefully, on top of the podium."

He took a swig of water before leading me to our starting spot on the ice. Our music began, and the other three teams gave us clearance as we performed the opening section of our program with the triple twist and the side-by-side Lutzes. The piano concerto continued, but we eased up and just coasted hand-in-hand, waiting for the time in the music where we'd do the throw Lutz.

When the tempo of the piece started to increase, we picked up our choreography and worked up speed for the throw. Skating backward with Chris behind me, his hands on my hips, I jabbed my toe into the ice as he vaulted me upward.

And then I saw Damien passing behind us.

He was close. Too close.

Panic tightened my muscles, and I couldn't open up quickly enough for the landing. My right hip slammed onto the ice with the cold impact jolting my entire body. I sucked in a breath, and my hand flew to my stomach.

Chris crouched next to me. "You okay?"

Only my hip was still throbbing. Everything else felt normal. I exhaled and nodded.

He helped me stand, and Damien circled around us. "Sorry about that," he said.

Chris dropped my hands and charged toward him. "How could you not see us?"

"Chris!" I hurried forward and grabbed his waist. "Let it go."

He glowered at Damien as we skated away. Our music was just about to end, so we drifted to center ice and struck our final pose.

"He did that on purpose," Chris said through gritted teeth.

"Probably." I touched my abdomen again. *You're fine. The baby's fine. Just one more program to skate tomorrow night.*

We went over to Sergei, and he grasped my shoulders. "You're alright?"

I gave him a reassuring smile. "Yeah, I'm okay."

"Let's cut this practice short. I don't want you out there with people who are being reckless."

We left him and did a quick cool down, during which Chris sent more scowls in Damien's direction. I concentrated on stretching my hip, calming my heart rate, and leaving the ice with a positive feeling. I didn't want the fall to be my last memory from the practice.

When we returned to the dorms, Sergei suggested I rest,

but I asked Chris to sit with me in the common room instead. There were some things I needed to say to him before our final competition.

"Since we'll be in competitive mode tomorrow, I thought we should talk today," I said as I tucked my legs under me on the couch.

"What are we talking about?"

"Our partnership. I know I've told you many times how blessed I feel to have you as my partner, but I want to say it again. You took a big chance on me, someone with no pairs experience and a history of being a head case on the ice. I can never, ever thank you enough for that."

"I knew when you laughed at my jokes that you were the one." He grinned. "The rest was just details."

"We needed a lot of jokes in the beginning." I laughed. "There were some tough days, but you always encouraged me and made me feel like things would get better."

"I never doubted that you would master it all. I could see how determined you were."

I propped my elbow up on the back of the sofa and rested my head on my hand. "It's going to be so weird not seeing you every day."

"You'll probably be too busy changing diapers to notice," he joked.

*Changing diapers.* That was one of those baby-related things I hadn't allowed myself to think much about yet.

"We would've had the summer tour to hang out and wind down our career, but now that's not possible," I said. "I'm sorry about that, by the way. It's a lot of money you're missing out on because of me."

"Don't sweat it. I can think of better ways to spend my summer than traveling on buses for weeks."

"You've been so great about this whole baby situation. No one else would've handled it as well you have."

He scratched the back of his head. "Honestly, it still

freaks me out a little when we skate, but I've been trying to keep my mind on just doing my job."

"Well, we only have one more practice and one more program to skate." I shook my head as a lump lodged in my throat. "Can you believe it?"

"Uh oh, are you getting ready to cry?"

I laughed as tears did indeed mist my eyes. "I can't help it. I'm just feeling very sentimental about everything right now."

He reached out and brought me into his arms, and the tears trickled down my cheeks. We hugged for a minute before he spoke, "Since we're being mushy, I should tell you that you've helped make the last seven years the best time of my life. I've loved every minute of skating with you, even with all the craziness we've been through."

I began to cry harder, and I clutched his shoulders tighter. "I feel the exact same."

He didn't let me go until my sniffles subsided. I wiped my face with my hands and stood from the couch. Chris dabbed at his own eyes with his thumb and forefinger, and I smiled.

"I'm looking forward to seeing you cry again tomorrow night," I said.

He stood and hugged me again. "I will gladly bawl like a baby if I have a gold medal around my neck."

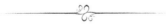

AUBREY FLOPPED DOWN ONTO her bed and watched as Em set the alarm on her phone. "Do you think you'll be able to sleep tonight?"

"Under normal circumstances I wouldn't, but the good thing about being pregnant is the exhaustion will probably knock me out."

"You're so lucky the pairs event is first on the schedule. I hate that I have to wait five more days to compete."

Em placed the phone on the nightstand between their beds. "Once I'm done, Sergei and I will come to your practices and be your cheering section."

She smiled. "Nick and Zach are bringing lots of obnoxious noisemakers to cheer you on tomorrow night, so you should be able to find us in the stands."

"Tomorrow night at this time, I could be an Olympic gold medalist." Em put her palm to her forehead and then rose to her feet. "It's hard to not keep thinking that."

"I have a good feeling about it."

Em stepped halfway into the bathroom and turned to look at her. "After last night and getting through the short pretty well, I've been feeling good about it, too, which makes me nervous."

"Don't be. You guys are gonna be awesome. I know it."

Em grinned and shut the door, and Aubrey reclined against her pillows. She was about to shut her eyes when Em rushed out of the bathroom with her hand on her stomach, a panicked look in her wide eyes.

"I'm spotting!"

# CHAPTER TWENTY-FOUR

"WHY AM I SPOTTING?" I CRIED as I sat on the bed. My legs had begun to tremble, and I didn't trust them to hold me.

Aubrey jumped up and sat beside me. "Are you cramping?"

I shook my head and clutched my abdomen with both hands. "Do you think it's because I fell today?"

"You said you fell on your hip, right?"

"I know, but what if the impact hurt something else?"

Aubrey put her arm around me. "Do you want me to call Dr. Parker for you?"

I didn't want to call our team doctor. I wanted to wake up and realize this was just a horrible nightmare. I squeezed my eyes shut and then opened them, but nothing changed. My stomach turned with sickening dread.

"I'll call Sergei first," I said.

Aubrey handed me my phone, and I dialed and waited with shaky breaths for Sergei to answer.

"Hey, did you want to say goodnight again?" he asked.

"I think something's wrong." Tears quivered my voice. "I'm spotting."

He was quiet for a few moments before bursting into action. "I'll call Dr. Parker. Do you have any pain?"

"No, I don't know why this is happening."

"As soon as I talk to Doc I'm coming over. Everything is going to be okay, Em."

I nodded, but I couldn't stop the tears from escaping my eyes. All the stress the past few weeks, the fall at practice earlier… had they taken their toll?

I changed from my pajamas into a T-shirt and yoga pants, and Sergei arrived a few minutes later wearing his jacket.

"Doc's going to meet us with a car downstairs. He'll go with us to the hospital, where they can do an ultrasound."

"Okay," I said quietly.

He enveloped me in a full body embrace and then held onto my hand as I grabbed my jacket and purse. Aubrey gave me a hug as we prepared to leave.

"Call me if you need anything," she said.

Downstairs in the lobby, we found Dr. Parker already waiting. He wiped his glasses on the sleeve of his coat and gave me a kind smile. "The van's outside."

Sergei and I climbed into the seat behind the driver while the doctor sat up front. Being whisked to the hospital wasn't how I'd pictured spending the night before my Olympic free skate. But maybe that was the problem. I'd spent too much time thinking about skating and not enough thinking about the child I was carrying. I teared up again as the terror in my gut became excruciating.

Sergei didn't say anything during the ride. He just kept me huddled to his side, his hand stroking my hair. I knew he had to be wondering if we'd made the right decision. He'd had doubts about me continuing to skate, but I'd kept insisting I'd be fine. Why did I have to be so stubborn?

When we arrived at the emergency room, I looked around and counted only five people waiting. Dr. Parker spoke with the desk and told us, "It'll just be a few minutes."

We sat in a row in the plastic chairs along the wall, and I flashed back to the last time the three of us had been in the ER together — five years earlier in Tokyo when I'd sprained my wrist. I'd give anything to have a sprained wrist instead of—

My whole body clenched with fear. I couldn't even think the words. *God, please, please, let the baby be okay.*

The nurse called for me after the promised short wait, and Sergei accompanied me to a small room at the end of a mint green corridor. After answering a few questions with a mixture of English and my limited Italian, we were led to another room with an ultrasound machine. I undressed and put on a hospital gown, and Sergei stood in front of me as I sat on the examination table. When he took my hands and kissed them, I broke down into a shuddering sob.

"I'm so sorry," I gasped.

He caressed my cheek, wiping my tears with his thumb. "There's nothing for you to be sorry about."

"I should've been more careful. I should've put the baby first."

"Em—"

"You felt it from the moment I told you I was pregnant. You fell in love with our baby. But I didn't feel it, not until now. And it might be too late." A cry strangled me, and I bent forward.

Sergei kissed the top of my head and gathered me in his arms. "It's not too late."

He repeated it again and placed soft kisses on my hair as I cried on his shoulder. When the doctor opened the door, Sergei reluctantly released me. I used the sleeves of my gown to wipe my face.

"Hello," he said in a heavy accent, giving me the same smile I'd received from Dr. Parker. "I am Dr. Silvia."

Sergei and I both shook his hand. He reminded me of Uncle Joe with his salt-and-pepper hair, hefty size, and deep voice.

"I speak with your doctor outside," he said. "You are here for Olympic Games?"

"Yes." I nodded.

"And you are eleven weeks pregnant." He looked down at the chart he carried.

"Yes."

"The blood you see… it is light, not dark?"

"That's right," I said, repeating what I'd told the nurse.

"Some bleeding is common in first months of pregnancy." He set the chart on a small table next to the machine. "We will look at the baby."

He spread a thick, cold gel on my abdomen, and I shivered. "This is your first ultrasound?" he asked.

"Yes. I'm scheduled for one with my doctor at home in two weeks."

Sergei clasped my right hand between both of his, and I took a deep breath and said another silent prayer. I'd said about a hundred of them the past thirty minutes. If the baby was healthy, I'd get on my knees and say a thousand more of thanks.

Dr. Silvia placed the machine's probe below my belly button, and a fuzzy black-and-white image came onto the monitor. I strained my eyes to see anything that looked recognizable.

The doctor pointed to a little blob surrounded by black space. "Do you see this?"

"Is that the baby?" Sergei leaned forward.

"Yes. That is—" He turned more toward the monitor and looked closely as he shifted the probe. "Oh."

The blood rushed from my head, and I squeezed the life out of Sergei's hand. "What's wrong? Is something wrong?"

He turned back to us. "There are two."

"Two what?" I sputtered.

"Two babies."

I may have stopped breathing for a full minute. I tried to

speak, but I couldn't form any words. Sergei stood frozen beside me. I stared at the screen as the doctor pointed to the now two blobs showing, each in their own little oval sacs.

"Do you see? I let you hear the heartbeats."

He faced the machine, and I tore my eyes away from the screen to look up at Sergei. His mouth still hung open.

"We're having twins," I croaked, not even believing what I was saying.

He looked at me, but his voice had disappeared. Dr. Silvia pressed a button, and a loud pulsating noise took over the silence.

"This is first baby's heartbeat."

I gazed at the monitor and the squiggly line bouncing up and down in rhythm with the noise. The heartbeat was so fast, so strong. And coming from inside me. There was another person *inside me*. *Two* little babies! My hand flew to my mouth, and I dissolved into tears once more. But these weren't rooted in fear. They were tears of wonder, of amazement at the most beautiful sound I'd ever heard.

Sergei's moist eyes shined as he turned to me. "That's the heartbeat."

I laughed while more tears spilled down my face. Sergei bent and pressed his lips to my forehead.

"Heart rate is very good." The doctor clicked something and then moved the probe slightly. "Look here — you can see baby's head, and here are where arms and legs will be."

I squinted at the blurry figure. The head was clear, and I could make out four little nubs for limbs.

"I see it! Do you see it?" I pumped Sergei's hand.

"It's amazing," he said hoarsely.

"We listen to second baby's heartbeat now," Dr. Silvia said.

He maneuvered more buttons, and the same thumping sound as before came through the machine. Just as fast, just as strong. And equally as beautiful.

"Very good, also," Dr. Silvia said as he peered at the image and slid the probe to the left. "This one curl in little ball… not as clear to see. He must be sleeping."

"He?" Sergei's eyes widened.

"Well, I just say he." The doctor smiled. "We do not know this yet."

"Can you tell if they're identical twins?" I asked.

"I cannot tell this yet, but do you see how they are separate here?" He pointed to the white fuzzy line dividing their sacs. "It is most likely they are not identical, but you know more when you can see sex of the babies. If boy and girl, obviously not identical."

Sergei and I both gawked at the monitor. Two babies. Oh my goodness. How were we going to take care of *two* babies at once?

"Everything look very healthy. They are right size, have good heartbeats." Dr. Silvia took the probe from my stomach and wiped off the gel. "As I say, light bleeding is very common in early pregnancy. If it continues, you should rest more and see your doctor when you return home."

Sergei rubbed my shoulder as his look of astonishment changed to concern. "Emily is supposed to compete tomorrow. What do you think she should do?"

"You are skater?" he asked me.

I nodded.

"You are good skater or you fall many times?"

"I don't fall much, but I fell today, so I was scared that's why I was bleeding."

"Was it hard fall? On stomach?"

"No, I fell on my hip."

He crossed his arms and studied me. "I do not think this caused it. If you feel good tomorrow with no spotting, I say you can skate. Take good rest before and after, though."

We thanked the doctor, and he left so I could get dressed. I swung my legs over the side of the table and sat facing

Sergei.

He shook his head and took my face in his hands. "This is incredible."

"Twins," I said as my chin started to quiver.

Sergei softly kissed my lips and rested his forehead against mine. The images from the ultrasound of the two little miracles played over and over in my brain. The babies were bigger than I'd expected, but they were still so tiny, so fragile.

"I don't wanna hurt them," I whispered.

"Do you not want to skate?"

I'd been through such a gamut of emotions that night, and the strongest emotion was my desire to protect our babies. I hadn't reconciled that yet with my lingering desire to compete.

"They're so much more real to me now. I don't know if I can skate without being afraid."

Sergei hugged me for a long minute and then pulled back to look into my eyes. "This is what we'll do. If you're okay in the morning, we'll have a very easy practice, one or two jumps, and we'll see how you feel."

My head bobbed slowly. "Okay."

He embraced me again, and I lifted my gaze to the ceiling. *Thank you, God. Thank you, thank you, thank you for answering my prayers! I know I've asked for a lot lately, but can I ask you to continue to watch over the babies and to help me be strong tomorrow? Please keep us all safe.*

AUBREY PUNCHED HER PILLOW and rolled onto her side. She had to practice the next day, but there was no way she could sleep until she knew Em was okay. She'd never seen her look so frightened. She couldn't imagine what she was going through. It had to be one of the most helpless feelings.

A quiet knock on the door made her sit up in bed. Had

Em forgotten her key? She rose and straightened her tank top over her flannel pants as she went to the door.

Chris stood in the hallway in his own pajamas — the faded black Orioles T-shirt and soft gray pants she remembered well from their nights cuddled in front of the TV.

"I'm going crazy staring at the walls, waiting for Em to come back," he said.

"Me, too." She hesitated and then opened the door wider. "You can wait here if you want."

He moved past her in the narrow space, and his arm brushed against hers, springing goose bumps down the back of her neck. She shut the door and stayed near it while Chris moved further into the room. He sat on Em's bed and bent forward, shoulders slumped, with his elbows on his thighs. She quietly sat across from him and watched him wring his hands while staring at the tile floor.

"She has to be alright." He put his head down and raked his fingers through his hair. "I should've seen Damien behind us this morning. I could've stopped the throw if I'd turned around and seen him."

"It wasn't your fault. Em said he came out of nowhere."

"If she loses the baby because of that fall, I'm gonna rip him apart with my bare hands."

That was an appealing image, but as much as she'd love to see Chris beat the crap out of Damien, she didn't want it to be because Em was hurt.

Chris shook his head. "She can't lose the baby. It would destroy her."

"She's gonna be okay. We have to believe that."

"I'm trying. I don't pray much, but I've been praying a lot since she called Sergei." He folded his hands together. "And I'm trying not to think about tomorrow and what happens if we can't skate. It just feels so selfish to be thinking about that right now."

She got up and sat next to him. "It's not selfish. You've

worked your whole life to get here. Em wouldn't think you're selfish either."

Chris turned his head, and their eyes locked. She told herself to look away, but she couldn't. The sincerity in his eyes pulled her in like it always did.

He held her gaze as he sat up straight. "It's so good to talk to you again," he said softly.

Her heart pounded harder with each second Chris looked at her. He slowly leaned forward, and she drew in a breath just as their lips touched. His kiss was as tender and sweet as she'd remembered.

She parted her lips, and his tongue slipped inside, stirring the desire she'd tried to bury. All the feelings she'd longed to forget rushed to the surface, including the pain of having her heart crushed. She tensed and broke away, hurrying to the window, the furthest she could get from Chris in the small room.

"I can't do this." She hugged her arms. "I can't be your rebound or your fun fling or whatever this is to you."

He jumped up and came toward her. "That's not what this is. That's never been what you are to me."

She turned so she faced him squarely. "You said what happened between us didn't mean anything."

"I thought that was what you wanted to hear. I thought if I told you how I really feel, it would freak you out."

Her pulse took off on a sprint, and she stared at him, searching for any clue of what he was about to say. "Why would it freak me out?" she asked quietly.

"Because you said you didn't wanna get serious. You've never let anyone get close to you. But I don't care anymore if it scares you. I need you to know how I feel."

This was just like the dream she'd had. Except Chris wasn't half naked. And this was achingly real. *Oh, please don't let me wake up alone again.*

He closed the space between them and put his hands on

her waist. She slowly tilted her head up to look into his eyes. The intensity in them made her heart race even faster.

"It was the night we went on our date and you did that ridiculously cute and sexy victory dance. That was the moment I knew." His hands pressed on her hips, bringing her closer to him. "That I'd fallen in love with you."

The warmest, most soothing feeling spread over her, like a part of her that had been empty for so long was finally filled. She couldn't speak. She just wanted to continue gazing into Chris's eyes and experiencing the wonderfulness of this feeling.

"I guess I'm not very good at keeping things casual," he said.

She unfolded her arms and squeezed her hands around his biceps. "I'm glad you're not good at it."

His face stretched into a slow smile. She reached up and ran her finger over his left dimple and then across his lips. His mouth opened slightly, and a heated breath escaped. She brought her hand down to his chest and leaned into him, stopping just before their lips met.

"It was the night I slept in your bed, and you held my hand all night. That was when *I* knew." Her voice broke with emotion. "That I am so in love with you."

Chris wrapped his arms completely around her, and they dove into a passionate kiss. The dizzying, floating sensation overwhelmed her, but she didn't fight it as she had so many times before. She let herself breathe in all the love in Chris's embrace.

He bumped his nose against hers. "Does this mean we're going steady?"

She grinned and hugged him. "I've missed you so much."

They clung to each other, hearts rapidly pounding. The silence gave her a moment to realize how much sweeter her world had just become.

"I always hoped that you felt something more," he said.

"I didn't wanna push, but I didn't know how much longer I could let you ignore me."

"When you said I didn't mean anything to you, it really threw me. It was so hard ignoring you, but it hurt too much to be around you."

"I'm so sorry I said that." His hands caressed her back.

"It doesn't matter now." She pressed her face to his neck and kissed her way up to his mouth.

His lips covered hers, and she heard the lock on the door opening. They looked toward it as they held onto each other.

Em and Sergei walked in and gaped at them. After taking a second to collect herself, Aubrey flew toward Em and gently grasped her shoulders.

"Are you okay? Is the baby okay?"

Em glanced at Chris and then back at her. "I had an ultrasound and everything looks fine."

Aubrey let out a long breath and circled her arms around her. "That's so wonderful."

"It was amazing to see the ultrasound," Em said. "The umm… the babies look really healthy."

"Babies?" Aubrey's jaw dropped and she stepped back.

Sergei grinned behind Em, who also broke into a wide smile. "We're having twins," she said.

"No way!" Chris exclaimed.

Aubrey squealed and embraced Em again, and Chris came up and gave Sergei a back-slapping hug.

"I can't believe you're having twins!" Aubrey cried. "Are you still in shock?"

"Shock, amazement, disbelief…" Sergei said.

"What did the doctor say about skating?" Aubrey asked.

Em's smile diminished, and Sergei put his arm around her waist. "If I'm not spotting anymore tomorrow, he said it should be okay for me to skate."

"So, we just have to wait and see," Chris said.

"I'm sorry this is such a fiasco." Em reached out and

touched his forearm.

Chris leaned down and hugged her. "We'll get through it. I'm just so glad you're okay."

He stood tall and turned to Aubrey, taking her hand in his. "Can you walk me out?"

She tingled all over just from the warmth of his hand around hers. Em and Sergei watched them closely as they walked out into the hall. Once the door shut, Chris drew her into his arms and held on tight.

"I don't wanna leave you," he said.

She looped her arms around his neck. "I wish you didn't have to go. But you have a big day tomorrow... trying to become an Olympic champion and all."

"You sound pretty confident we'll get to skate."

"I guess all your optimism has rubbed off on me."

He brushed his thumb down her cheek and under her chin, sparking even stronger tingles. "I knew I'd already found her."

"Who?"

"My Miss Brightside."

She smiled and pressed her lips to his. If she'd ever had a better night in her life, she couldn't remember it.

# CHAPTER TWENTY-FIVE

CHRIS AND I STOOD AT THE end of the long rink and watched the other pairs in our practice group fly around the ice. I wanted to stay far away from the traffic jam, more specifically Maddy and Damien.

I stifled a yawn and rolled my neck. I'd woken up every hour to anxiously check for any more spotting. It had stopped shortly after midnight, but I couldn't shake the fear that it would start again, especially once I began skating.

"Ready to warm up?" Chris reached for my hand.

The other skaters had slowed their pace, so now was as good a time as any for us to join the crowd. All the officials and volunteers gathered behind the boards looked at us curiously, surely wondering why we hadn't warmed up with the rest of the group. The thousand or so fans watching in the stands were murmuring, also.

I nodded to Chris but didn't move, and he tightened his grip on my hand. "I've got you," he said.

We set off with light stroking, slowly building up speed with deep edges. The gliding and the sweep of cold air over my face were such familiar sensations, but something felt different. All I could think about was how there were two little ones experiencing every movement along with me.

Sergei held up one finger as we skated past him, and we lapped the rink once more. My nerves twitched harder, anticipating the jumps we had to practice shortly.

Chris guided me around the spinning Chinese pair, and we kept a close eye on Maddy and Damien at the opposite end of the rink. They were talking to their coach, so they wouldn't be a danger to us. We stroked in tandem down the ice and then separated to do easy side-by-side double Lutzes. A double didn't scare me. It was the triple that had me panicky.

We circled the ice again, and my heart pounded. I *had* to do the triple. I needed to believe in my training and my ability. I couldn't bail now... not on myself and not on Chris... not after making it this far.

In unison we picked into the ice, and my body tensed as I went airborne and spun three times. I came down, and my blade hit the ice, scraping it hard on the tight landing. I exhaled and touched my stomach. The jump hadn't been pretty, but I'd stayed upright.

Sergei nodded energetically as we returned to him and came to a stop at the boards. He patted my hands and focused his eyes on mine.

"You're doing great. Just try to relax into it a little more."

*Relax.* I'd forgotten the meaning of that word the past twelve hours. The last time we'd competed at the Olympics I'd been a jittery mess the entire day, and I'd hoped I wouldn't feel the same this time around. No such luck. The anxiety gripping me now felt even worse, like someone had twisted my insides into a ball that couldn't be untangled.

I followed Chris back into the action, and he glided toward Maddy and Damien as they left the boards.

"Stay away from us," he ordered while skating past them.

Damien looked over his shoulder. "Protect your partner better."

Chris's hands clenched at his sides, and I grabbed his forearm. "Forget him."

We headed in the opposite direction to set up for the throw triple Lutz, and I watched the Canadians the entire way, making sure Damien wouldn't sneak up on us again. I was so busy looking out for possible dangers that I didn't have time to fear the throw. Chris assisted me into the air, and my muscle memory took over. I tightened up on the landing again, skidding my blade along the ice, but I'd gotten through the jump.

Chris put his arm around my shoulders, and we returned to Sergei for more guidance. He handed over my water bottle and rested his elbows on the boards so he was eye-level with me.

"Can you do one more jump and one more throw?" he asked.

I recognized his psychological strategy. He'd used it on me many times. He wanted me to gain confidence by giving him a positive answer. It had to be incredibly tough for him to be so poised when I knew he was worried about my physical condition, too. But no one would ever know from his bright eyes and calm voice. If he could show so much sureness, then so could I. The only way to conquer my fears would be to attack them. I'd never get through a four-minute program that night if I doubted myself every second.

"I can do it," I said.

I took two sips of water and didn't wait for Chris as I pushed away from the boards, pumping my legs. He caught up to me and said, "Loop first."

We passed Maddy and Damien doing their death spiral, and I centered all my thoughts on the technique of the throw triple loop, squashing my overbearing doubts. *You've done this successfully a thousand times. You are in control.*

On a big curve we sped into the throw, and I sailed through the air, the sparse crowd blurring around me. I came down on one foot and stretched my arms out to balance myself, securing the landing. I carried the same mentality into our side-by-side jump combination and earned the same result.

*I can do this!*

Chris gave me a wide smile, and Sergei treated me to an even bigger one as we rounded back to him.

"You're getting stronger with each jump," he said. "Let's finish with a couple of the lifts. You're more than ready for tonight."

We did the star lift and the press lift as directed and then cooled down while the rest of the couples still went hard. As we skated over the Olympic rings painted on center ice and bowed to the spectators, my chest swelled with emotion, and I bit down on my lip. I'd just finished the final practice of my career. All the years, the hours, the minutes of work I'd done on and off the ice... it would have to be enough. There was nothing more I could do before the free skate to prepare myself except rest... and not let the long wait mess with my head.

Before we left the arena, I spent a few minutes with my family and wasn't surprised when Mom questioned our abbreviated practice. I didn't want them to know about my hospital visit until after the competition, so I just said I was conserving energy for the free skate. Sergei and I had agreed to wait and surprise everyone with the twins news after the event. I was itching to tell them, so I was glad Sergei got me away from them and back in the Village before I let the secret slip. I especially couldn't wait to see Liza's reaction.

After a quick lunch in the dining hall with Chris and Aubrey, Sergei and I went to my room and lay on my bed for a nap. Chris and Aubrey had looked so radiantly in love it had made me grin like an idiot just watching them together. Their faces were going to hurt from smiling at each other. They'd gone to get coffee, and I didn't expect them back anytime soon. Competing for an Olympic gold medal was probably the only thing that could tear Chris away from Aubrey at the moment.

I snuggled my back against Sergei's chest, and he draped his arm over me, creating a warm cocoon. After my restless night, I thought I'd fall asleep easily, but too many demanding thoughts occupied my mind. Besides visualizing our long program again and again, I was also kept awake by the list of challenges in raising twins. Did we need to buy two of everything? I might have to jump on more of those endorsement opportunities in order to afford all the stuff. Would the babies have the same feeding schedule or would I be up all night taking turns with them? Was it even possible to breastfeed two babies at once? That sounded painful...

Sergei's measured breathing behind me indicated he'd had no trouble falling asleep. Totally not fair. Where was my pregnancy exhaustion when I needed it?

*It better not show up in the middle of the competition.*

I squeezed my eyes shut and tried desperately to quiet my brain, but visions of skates and medals and babies in matching outfits kept running on a constant loop. When the alarm on my phone rang, Sergei stirred and kissed my temple. "Did you sleep?"

"Not at all." I sighed. "I think I skated our program fifty times in my head."

He rubbed my hip and kissed me again. "As long as you don't actually *feel* like you skated it fifty times."

I had to do my hair and makeup, and Sergei had to get cleaned up and into a suit, so he left me alone staring into the mirror. I thought about the person I'd been at the last Olympics — the terrified girl who'd overcome crippling anxiety to perform the best program of her life. Remembering exactly how I'd felt that night, I was filled with inspiration. I'd stepped up big time when the moment had arrived, and I could do that once again. I wanted to match that performance and make a very special memory to share with the twins one day.

The next couple of hours I felt more focused than I had in months. My mind was completely zoned in on the task at hand. None of the potential distractions backstage at the arena bothered me, and I completed two solid jumps and throws in the six-minute warm-up. Since Chris and I were skating last, Sergei took us aside after the warm-up and sheltered us inside a small room so we wouldn't hear how any of the other teams in the final group fared. A strange sense of calmness had settled over me, and I prayed it would stay with me when our names were called to skate.

The time came for us to leave our sanctuary, and I kept my head down during our walk to the ice. I couldn't chance seeing the scores on the monitor or Maddy and Damien's faces in the mixed zone. My job was to skate a program I'd be proud to remember. How anyone else fared was irrelevant at the moment.

We stepped out of the tunnel, and I turned to Chris, gluing my eyes on his. He smiled and held my hands, and I fought another rise of emotion as I had at practice earlier. Now was not the time to get sentimental. If I started thinking about the finality of the occasion, I'd be a sobbing wreck.

The Chinese pair received a loud ovation as they finished their program, and the moment they left the ice, Chris and I burst onto it. I couldn't help but hear their second-place score as we circled the rink, but I didn't look up at the video board to see the current first-place total. Knowing the mark we had to beat wouldn't help.

*The only thing that matters is how WE skate.*

Chris drifted to my side, and we paid Sergei one last visit. I checked my tight hair bun for any loose strands and then brushed my hands down my velvet dress. Sergei watched me fidget before taking my hands and capturing my attention.

"You have never looked more beautiful," he said with a

soft glow in his eyes. "And you are just as strong as you are beautiful."

I smiled and took a few calming breaths, locking the word "strong" into the forefront of my mind. That was the most important word of the night.

Sergei turned to Chris and patted his shoulders. "There's never been a better, more dedicated partner than you. I never doubt where your heart is because you put it out there every time you take the ice."

Chris's expression deepened with determination, and Sergei looked at both of us. "There's not much left to say except have an incredible time. Enjoy every second of it."

We received our introduction, and boisterous cheers rang out, giving me an extra shot of adrenaline. I positioned myself in front of Chris to start the program, and he closed his arms around me.

The piano concerto began, and I mentally repeated "strong" as we commanded the opening sequence and easily completed the triple twist. My first jumping test was next, and I remembered the clean jump I'd done a short time earlier in the warm-up.

*You can do it again just like that. Be strong.*

I powered into the Lutz and reeled off three crisp turns alongside Chris. We landed on the same beat of the music, drawing a burst of applause, and I looked into the crowd with confidence. I felt their energy already fully invested in us. We just had to maintain our commitment to the spirit of the program.

Over the next two minutes, we threw ourselves into every single movement, letting our emotions shine through the soaring lifts and passionate choreography. It was just how Sergei and I had imagined it when we'd created the program together. As we completed our side-by-side jump combination, I buzzed with excitement, knowing we only had one lift and the throw Lutz remaining.

We turned the corner of the rink, and I worked my blades over the ice, but my crossovers didn't feel as deep as they'd been the entire program. I tried to press harder, but my legs shook in response and my breathing became shallower.

*No, no, no! Only one minute to go. I can't lose steam now!*

My heart throbbed in my ears as I lost touch with my body. The shortened practices and lack of run-throughs had caught up to me. The throw loomed, and I could NOT chance falling. Any other time, I'd grit my teeth and dig a little deeper, but I couldn't take the risk. Not with my precious babies to protect.

"Double," I said to Chris. "Double!"

Just like at Nationals, we lost our big wow moment as we turned the throw triple into a double, but I didn't regret it. I'd done what I knew was best even if it cost us valuable points.

I used my last bit of energy to hold myself up in our press lift and to give our final steps the stretch and intensity they deserved. The piano notes quieted, and Chris dipped me downward, holding me in our final pose as the audience leapt to its feet.

Well after the music ended, Chris slowly lifted me and buried me in an embrace. The whole arena rocked with cheers, and flowers and stuffed animals flew onto the ice from all directions.

It was over. I would never skate another competitive program.

I couldn't hold back the tears. My chest heaved, and I clung to Chris's shoulders. He rubbed my back and kissed my cheek.

"I love you," I choked out.

"I love you too, Em," he whispered, his own voice wracked with tears.

We both had wet faces as we took our bows. I pivoted to see the entire building and to soak in the sights and sounds of the screaming fans. Our small mistake hadn't taken away from the audience's enjoyment of the performance. That made my heart swell even more.

Chris held me close to his side as we skated to the boards, and when we reached Sergei he didn't wait for me to put on my guards. He picked me up and hugged me flush to his body, pressing his cheek to the top of my head.

"You are amazing," he said.

I pulled back to look into his glistening eyes, so gorgeous and swimming with passion, and I couldn't stop my emotions from taking over. I kissed him full on the mouth. *Forget the PDA rules.* He kissed me back and then hugged me again.

Sergei embraced Chris as we moved into the kiss and cry, and I sat between them on the short bench. Our jumps replayed on the monitor, showing the perfect unison with which we'd executed them. Our positions in every part of the program matched exactly, like we were truly skating as one unit.

Chris clasped my hand and laced our fingers together, giving them a warm squeeze. We'd done everything we could except for the one blip on the throw. Two and a half points. That was the difference between a triple and a double. If Maddy and Damien had skated well, we'd need those points to beat them. But I still had no regrets about my decision. I'd kept my babies safe.

"The score please for Emily Butler and Christopher Grayden of the United States of America."

The announcer paused, and Sergei grasped my other hand. I bobbed back and forth, drawing in deeper breaths with each second of silence.

The announcer returned and read our technical score first then our program component score and the free skate total. It was lower than our season's best. She paused again, and my heart hammered against my chest. A lifetime of work, all down to one moment. One agonizing drawn-out moment.

*Please be good enough for first. Please be good enough for first.*

"They have a combined total of two hundred and two point one four, and they are in first place!"

My body went momentarily numb, and then I burst into tears. Chris yelled, "Yeah!" and jumped up, pulling me with him. He lifted me off the ground and swung me around in a dizzying circle. I was laughing and crying so hard I couldn't find my breath.

"We did it!" he cried. "We did it!"

He set me down, and I went right back up into Sergei's arms. Tears blinded my eyes and choked my throat, and my head spun from the whirlwind of Chris's embrace. I held onto Sergei with all my might.

"Is this really happening?" I whispered.

He touched his forehead to mine. "You made it happen."

I kissed his lips and hugged him a little longer before taking a step back to look around us. Chris stood with his hands on his head, tears trickling down his cheeks. He stared up at the crowd, taking it all in. I heard a group of voices shouting my name, and my head swiveled to find the source. Sergei pointed to the corner section of seats, where my family and his mom were on their feet, clapping and thrusting their fists into the air. Liza bounced into the aisle and screamed along with them. I hopped up and down and frenetically waved my arms to let them know I saw them.

We were ushered backstage, and I blabbered incoherently through the television interviews. The reporters informed us that Damien had made a tiny misstep on their jump combination, explaining their slightly lower score. Less than two points separated our totals. I made no comment to the media, but I felt like there may have been some karma involved in his mistake.

There were only a few minutes until the medal ceremony, so I hurried from the mixed zone to the locker room to dry my eyes and touch up my makeup even though I fully expected to bawl my eyes out on the podium. When I rejoined Chris near the ice door, he wrapped me in a hug and we held onto each other until the regal music began playing, signaling the start of the presentation.

The bronze medalists, the Chinese pair, were introduced first, and then Maddy and Damien took their designated place on the second tier of the podium. The Canadians looked like they'd rather be anywhere else in the world.

"The gold medalists and Olympic champions, representing the United States of America, Emily Butler and Christopher Grayden!"

Goose bumps covered my arms, and Chris and I gave each other the biggest grins. We skated to the middle of the ice and bowed to each side of the arena, blowing kisses in the direction of our families. Gliding to the podium, we exchanged congratulations with each of the medalists, receiving scowls from Maddy and Damien, but nothing could ruin my moment of total bliss. Chris stepped up onto the top tier and assisted me with the steep climb, and I looked over at Sergei behind the boards. His beaming proud smile sent another chill down my spine.

The official presented the two other pairs with their medals first and then stepped toward us. I bent forward, and he looped the red ribbon around my neck and shook my hand. The shiny gold medal had a hole in the center, making it look like a compact disc, but I didn't care if it had ten holes in it. It was an Olympic gold medal. And it was mine.

As Chris received his medal, I tipped my head back and looked skyward. *Thank you, God, for being with me today. You have blessed me so much!*

After we all had our medals and bouquets of flowers, the announcer asked everyone to stand for our national anthem. I put my hand over my heart and gazed at the American flag rising above the ice. My shoulders trembled with a quiet sob, and tears rained down my face. This was the moment I'd dreamed of the first time I'd competed at seven years old. It was what I'd dreamed of every step of my career. When I'd almost quit the sport because I couldn't overcome my competition anxiety, I'd wondered if my dream would stay unrealized forever. But then I'd met Sergei and Chris, and they'd given me new confidence. They'd given me a reason to believe again.

The final notes of "The Star-Spangled Banner" boomed through the arena, and my hand went to my stomach. My babies were gold medalists, too. That's what I would tell them when we'd talk about this night. I wanted them to know how much they were always on my mind... how much they were in my heart. They'd made this night even more special than I'd ever dreamed.

# CHAPTER TWENTY-SIX

CHRIS AND I DIDN'T HAVE A chance to breathe over the next hour as we were hustled between photos and interviews. Finally we were able to change out of our costumes and board a van to the USA House, where we would see our family and friends. I was as excited to tell them about the twins as I was to celebrate our victory.

We walked into the pub, and the packed room erupted with cheers, rattling noisemakers, and swishing red, white, and blue pompoms. Chris spotted his parents, and Liza broke away from the front line of the crowd and tackled me with a hug.

"You were so-o-o-o awesome!"

I unzipped my jacket, and her eyes widened as she touched my medal. "Do you want to try it on?" I asked, reaching for the ribbon.

Her mouth hung open, but then she quickly shut it and shook her head. "I want the first Olympic gold medal I wear to be the one I win myself."

I smiled and set my hands on her shoulders. "If you keep working as hard as you have been, I know you can do it."

My parents and Aunt Debbie and Uncle Joe came forward next, and their teary eyes set me off again. None of us said very much as we shared long hugs.

"We're so proud of everything you've done, Em," Dad said, his voice thick with affection. "Not just the medal but how you've handled all the obstacles you've faced."

I swallowed hard. "I had great role models growing up."

Sergei's mother Anna beamed at me over Dad's shoulder, and I reached out to embrace her. I didn't get to see her often, but Sergei and I talked to her at least once a week on the phone. Her English and my Russian were close to meeting in the middle.

"This is most wonderful night," she said. "To see you skate like this when you carry baby... it is amazing!"

"I'm so glad you could be here."

Sergei slid next to us and put his arm around me. "I wish Papa could've gotten away from work."

"He watch on TV and he call me soon after," Anna said. "He want me to tell you he is very proud."

One of the federation officials motioned he needed Chris and me for pictures, but I asked for a few more minutes with my family. Sergei grinned at me, and I huddled everyone closer to us.

"So, we have something else to celebrate tonight," I said. "We have some baby news."

"You found out if it's a boy or a girl?" Liza asked.

"Not yet. This is even bigger." I paused and glanced at Sergei with a smile. "We're having twins!"

The jaws of all the adults dropped, and Liza shrieked, "What?"

Out of the group, Aunt Debbie collected herself first and corralled both Sergei and me into a hug. "That is definitely big news!"

"Wow," Dad said and kissed the top of my head. "I was not expecting that."

"How did you find out?" Mom asked.

"I had an ultrasound last night because I was spotting a little." I saw alarm pale her face and I waved my hands. "Everything is totally fine. The spotting stopped, and the ultrasound showed the babies are right on schedule."

"We got to hear their heartbeats." Sergei grinned even wider.

"You have two baby?" Anna touched my face and then Sergei's. "This is miracle!"

It was indeed. The fact that I'd gotten pregnant at all while on the pill had been a miracle. Twins… well, God had really worked overtime on that one.

Mom rubbed my arm. "Sweetie, thank goodness you're okay."

"Will they be identical or fraternal?" Liza asked. "There are two girls at my rink who are fraternal twins."

"We don't know yet," Sergei said. "They could be two girls, two boys, or one of each."

"Ooh, I want one of each!" Liza said.

"We're going to have a lot of fun planning this baby shower," Aunt Debbie said.

"Em!" Chris called from across the room and pointed to the photographer waiting with him.

"I guess that's my cue. We'll have more time to celebrate tomorrow," I promised.

I scurried over to Chris and ran into Aubrey along the way. We only had a minute to laugh and cry together before the photographer interrupted us.

"Sorry," Chris said as he posed next to me. "I figured the sooner we do our duties, the sooner we can get back to the party."

"You mean you can get back to Aubrey." I poked his arm.

His mouth stretched into a huge smile. "She has to go back to the dorm in a little while since she has early practice, so… yeah, I'm trying to get in as much time with her as I can."

"Have I told you how much I love seeing you together?"

"How many guys get the girl of their dreams and an Olympic gold medal all within twenty-four hours? It seems too crazy to be real."

"How many women find out they're having twins and win an Olympic gold medal all within twenty-four hours? I think we've both been hit by some magic spell."

The photographer pointed his camera at us. "Keep smiling just like that."

After we finished with the photos and did all the necessary mingling with the officials and sponsors, Sergei took me aside and asked, "Are you getting tired?"

The exhaustion I'd felt on the ice had been replaced by euphoria, and I'd been flying high on it since the medal ceremony. I had to make sure I didn't overextend myself, though.

"I'm still pretty wired, but I know I should probably rest. Tomorrow's going to be a long day with all the press we have to do."

"Well, I have a place we can go that will be very comfortable and quiet and private." He slipped his hands around my waist. "Just the two of us."

"I like the sound of this place."

"There's a hotel room not far from here waiting for us. Kristin helped me set it all up."

"So we don't have to go back to the Village tonight?"

He pulled me closer. "We don't have to go back the rest of the week."

I smiled and clutched the lapels of his dark suit. "Can we leave now?"

"I'll see if the car's ready."

While he went to find Kristin, I bid goodnight to my family with promises to see them the next day before they had to fly home. I met Sergei at the door of the pub, and we hopped into the van and sped off to the hotel. *What a difference a day makes*, I thought as we traveled the dark roads of Torino. The previous night when I'd taken a similar ride, I'd felt more frightened than I'd ever been in my life. Now I had nothing but joy in my heart.

The van dropped us at the Grand Hotel Sitea, and I gaped at the luxurious lobby and the old-world European charm of our room. "This place is gorgeous. How did you get a room here? Everything in the city is booked up."

"It pays to have an agent with great connections," Sergei said as he took off his suit jacket.

I went over to the marble-topped table and uncovered the silver bowl next to the bottle of sparkling water. "Chocolate-covered strawberries!"

"I thought you might be hungry."

I bit into one and savored the juicy sweetness. "Mm… so good."

Sergei stood behind me and gently removed the pins from my hair, brushing my long curls over one shoulder as they tumbled down. He kissed my neck and nipped on my earlobe, and my knees weakened. I sighed and leaned back against him.

"My Olympic champion," he murmured as his lips grazed my hair.

I smiled. "I'll never get tired of hearing that."

He turned me so we were face to face. "You were so brave tonight. I've never been more proud to be your coach and your husband."

I stared into his adoring eyes and thought of all the tough days of training when he'd been by my side, encouraging me and showing me nothing but patience and support. There weren't enough ways to express my appreciation for everything he'd done for me.

"You give me so much strength. I couldn't have done any of it without you. Thank you for believing in me and teaching me and loving me." I took the medal from my neck and slipped it around Sergei's. "You deserve this just as much as I do."

His eyes shined with his own gratitude, and he cupped his hands under my chin and kissed me deeply. I pressed against him, moaning softly as his lips stroked mine.

He broke our kiss and removed the medal, placing it on the table. "We don't want this to get damaged."

I unknotted his tie and started on the buttons of his shirt. "That's not the only thing that needs to come off."

He sank his fingers into my hair and claimed my mouth once more. Together we moved toward the bed, and I pulled off his shirt as he eased me down onto the pillows. I flattened my palms against his chest and slid them across his warm skin and over his broad shoulders. Oh, how I'd missed the feel of him, the heat of his body next to mine.

He untied my wrap dress and spread it open, and his gaze traveled slowly over me, filling me deeper with desire. Bending his head, he touched his lips to my stomach, and I shivered from the softness of his kiss.

His mouth brushed below my navel, and he whispered, "I love you."

My heart melted, springing tears to my eyes. I didn't know if it was possible for the babies to hear Sergei, but I believed the love in his voice was strong enough to reach them.

He lifted up and kissed my mouth, and I grasped his face between my hands. "I love you so much."

Our bodies came together, and he professed the same to me, showing me time and again that night just how much.

AUBREY CIRCLED HER ARM around Chris's waist and flashed a smiled to the line of clicking cameras. They finally had a chance to hang out after Chris's whirlwind day with the media, but his obligations hadn't ended. He had one last appearance to make, so they stood among a crowd of athletes, celebrities, and sponsors at Club Bud, a big party spot at the Games. She had another practice the next day, so she couldn't stay long at the event, but she wanted to see Chris, even if just for a little while.

"How was practice today?" he asked as the second-ranked American pair Candice and Shawn took their place in front of the photographers.

"Not bad. We're trying to pace ourselves since we still have three more days until the competition, but it's getting harder. We're both just so ready to get on with it."

"I'm gonna do my best to come watch you guys tomorrow. Since it's in the morning, I might be able to do it before the craziness starts again."

"Do you have another full day of press?" she asked.

"Think so. I know we're doing a skit for *The Tonight Show* and a couple of photo shoots. Kristin said we might be on a Wheaties box."

"My boyfriend, the superstar." She grinned.

Having never been in a relationship, she was surprised how easily the word "boyfriend" slipped off her tongue. It felt amazingly natural... and wonderful.

"Posters of you will be hanging on the bedroom walls of teen girls everywhere," she said. "Next you'll be in *Tiger Beat*."

He laughed. "If it pays well, I'm all over it. I don't wanna have to worry about money for a long time."

"I know. The money I make on tour this summer is going to help my college fund greatly."

"It really sucks you'll be gone almost all summer." Chris hugged her against him.

"You can come visit me at some of the stops."

His face lit up. "I won't tell you which ones so you'll never know where I'll pop up next. It'll be the most fun surprises ever."

His wide-eyed enthusiasm made her giddy. She kissed him and gave him a bear hug, but her smile quickly disappeared when Damien slithered through the crowd toward them.

"Let's get some drinks." She tugged on Chris's hand.

But she couldn't get him through the jumble of people quickly enough. Damien folded his arms and smirked at them.

"I should've known you two were together, the way you're always trying to act like her hero," he said.

"Just leave us alone." Aubrey dragged Chris away from him.

"Hey, I can give you some tips on what she likes," he said, raising his voice over the music. "She likes being on top, I remember that."

She froze and sucked in a breath.

Chris wheeled and stormed into Damien's face. "What did you say?"

"She didn't tell you we hooked up in Paris?"

Chris looked back at her, his eyes now wide with confusion and disbelief. Her throat turned sour with bile, and her whole body began to tremble.

She shook her head vehemently. "It wasn't…" she choked as tears of shame mixed with the bile. "I was drunk…"

"You knew what you were doing," Damien said and then turned to Chris. "I'm just trying to help you out, man. You might think you're getting something special, but she's just another slut."

Chris's jaw clenched and he slammed his fist into Damien's mouth, sending him stumbling backward. Aubrey watched numbly as Damien touched the blood oozing from his lip and then charged toward Chris, swinging his own punch. Chris ducked and shoved him, setting him up for another hit, but Shawn jumped between them.

"He's not worth it," Shawn said, pushing Chris in Aubrey's direction.

Damien grunted and held his hand to his mouth. "You deserve each other."

He disappeared into the darkness, and Aubrey clutched her stomach. She thought she might be sick. The people standing around them whispered to each other and glanced at her with raised eyebrows. Everyone nearby had heard what Damien said about her.

Chris stared at his bruised knuckles and then slowly lifted his head. She didn't want to see his eyes. Her heart couldn't take it if he looked at her with disgust.

Before he could turn to her, she raced toward the door, pushing her way through the crowd. She burst out into the frigid night and flagged down the first taxi she saw. As they took off for the Village, she slunk down in the backseat, still holding her stomach.

*She's just another slut.*

She bit down hard on her lip, holding in the suffocating cry. She kept it in during the ride, but as soon she reached her dorm room, tears flooded her eyes. How was she ever going to face Chris? Would he be able to look at her without thinking of her with that piece of slime?

She sat on the edge of her bed and dropped back onto the blanket. She should've known things were too good between Chris and her. The stupid mistakes she'd made in her past were bound to come back and screw her over.

A knock rapped on the door, and she shot upward. That had to be Chris. But she wasn't ready to see him. She didn't know when she'd ever be ready to see him.

"Aubrey?" he called.

Just hearing his voice brought another round of tears. She covered her mouth and turned toward the window.

"Aubrey, please open the door," he said lower.

She stood motionless, trying to catch her breath. His pleading tempted her to throw open the door and wrap herself around him, but she couldn't make herself move.

"Please talk to me." His voice grew even deeper with emotion. "I'll stand here all night if I have to."

She had to say something because she believed he *would* stay out there all night. She crept to the door and leaned her head against it.

"I don't want you to see me right now," she said, sniffing back tears.

"I really need to talk to you."

She rubbed her forehead. It might be better to face him now and get it over with. Air all her dirty laundry so he'd know just the kind of girl he was dating.

She turned the knob and retreated with her back to the door. *Okay, so I'm not quite prepared to literally be face to face with him.*

His footsteps stopped a few feet behind her, and he took a moment before he spoke. "I'm so sorry you had to hear that… garbage."

"I'm sorry you had to hear it, too."

He hesitated and then asked quietly, "What happened in Paris?"

She hugged her arms over her chest and stared at the floor, still not turning around. "Even though we won, I was upset because I didn't skate well, and I drank way more than I ever have. I don't remember much except Damien buying me shot after shot. Everything else is a blur."

"He took advantage of you," Chris seethed.

"I don't remember how things happened…" She pressed her temple. "I never should've drank so much. It was my own fault for staying in the bar so long."

"It's not your fault that jerk didn't have the decency to walk away when he saw the condition you were in."

"I wish I could blame it all on him, but I can't." Her head swayed back and forth as she walked further away from Chris. "Maybe it's good this came out now. I don't want you to be mistaken about who I am."

"What are you talking about?"

"You've only dated two girls. I've dated half of Cape Cod."

"Aubrey…"

"I've made lots of bad decisions when it comes to guys, and I'm not—"

"I don't care about any of that."

She felt him come up behind her, and he put his hands on her waist. "Look at me," he said softly.

It had taken her so long to find a guy she could trust — someone who made her feel safe and cherished. She wanted to believe more than anything that something so good could last, but those old fears, those walls she'd had around her heart for so long… they hadn't completely gone away.

Chris moved in front of her, but she kept her head down. He gently pushed the curtain of hair away from her face and tilted her chin up to him, and her eyes were forced to meet his. She carefully looked into them and let out a tiny exhale. They held the tenderness she'd come to know so well. Not a trace of disappointment.

"I know exactly who you are," he said. "You are the most beautiful, lovable, funniest, exciting woman I've ever known."

She relaxed into his touch, and he continued, "I don't care about anything that happened in the past. The only thing that matters to me is who you're dating now. I know the guy pretty well, and he's head over heels, wants to be with you day and night, beyond madly in love with you."

The smile she felt on her lips came from a place deep inside, behind the walls that were slowly crumbling. There was no reason to be afraid anymore. It was time to look only to the future and to the happiness waiting for her with Chris.

She reached up and gave him a feathery kiss. "You've made me a believer."

"In what?"

She wrapped her arms around him and kissed him again.

"Everything."

# CHAPTER TWENTY-SEVEN

AUBREY LOOKED UP INTO THE CHEERING crowd and felt the sense of satisfaction she'd hoped for after her final competitive skate. The audience was on its feet, wildly applauding the perfect free dance she and Nick had just performed. They'd skated perfectly in all three phases of the ice dance event, ending their career with no regrets. She couldn't ask for anything more.

Nick took her hand after their bows, and they met their smiling coaching duo at the boards. Natalia swept her into her arms while Peter embraced Nick.

"Beautiful! Magnificent!" Natalia exclaimed.

"I don't think we could've given any more," Aubrey said.

Peter put his arm around her shoulders as they walked to the kiss and cry, and she peered into the stands for Chris. He said he'd be near the top of the closest section of seats. His waving arms caught her eye, and she smiled and blew him a string of kisses. He did the same until she had to sit to wait for the scores.

She and Nick linked their arms and their hands together and stared at the small monitor. They were currently in fourth place after the compulsory and original dances, where she'd expected them to be. Marley and Zach had skated amazingly so they were right ahead of them in the standings. The Russians were in first, and the second-place Italians would skate next.

The announcer read the marks, and Peter and Natalia clapped at the high score, their best of the season. Aubrey held her breath, wondering if it could be enough to pass Marley and Zach. It wasn't likely, but she had a sliver of hope.

"…and they are in third place," the announcer declared.

Her shoulders dropped. They'd almost certainly be bumped down to fourth once the Italians skated, so their podium dreams were pretty much dead.

"We did everything we could," Nick said while hugging her. "We went out with our best."

She squeezed him hard. He'd had nothing but a positive attitude since she'd messed up at nationals. They didn't usually get very emotional with each other, but she'd been more sentimental lately than she'd ever been.

"You're awesome," she said, her voice wavering. "I just want you to know that."

He cleared his throat. "Of course I know that."

She laughed and slapped his back, and he held her tighter. "You'll always be my girl."

They stood and she waved at Chris as they left the kiss and cry. He patted his heart and pointed at her, bringing a huge smile to her face. She might not win a medal, but she'd leave the Games with an even bigger prize.

A long line of media awaited them in the mixed zone backstage. They started at the head of the line and saw Marley and Zach further down amid the chaos. Aubrey wanted to go congratulate them, but the NBC reporter started firing questions at her.

She and Nick moved slowly along the line, repeating their happiness with their performance to every member of the

press. As one of the print journalists prepared to interview them, a buzz spread through the area, and Marley rushed up to them and grabbed her arm.

"You got bronze! The Italians fell!"

Aubrey stared at her, unable to process what she'd said or form a coherent response.

Nick gaped at Marley, too. "Are you serious?"

Peter and Natalia pushed past the reporters, and Natalia cried, "You win medal!"

Aubrey's head spun in all directions. This couldn't be some kind of mistake, could it?

Nick began whooping and laughing, and Marley choked her with a hug. Peter and Natalia swooped in for more hugs, and the news finally sank in. They'd won a freaking Olympic medal!

They did more laughing than talking during the rest of the interviews. Neither of them could put into words what they were feeling besides shock. They learned the Italians had fallen on one of their footwork sequences, similar to the mistake she and Nick had made at nationals. She knew how awful they must feel, especially screwing up in front of their home crowd. But she and Nick had earned their spot on the podium with three stellar performances. No one could deny that.

When they stood on the podium a few minutes later, she couldn't stop smiling and staring at the medal hanging around her neck. It was so much more than just a shiny piece of metal. It was the culmination of all the early mornings at the rink, the cuts and bruises, the political games they'd had to play. She and Nick had battled through it all together and had thrown down the best performances of their lives at the biggest event of their career.

After they posed for all the official podium photos and took a victory lap, they scooted off the ice and Aubrey saw her parents, Chris, Em, and Sergei standing in the first row above the kiss and cry. Chris climbed over the railing and jumped to the ground, and he lifted Aubrey into his arms for a long embrace.

"I'm so happy for you," he said in her ear.

She pressed her face to his neck and left a tiny kiss. "It makes it even better having you here with me."

He set her down, and she looked up at her parents. They wore genuine bright smiles, something she didn't see on them often.

Her mom leaned over the railing, stretching to grasp her hand. "We're so proud of you."

Aubrey squeezed her hand and gave her the bouquet she'd received on the podium. "These are for you."

She held the flowers to her nose. "Thank you, honey."

Her dad angled forward and reached out for her hand, too. "You deserved this. I know how hard you've worked."

Her throat tightened as she felt the warmth of his gesture. "Thanks, Dad."

She took a deep breath and made her way over to Em and Sergei. Em bounced up and down and then tried to hug her through the bars of the railing.

"We'll see you at the USA House. I get to be a cheerleader this time!" Em shook her red and blue pom pom.

"Gold and bronze for Team Cape Cod," Aubrey said. "Not too shabby."

Chris hooked his arm around her. "Best team on the planet."

"Will you wait for me to change so we can ride to the party together?" she asked him.

"I'll wait for you anytime, anywhere."

She smiled and rested her head on his shoulder. She knew every day couldn't be as perfect as this one, but with Chris by her side, she had a feeling they'd come pretty close.

"THAT WAS SUCH AN incredible race," I said as Sergei and I walked through the Village five nights later on our way back from the Palavela Arena. "But I will never allow our kids to do short track speed skating. It scares the living daylights out of me watching people I don't even know. I couldn't imagine if my kid was out there, about to get his hand sliced off by somebody's skate blade."

"It is nerve-wracking." Sergei chuckled. "We'll encourage them to stick to figure skating. You know, if we have a boy and a girl, they'll be a ready-made pairs team."

"No, no." I shook my head. "I've told you my feelings on sibling teams. I want our kids to have a normal brother-sister relationship and not have all the stress of being a pair team."

"Think how much they'd probably be in synch, though, since they're twins. The Petrov kids would be unstoppable!"

I laughed. "Nope, I'm not changing my mind."

We drifted toward one of the benches along the path, and Sergei cuddled me against him as we sat. We only had one more day in Torino, and I was prepared to be an emotional basket case at the Closing Ceremony. These Games had been the two most memorable weeks of my life for so many reasons.

"Speaking of the twins, we haven't talked about names yet," Sergei said.

"I've been thinking about some the past few days. What if we do one Russian name and one American name?"

"I like that."

"I've been trying to think of names that have special meaning to us, and I thought of Aquinnah, where we had our first kiss. We could call her Quinn."

"Quinn Petrov." Sergei smiled. "I like it a lot."

"I was having trouble coming up with a boy name with special meaning, though."

Sergei gave me a pensive look and then started laughing. "Well, there's always our favorite artist and the first concert we went to."

I threw my head back with laughter. "I'm not naming my son Sting."

"As amazing a singer he is, I whole-heartedly agree. So, let's move on to the Russian names. What do you think of Alexander?"

"Alex Petrov," I stated, and the image of a little boy with blond hair and Sergei's big blue eyes flashed through my mind. "I love it."

"Now we need a Russian girl name and an American boy name."

"I like Anastasia," I said. "Stasia for short."

Sergei nodded. "That's a good one."

"Maybe we can just stick with one boy name for now."

"You're hoping we don't have two boys." He ruffled my hair.

"I just want two healthy babies, but if I had a choice, I'd love to have at least one girl." I smiled. "I have so many dolls and books to give her!"

"I've seen the boxes of books in your parents' attic. We're going to need a library in our new house."

I tapped my fingers on his thigh. "And where will that house be… that's the big question."

"Should we revisit our pros and cons list?" Sergei asked.

"I don't know… I've been thinking a lot about it, and as convenient and better for our careers living in Boston would be, every time I picture our future, I see us on the Cape, living on the water like we've always dreamed."

"I have the same picture in my head."

I turned to look into his eyes, and I saw the certainty I was feeling. "Then I think we have our answer."

Sergei kissed my forehead. "I'll find a realtor on the Cape, and as soon as the rink is rebuilt, we can move home."

"Home." I sighed.

"Fresh air, lots of land for the kids to run around, maybe

a romantic terrace for Mom and Dad to escape to after the kids are asleep." He grinned.

"I'm loving this house already."

"We might not find one that has everything we want, but as long as you and the twins are there, it'll be my dream house."

I smiled and softly kissed his lips. "I feel exactly the same. You and our babies... you're the best dream come true I could ever have."

# EPILOGUE

THE LIGHT, LATE SUMMER BREEZE FANNED through the trees and across the back deck of the house. I swaddled the blanket tighter around my perfect baby boy and gently rocked my chair, lulling Alex to sleep. My own eyes drooped a little, and I rubbed the corners with my fingers. We had company coming, so I had to stay awake.

Sergei opened the sliding door from the kitchen while cradling Quinn in one arm. She looked so tiny when he held her, which was often since he seemed to calm her fussiness much quicker than I could. She was already a daddy's girl for sure.

"Who was at the door?" I asked.

"The mailman. It was another package from your Aunt Rafi."

"She must be knitting hats and blankets twenty-four hours a day."

The doorbell chimed, and Sergei turned back into the house. "That's probably Aubrey and Chris."

I smiled as the breeze tickled my cheeks again. This was my favorite spot in our new house — under the shade of the covered part of the deck with a view of the sparkling blue pond just beyond our yard. We'd found our dream house on the water, and it even had the terrace off the master bedroom and a library with the window seat we'd wanted.

Sergei reemerged with Aubrey and Chris close behind. Aubrey peeked over my shoulder at Alex and touched the fuzz of his golden-colored hair.

"He always looks so peaceful every time I see him," she said.

"He's definitely the calm one of the two. Even though he's technically older, I think Quinn will be bossing him around. She makes her presence known."

Sergei sat next to me while Aubrey and Chris took seats on the big swing. Quinn stirred in Sergei's arms, and he placed a soft kiss on her forehead.

"Look at the proud papa." Chris grinned.

"It doesn't get much better than this," Sergei said. "You'll find out."

Aubrey laughed nervously, and Chris said, "Not any time soon. Your kids will be in college by the time we finish."

"It won't take you that long," I said.

"No, but it'll be awhile. Six or seven years for you to get a masters in design?" He put his arm around Aubrey and she nodded. "And the same for me to get my physical therapy degree."

"How was your first week of classes?" I asked.

"It's weird being back in school," Aubrey said. "I feel like I have to relearn how to study."

"I feel like an old man," Chris said. "I walked into my Intro to Psych class and all the other students looked like they were twelve."

I laughed. "You *have* to take my mom's English class next semester."

"No way. She'd probably call on me all the time."

Sergei's phone vibrated on the patio table, and he reached

for it to read the text.

"Court's at the seamstress," he said. "She says their short program costumes came out great."

"When are you going back to work, Em?" Aubrey asked.

"In a few weeks. Courtney's aunt is actually going to watch the twins for us. She used to have a little daycare in her house, so she has a lot of experience."

"What are you gonna do when you have to travel to competitions?"

"Aunt Deb is coming with us to Skate America in Hartford and probably nationals, too. She's all excited to play nanny." I pushed a strand of hair out of my eyes. "I don't think I'll make any of the overseas trips this fall."

"I bet you're itching to get back to the rink," Chris said. "I know you. You've always been a rink rat."

I smiled. "I do miss it a lot, but it'll be hard leaving the babies. Good thing is, I'll be done in the afternoon every day at the rink, so I'll only be gone from them half the day."

A flock of seagulls squawked as they flew over the pond, and Chris gazed out at the water. "I miss the sounds of nature. All we hear are honking horns outside our apartment."

"We've been talking about buying a summer house out here, so if you hear of anything reasonable nearby…" Aubrey said.

"Buying property together? Should we expect a ring soon?" I asked with raised eyebrows.

They gave each other little smiles, and Chris said, "You'll be the first to know."

As the four of us talked and the twins slept, I thought about how far we'd all come since our early days on the Cape. I never would've imagined us like this — two couples starting blissful new lives together. The future held so many amazing possibilities for all of us.

# MORE BOOKS BY JENNIFER COMEAUX

Edge Series
*Life on the Edge (Edge #1)*
*Edge of the Past (Edge #2)*
*Fighting for the Edge (Edge #3)*

Ice Series
*Crossing the Ice (Ice #1)*
*Losing the Ice (Ice #2)*
*Taking the Ice (Ice #3)*

To stay up to date on Jennifer's new releases, join her mailing list:
http://eepurl.com/UZjMP

Jennifer loves to hear from readers! Visit her online at:
jennifercomeaux.blogspot.com
www.twitter.com/LadyWave4
www.facebook.com/jennifercomeauxauthor
www.instagram.com/jcomeaux4
jcomeaux4@gmail.com

Please consider taking a moment to leave a review at the applicable retailer. It is much appreciated!

# ABOUT THE AUTHOR

JENNIFER COMEAUX is a tax accountant by day, writer by night. There aren't any ice rinks near her home in south Louisiana, but she's a diehard figure skating fan and loves to write stories of romance set in the world of competitive skating. One of her favorite pastimes is travelling to competitions, where she can experience all the glitz and drama that inspire her writing.

Printed in the USA
CPSIA information can be obtained
at www.ICGtesting.com
LVHW051620110124
768548LV00068B/2098